DON'T FORGET YOU LOVE ME

ROSEMARY AUBERT

DON'T FORGET YOU LOVE ME

Rosemary Aubert

ISBN: 978-1-927114-98-8

**CARRICK
PUBLISHING**

Kindle Edition

Carrick Publishing

Cover Photo Gord Jones

Cover Art and Design Sara Carrick

Critical acclaim for Ellis Portal and the Ellis Portal mystery series:

The New York Times

"…in Ms. Aubert's sensitive treatment, a character with great dignity and unusual moral depth."

Washington Post

"Rosemary Aubert has a touch of the poet."

Kirkus Reviews

"Heartfelt and often piercing in its portrayal of life on the edge."

New Brunswick Reader

"An absorbing read that stays with you long after you put it down."

The Globe and Mail

"Aubert has done a fine job…taking on some of the social issues that bedevil a big city…"

I'd like to acknowledge the assistance of Peter Moon and Pat Capponi during the early stages of research for this book. And I'd like to thank Donna Carrick for her invaluable help during the preparation for publication of the manuscript, including her help in recruiting the excellent cover artist, Sara Carrick.

As always, I thank my husband Doug Purdon for his continuing support in all ways at all times.

This book is dedicated to my sister, Linda Proe.

ONE

It's nothing but a skeleton now. If you look up from the parkway at just the right moment, you'll see a ten-story curve of concrete, its insides gutted. That's the latest thing here. Take an old building, eviscerate it, plunk something new inside and call it restoration. But if you haven't got the patience for that, build fresh. Beside the old Riverside long-term-care facility, is the brand-new building, a twenty-story wedge of shining glass. I don't know how they're going to keep all the sadness inside from the view of cars stalled in traffic in front of it on the highway.

I knew Queenie had gone over to the other side long before the day she died. She lay motionless in bed, no longer asking me to wheel her to the window of the old building, where she had been one of the last patients.

We had spent her final days of full consciousness looking out over the lush green park below, reminiscing about our days in far wilder parts of the valley of the Don River that cuts through downtown Toronto the way the blood system cuts through the body.

"I'll never go down there again, will I?" She asked me.

"No," I said, keeping my voice as light as I could, "and a good thing, too!"

She laughed. It nearly broke my heart to realize she had got the joke.

"I liked running the tent city best," she said. Her voice, always deep and throaty had grown so faint that I had to bend close to hear her. She paused, as much to catch her breath, I thought, as to let the memories flow over her, memories of the time she spent catering to the poorest of the city's poor, people who had nowhere to live but in rough canvas hovels set up at the very brink of the Don in its lowest reaches.

"And I liked sleeping under the stars," I responded as if the years I'd myself been homeless in the valley had been some kind of glamorous camping trip.

But all those days were gone. Our days in the valley. Our last days by the window.

The day she died, there was so little left of her! Silent, tiny, pale. I felt as if I were trying to hold smoke in my hand.

There were no visitors now. At first there had been so many that I had considered asking the hospital to put some kind of hold on them. There were well-dressed people from Queenie's church and from among her co-workers at the downtown shelter of which she'd eventually become the administrator. There were Native friends from the Cree reserve in Moosonee, the settlement far north of Toronto near James Bay, an offshoot of Hudson's Bay. These were people among whom Queenie had spent her childhood and to whom she returned for a while to heal herself after her long bout with homelessness and despair. They uttered what sounded like prayers over her in a language I couldn't understand. And twice they were kicked out for burning sweetgrass in Queenie's room.

And there were clients of the shelter who came, too, shabby unfortunates who, I could tell, had polished themselves up the best they could to come and pay their respects to the woman who had always respected them. At first the hospital staff was appalled at the appearance of these people. But after I lost my temper and set the record straight with the head nurse as to who they were and why it was essential to Queenie that they be allowed to visit, they came unimpeded.

But they were all gone now. No one was left except the Reverend Kathryn Whittaker, the pastor of St. Ambrose, the Anglican Church of which Queenie had been a member for a longer time than I remembered.

Kate, as her parishioners called her, was the nearest thing to an angel I'd ever seen, patient, kind, gentle and still beautiful with silver curls framing her smiling face.

"The Lord is my shepherd; I shall not want."

Kate glanced at Queenie, who lay still, her eyes closed as if they'd never open again. She waited.

And then, as if breathed rather than spoken, Queenie's voice responded, "He maketh me to lie down in green pastures: he leadeth me beside the still waters."

I felt the hot sting of tears and fought to hold them back. Still waters. There had been a time, only a few short years it seemed now, but there had been a time when Queenie and I had been the still waters beside which each of us had finally found peace.

Try as I might, I couldn't suppress a sigh. Without looking up from Queenie, Kate reached over and squeezed my hand where it lay on top of the covers of Queenie's bed.

They proceeded that way through almost the entire psalm until they reached the phrase, "mine enemies". It was there that Queenie opened her eyes, raised her pale, thin hand and stopped Kate.

"Your Honor," she said. It was her nickname for me and she had always called me that in my years of disgrace as a former judge and in my years of triumph as one having returned to the bench. "Your Honor, you gotta make a promise to me before I meet the Lord."

I would have promised Queenie anything, not just in this sacred moment of our final goodbye, but at any time I'd ever known her.

I was afraid to touch her, afraid I would break the fragile thing that she had become, but she reached out and touched me. Even in her so lessened state, her touch brought back a physical memory of all we had shared as husband and wife despite the fact that we had never been young together.

"Anything."

"You ain't gonna like this," she said, her voice becoming stronger. When I had first met Queenie, she spoke the language of the streets. She was tough, illiterate and a master at the slang that the people of the street spoke. But we had worked together to help her to learn to read and then she went back to school and became a professional and learned to speak like one.

3

But in the past few days, I'd noticed, she'd slipped back to her old way of talking. It just wrenched my heart, thrusting me back to our earliest days together, our days of sleeping in doorways and eating out of the trashcans behind McDonald's…

"You heard about the Juicer?"

I'd heard, over the years, about a great number of the reprobates that Queenie had saved in her work at the shelter. I assumed that this was just one more, that her mind was wandering back to the days in the not-so-distant past before she had retired from her position there.

"What about him, Queenie?" I asked gently, willing to hear whatever she had to say whether or not it made any sense.

She gasped then, terrifying me, making me fear that that terrible sound might be her last. She looked up at Kate, who, by the grace of God, seemed able to read Queenie's mind.

"She means the homeless man they called the Juicer because he practically lived on orange juice," Kate said, making a face that made me think this was not as strange as some things she'd heard about. "He's the man who died recently after being briefly apprehended by four Toronto police officers. There's some question as to whether the so-called take-down was the cause of death…."

"Murdered." Queenie gasped again.

"Sweetheart," I said, not hesitating to take her hand this time, "You don't have to worry about these people anymore."

"Promise me," she said, so feebly that I wasn't sure I heard correctly.

"Promise what? What do you want me to do?"

"Find out who killed him." And this time her voice was as clear as it had ever been.

"Don't worry, my love, the police will look into it if there's any question of…"

She terrified me by struggling to rise up, lifting her head and shoulders from the pillow. "Your Honor, you gotta. You gotta promise me."

I touched her shoulder and she lay back down. I glanced at Kate. She nodded.

"All right, Queenie," I said, "I promise."

I didn't really care what I was saying, but the sense of relief I felt when she lay back down, smiled and closed her eyes seemed about to equal the relief she felt at having elicited this ridiculous promise.

Kate nodded again, picked up her Bible, though I was positive she didn't need it to continue reciting the 23rd psalm.

"Surely goodness and mercy shall follow me all the days of my life: and I will dwell in the house of the Lord forever."

"Amen," Queenie responded.

It was the last thing she ever said.

TWO

I forgot about the promise. The days after Queenie's death were at first filled with the busy tasks that, I have come to think, are designed to distract from the coming pain of grief, the way an aspirin will push away a throbbing headache for a little while.

First there was the arranging of her funeral, which had the biggest turnout of mourners that little St. Ambrose church had ever seen.

Rev. Kate kept it simple: traditional prayers, a short, sweet sermon, a number of touching testimonials. Queenie's Native friends performed several rituals, and this time, nobody stopped them. At the burial on a late summer day when the earth was still as soft as in full summer, I felt the rare urge to pray and I gave into it.

At the gravesite, I was surprised to see quite a few people I hadn't seen in a while, though I suppose I shouldn't have been. One person who turned up was a considerably cleaned-up Johnny Dirt, an old reprobate that I had sparred with on the street for years. One of the counsellors from Queenie's health center leaned over and whispered to me, "Isn't it amazing how far Johnny has come? He works with us now." When I went over to Johnny and thanked him for coming, I commented on the changes he had made in his life. He sneered at me and spat out, "If you could do it, what makes you think I couldn't?"

Another person who came to offer her respects was a mysterious middle-aged woman, quite attractive in a mature way, whom I didn't recognize at first. I caught only a glimpse of her and when I tried to recall her name, dizzied by the events of the day, I failed.

When the funeral was over, there was the straightening out of Queenie's financial affairs, which took nearly no time at all, since all her assets were in my name.

Ordinarily, there would have been family matters to deal with, but Queenie had no one and my own family, my brother and sister, my son and daughter, though they offered, could do nothing to really help.

So it was a couple of weeks before I got down to what I have since learned is often the gateway to grief: deciding what to do with Queenie's possessions.

Neither she nor I had many. Our long years of living on the skid had robbed us of the need for anything but essentials.

I gave her clothes to a women's shelter. I asked my daughter Ellen if she wanted Queenie's jewelry, but except for the golden wedding ring with which she had been buried, she'd had nothing of monetary value, and the beads and feathers of Queenie's necklaces and earrings did not appeal to a young woman whose own jewelry was modern combinations of silver and stone. In the end, the jewelry had been taken by Angelo, my precocious grandson, who used it in a school project on Native creative arts.

It wasn't until I discovered, at the very back of Queenies closet, a box made of quills that I came upon Queenie's most treasured belongings.

The feel of the quills against my fingers as I lifted the box reminded me so strongly of all that was Queenie—the exoticness of her, the evanescent beauty, the combination of strength and vulnerability—that I burst into tears.

I was so grateful that I was alone in her room, that there was no one else in the apartment nor likely to visit anytime soon. I felt I was alone with her, that I somehow held her in my hand, that for this moment, I had her back.

I sobbed. It had been years since I'd cried. I couldn't even remember the last time.

I had been through the disgrace of being removed from the bench because of criminal charges. I'd been in jail. I'd seen my worst enemy end up with my exquisite first wife. I had lived in a cardboard box in the valley of the river. I had survived shame and storms, regret and revulsion, but I had never cried.

Until now.

When I finally managed to calm myself, I put the box back where I had found it.

7

I made myself a cup of tea. Sat down. And stayed seated for six hours.

Then I got up and got back at it.

I recovered the box, lifted the lid, took a deep breath and peered in.

On top there was a copy of Queenie's and my marriage license. We'd only been married ten years, so the paper was crisp and the signatures on it bold and dark. I set it aside and lifted another paper, a little older. This was Queenie's first license as a nurse.

The real treasures were further down in the pile. There was a long, curled thatch of beautiful still-shiny black hair. I knew at once that this must have been from the head of Queenie's daughter, Moonstar, who had died at an early age, violently on the street. And, to my amazement, I found a lock of my own silver hair. How Queenie had gotten that, I had no idea.

At the very bottom were various tokens of Queenie's life— gifts of the street we used to call them. A colorful button, a little iron beaver, more feathers…

And then I found something I was astonished that she had saved. I found the index cards that she and I had used when I taught her how to read. They were carefully tied in a faded red ribbon. As I thumbed through them, I felt I held in my hand the history of our progression toward literacy. The first card in the stack, printed boldly in my handwriting and beneath that in an awkward scrawl in Queenie's, said. "I am Queenie and you are Ellis." The last card, in her hand only, now confident, said, "Between you and me, a promise made is a promise kept."

THREE

The Juicer.

I vaguely remembered the man. On the whole, I had stayed away from the shelter where Queenie worked. There had been a few reasons for this. I had street people I was helping on my own down in the valley, and I didn't think it was a good idea to mix the two groups. Also, Queenie and her staff had their own routines, their own rules. I didn't want to step on any toes.

And of course, for reasons of confidentiality, Queenie didn't talk about her clients or their problems.

Except that once in a while she mentioned with gentle laughter that the Juicer had said this or done that. She found him amusing, charming, even. I was soon to learn that she had probably been the only person in the world who did.

I saw him a couple of times, too. He was pale and he was pudgy and he was hairless. Not Native. Not at all like everyone else Queenie's shelter served. The times I had run into him, he had made a great show of bowing and calling me Your Honor. It wasn't, of course, affectionate like when Queenie used the term, but nor was it colored with tones of disrespect like it was when Johnny Dirt sarcastically called me that.

I could have been forgiven for having lost track of the news over the past few weeks. I quickly learned that the story of the death of a homeless man less than an hour after he had been subdued by four police officers in the presence of twelve other officers had slipped quite a way down into the back pages of the paper from the headlines it had occupied a few days earlier.

Less than an hour at my computer, though, got me up to speed. The Juicer had originally been apprehended several days before his death because he had "lost it" in front of a house in a run-down neighborhood, a house into which he had finally been able to move after years spent sleeping in doorways and shelters.

9

There was no mention of what, exactly, had caused this sudden lack of all control.

At the time, he had been taken to the mental hospital on Queen Street, had been treated and was believed to be improving.

The articles I read made no mention of the possible reason for what happened next. The man came to the attention of the Toronto police when he was seen parading in front of the hospital on a cold night with nothing on and brandishing weapons in each hand. These turned out to be pieces of a broken towel rack, but the sight of him had resulted in the staff making a frantic 911 call. As soon as he saw the police, the man went completely berserk.

After a brief but violent struggle, he was subdued. No shots were fired. One witness later said that she had seen one of the police officers use a Taser, but it was quickly established that that was not possible because none of the four officers was a supervisor and only supervisors had been allowed to carry and discharge so-called "stun guns".

Several of the articles I read noted that the incident would probably have been unremarkable, an incident similar to scenes played out across the city night after night. An old guy goes nuts. He runs around with nothing on, swearing he'll get his own back for whatever reason and brandishing the feeble weapons of the disenfranchised. Somebody calls the cops. They come. They calm him down. Somebody puts him to bed. The end.

I thought, as I read, that it would have been like that for the Juicer, too.

Except that within an hour of the incident, he was found dead in his hospital bed. Dead of apparent heart failure, possibly as a result of his recent "misadventure."

Again, it might have ended there. But the chief of police, sensitive to public demands concerning security issues around the upcoming International Seminar of Global Partners had, in an unusual move, asked PIC, the Police Investigative Committee, to look into the incident, the same way they would have if a citizen had clearly been harmed as a direct result of police action. Apparently the chief was still smarting from the negative press his force had received over their part in the mishandling of security at the recent G20 summit.

I read all this with not much interest but with a good deal of relief. Because it seemed to me that this was going to be an open and shut case. A simple matter of over-diligence on the part of the force. Commendable perhaps, but unnecessary.

My years on the bench had taught me a lot of things about the Toronto Police—some good, some bad. But nothing I had experienced so far had ever convinced me that any member of the force had been a murderer.

Was this conviction about to change?

I hoped not. I had enough to deal with without returning to the thankless job of being some sort of part-time amateur private detective.

Nonetheless, just to play it safe, I decided to visit my friend Matt West.

Matt and I went way back, and he had always been accessible to me if I dropped by police Headquarters on business—legal business, friendship business, or just the business of being in the neighborhood and looking for somebody to have a coffee with.

But I knew the minute I entered the lobby that things weren't the same at Headquarters.

For one thing, there was some sort of "community co-operation" campaign going on.

This sort of thing had never been necessary in Toronto in the old days. People had trusted the police. That was before they were all bald. I knew I was being petty, like the old man I am, but I couldn't understand how the complete removal of hair from a young man's head made him feel like a hero. To me, all these bald police officers just looked like feeble knockoffs from American cop shows.

But of course, that was just my opinion, and it apparently wasn't shared by everybody—or even by many, judging by the scene that met my eyes. The entire lobby of Headquarters—a large room that took up a great deal of the first floor of the station—was filled with screaming children, many of them jumping up and actually grabbing at the five or six young cops who were trying—without much success—to get them to calm down. I couldn't help wondering where the Tasers were when you needed them.

It took me a minute to figure out what was going on and that was only possible because my eye caught a giant banner—it must have been ten feet long—hanging somehow from the two-story-high ceiling. It depicted a friendly cop—a female—showing some sort of crime-fighting device to a child. The photo was gigantic, much larger than life. The banner read, "We're all in this together—young and old."

"Can I see your gun?" some little voice called out. And half a hundred others joined in with the same question, "Can we? Can we?"

As the officers herded the children toward several exhibits, including a police car with huge eyes and a mouth, I made my way toward the duty desk to ask for Matt. For the first time in a long time, I couldn't see anyone that I knew. Several officers behind the desk were carrying on an animated conversation that my presence did nothing to interrupt. I cleared my throat. Nothing. I coughed. Nothing. I ventured to say, "Excuse me," Still nothing.

"Ellis, long time…" I heard Matt's deep voice behind me and turned to see the handsome, huge black cop. "What's up, man?"

"Lots," I answered. "Got a minute?"

In the old days, I wouldn't even have had to ask for Matt's time in that casual manner. He'd always been happy to see me. But things were different now, and I could tell the second I saw him that my presence was going to be an annoyance unless I kept it really short.

"How's life as Deputy Chief?" I asked.

"Busy, my man. Busy. What can I do for you?"

I expected, as always, to be escorted to his office by a quick wave of his hand toward the stairs to the second floor.

But this time, he just stood there as if he wanted to conduct our business, whatever it might be, right there in the lobby.

"Uh, could we go upstairs?" I asked, feeling awkward, feeling, I soon realized, like some ordinary citizen who had the temerity to disturb the second-in-command of the Toronto police with a personal question of little importance.

"Sure, Ellis, sure."

In the old days, Matt's office had been a homey sort of place with an old wooden table instead of a desk, with antique bookcases lining the walls. It had been small, cozy, almost comfortable, and I used to feel that if I were a homeless person—one of the "clients" Matt used to help in those days, I wouldn't have felt afraid.

But that was all changed now. Matt's new office was huge. A wide window overlooked College Street. There were no books, no pictures on the wall. The desk was a big metal thing. When I sat in the chair in front of it, I had the feeling that Matt was interrogating me before he even sat down some distance beyond me behind it.

Before he said anything, he looked at his watch. "What can I do for you?"

I told him about Queenie.

"Oh, man, I'm sorry. I'm so sorry," he said in a way that reminded me of the old Matt. "She was so good. She was a saint." He shook his head. "I went down to her shelter a number of times. Just to check on her. Just to make sure she was doing okay."

"That was good of you, Matt, I—"

He shook his head again. "She didn't need any help, did she? She ran that place like a clock. And man, that couldn't have been easy with some of the people she had living there!"

"Matt," I said, "that's what I came here about."

"About the shelter? I heard the man who replaced Queenie when she retired is very good. Plus," he looked up at me as if he were about to say something that he knew was bound to upset me, "It's closed now."

Of course I knew this already. "Moved," I said. "It's moved. But that's not what I want to talk to you about."

He hadn't been made deputy chief for nothing. Matt West was a top-notch investigator, a cop's cop. He knew damn well what I wanted to talk about.

"Look," he said, "I know Queenie really cared about all those people she helped. I know she would have been upset about…"

"Yes," I interrupted, "upset about the Juicer. And so am I."

"You? What did you have to do with him? I always thought Queenie was very careful about confidentiality."

"Of course she was. But as you know, Queenie had strong views about everything, and once she made up her mind about something, there was no changing it."

"Made up her mind?" Matt's handsome face was screwed up with, I thought, suspicion. "What exactly has—I mean did—she make up her mind about?"

"She thinks the Juicer was murdered."

I didn't have to say anything more about the case. I was sure that Matt knew every detail. Especially since the minute I mentioned the "victim" by name, I could feel him shut down the way a machine shuts down when you pull the plug.

He was silent for a moment. "Listen," he finally said, "I don't think I have to tell you that the minute PIC gets involved, nobody here—and nobody in the divisions or on the street--is going to tell you anything about him."

"So the PIC is involved?"

Matt was too good a cop, too experienced an officer, to let the completely neutral expression on his face change, but both he and I realized he had just made a mistake. He had just revealed something about "the case" that I hadn't been sure about before. Unfortunately, it wasn't good news for me. How could I find out anything if I couldn't even talk to the people most involved in the Juicer's death?

There was a moment's silence. Matt looked at his watch again.

"Matt," I finally said, "I've got no stake in this myself. I'm sure your people did the job they had to do. I'm sure the Juicer's death was just what the hospital said it was, a heart attack, but Queenie thought otherwise."

He looked at me as if I were crazy. I could almost read his mind. *She's gone. What difference could it possibly make what she thought about a police matter?*

"Matt, she was convinced that the Juicer was murdered. She was so sure, that she made me promise that I would look into the possibility—the certainty." I was afraid to look up at him. "I'm not at all convinced myself, but to honor her last wishes…"

"Forget it," he said. It was his cop voice, his "I'm in charge here and I'm telling you to leave and be about your own business" voice.

But then he softened. "Listen, Ellis," he said, "I can see you're hurting. I know you would have done anything for Queenie. Anybody who knew her felt the same. But sometimes we make promises we just can't keep. I gotta tell you, my friend, this is one of them."

FOUR

I didn't know what to make of what Matt had said and I didn't have one minute to think about it because on the way out of Headquarters, I ran smack into the mysterious woman I'd seen at Queenie's funeral.

Aliana Caterina.

I'd known her since she was a girl. My father, a bricklayer with skills acquired in the old country, had hired her father, Vincenzo Caterina, to help him cater to clients in wealthy neighborhoods of the city who wanted artisans to build their mansions from brick and stone. Nowadays, glass and some sort of pressed-wood chipboard is what's used in the construction of even the finest homes, but in the days of Vince and my father, only the best would do for the best.

Aliana was at least fifteen years younger than me, which put her well into her fifties, but she still looked lovely, a classic Italian-Canadian beauty. The years had strengthened her features, and her thick black hair was now touched, I saw, with silver, but she had remained thin and graceful.

"Ellis," she said with a warm smile and extending her hand, which I noticed at once held her wedding ring, showing she must be a widow, "I'm so happy to run into you!"

"It's been a long time." I wasn't exactly thrilled to see Aliana. I had always felt that she wanted something from me that I wasn't prepared to give. In her work as a journalist, she had followed my decline and had reported on it in her capacity as the chief city correspondent for the *Toronto Daily World* with compassion. Over the long years, I had completely lost track of her as a person, though I read her work from time to time.

"I am so sorry about your loss," she said. "I tried to talk to you the day of the funeral, but of course…"

"It's fine, Aliana. Thank you for your consideration."

She nodded toward the door I'd just exited from and smiled again. "Police business today?" she asked pleasantly.

"Just checking on some unfinished business for Queenie," I said, not really wanting to give Aliana any information. She wasn't an award-winning reporter for nothing. One wrong word and I'd find myself staring up at me from the pages of the *World*.

"Yes." She hesitated, "Listen," she said, "I know there are some questions about the police involvement in the death of that man that was Queenie's client…."

"Still on the prowl, Aliana?" I couldn't help myself. There was a time when nobody knew more about what was happening around the city than she did.

She looked at me with a serious expression. "Ellis," she said, "like you, I haven't been idle in the years since we last talked. I've been in Italy most of the time, but now that Eduardo is dead, I've come back. I'm working on a couple of things here right now."

"Good, Aliana," I said, trying to sound interested.

"I assume you're here to talk to Matt West?"

"Just to say hello," I answered.

"If you're trying to get anything out of him about that client of Queenie's, you're wasting your time, you know that."

I glanced at my watch, just like Matt had glanced at his, and for the same reason. "I'm sorry, Aliana, but I'm on my way to…"

"I can help you. I've got workarounds when it comes to PIC." She reached into her bag. I recognized the label—a top Italian designer. It must have set her back a few thousand euros. She pulled out a business card, finely printed in English and Italian. "Give me a call."

I didn't have anything to hand back to her, not that I wanted to anyway. The last job I'd had was as a judge. After I had been restored to the bench, I had thought it unseemly for a judge to have a business card.

"Yeah, well, thanks," I said. "Nice to see you."

I felt guilty to be happy to get away from her. Aliana had always been a bit of a pest with her constant sniffing around for a story.

But considering how things had just gone with Matt West, if she really had ways of getting around PIC, maybe I shouldn't be so fussy about becoming "friends" with her again.

***

Whether or not I had the help of Matt and Aliana, I decided I'd better get as many of the facts of the case myself as I could. When I think back on this now, I wonder if my "investigation" was just one more way of pushing away my grief. But every time I thought of giving up the whole ridiculous "case", I felt as though I heard Queenie's voice saying, "Don't forget you love me."

To tell the truth, I felt the same way about the city. I knew that to get any information of real value, I'd have to go back to the streets. And the prospect frightened me. There had been a time when I felt like a free man, despite my destitution, just because I could walk the streets without hindrance. Now, even the best neighborhoods, even the most popular and well-peopled shopping plazas, even the schools, for heaven sake, were places where a man could be shot dead on the spot.

By rival gangs who didn't care if a few people got between them and their intended victims. By a gunman who had mistaken an innocent bystander for his real target. By an enraged spouse or a despondent mother. By a bank robber or a person who had decided to snatch the till of the subway token-seller. It was mean and it was mine and a lot of the time, I didn't know how to think about what the city had become. Especially on a September morning when the trees were hinting at the coming autumn, and the Don flowed clean and as pretty as the river that runs through the city of God.

One material thing that Queenie and I did care about was our wardrobe. Before my fall, I had been quite the dandy. I'd had my suits made to measure. And there were a lot of them. I had a separate closet for my shirts: Turnbull & Asser, Thomas Pink… Ties, ascots…

I never went back to dressing like that. But after several years of wearing things that were literally rags, when I returned to respectability, I developed a style that was comfortable and somewhat casual but still appropriate for anything from a dinner at the home of the chief justice to a holiday party at Queenie's shelter.

I tried to choose something nondescript for my foray. A faded worn blue casual jacket, old jeans, scuffed shoes that I had intended to polish the last time I'd worn them, but had apparently failed to do. The thought of actually going out like this made me queasy, but looking at myself in the mirror, I realized that my most worn and least formal clothes would still look better than the clothes of anyone I was likely to meet if I went back to the haunts of the homeless and the bereft.

FIVE

I decided that my first stop should be the place where Queenie's clinic used to be. It had gone through several names during Queenie's reign as supervisor, sometimes because of City policy, sometimes because of donor requests, sometimes because of occasional volatility around Native issues.

As I neared the building on a corner of a street near Parliament and Queen, I saw that the most recent sign for the place had been taken down and was propped up against part of a brick wall that was clearly in the process of demolition. The sign, which was still pristine, said Wholeness Spirit Center. It showed an eagle—a very benign eagle—with wings spread, depicted against a stylized circle with its four quarters representing all the peoples of the earth: red, white, yellow and black.

Seeing this sign and the half-demolished building, I started to cry again. I had to stop this, not only for my own sanity, but because an old man standing on a street corner crying is just asking for it.

Thankfully nobody saw me. I collected myself and started to explore, being careful not to trip on the rubble. Except for a few workers on the site, I didn't see anybody at first.

Then I heard voices coming from down an alley behind the building. I had to climb over bricks and boards and hunks of smashed concrete as well as the spilled contents—including rotting food—of a dumpster that been tipped either by the workers or by people looking for a meal.

After nearly breaking my neck tripping over a bent rusted pipe and a discarded filing-cabinet drawer, I finally came upon four men who were, despite the coolness of the afternoon, sitting on the pavement and leaning their backs against the building next door to the construction.

I didn't know whether I should be flattered that they recognized me at once. I could see that they couldn't possibly have ever been in good enough shape to attend Queenie's funeral, but I was surprised when they offered their clumsy but sincere condolences.

"Sorry, Your Honor," one of them said in a slurred voice, sticking out his hand for me to shake. It was covered with oozing red and yellow sores. I couldn't afford to recoil if I was going to get anywhere in my investigation. I held out my own hand....

"Yeah," said another, rising awkwardly as, I was sure, a sign of respect. "She was a lady and they don't make 'em like that, anymore. That's for damn sure."

I nodded. And I stooped down to meet them on their own level, if only to prevent them from having to make the obviously difficult effort to stand up unsupported.

But I couldn't bring myself to actually sit on the ground, though, in a flash, I remembered how it felt to *sleep* on the pavement without a second thought.

Gradually, respecting the way of the street, I began a slow conversation with these men.

"How's it going down here?" I asked.

They all laughed. "It's goin', man. It's always goin'...."

"You heard about the Juicer?" One of them said.

"Course he did, you idiot," another answered. "He was Queenie's favorite, though only God knows why." He gave the matter some thought. "Still," he finally said, "it's a damn shame what they did to him. He was an asshole, but he didn't deserve to die right when he finally got a home and all...."

"Remember that time he robbed a nun? Took her purse or something?"

All four of the men found this recollection fairly hilarious. "Yeah, and Queenie made him sit with her at her computer until she found the nun's phone number and made him take the thing back to some convent or something like that."

"And," another added to the story, "When the nun saw him coming, she was afraid to answer the door. She didn't have no credit cards in that purse or maybe she already cancelled them.

Anyway, she talked through the door. She told him to keep the purse and whatever was in it. She said she didn't need it anymore."

"Queenie said it was an 'act of charity,'" someone commented. "But I think that nun didn't want to touch anything the dirty old Juicer had touched!"

This, of course, was cause for further laughter, to which I felt obligated to add my own guffaws.

"Yeah, what happened to that Juicer is a damn shame. Way worse than he deserved."

I kept my tone level and my voice low. I also shifted position. My knees were killing me, squatting as I was, "What do you figure really happened?" I said.

For the first time, I felt they were looking at me as if I were some sort of outsider, as if they knew things about this whole "case" that they didn't think it best to let me in on.

"Who knows?" one said, and they all shrugged their shoulders simultaneously as though they'd practiced the gesture.

I waited for a minute. Then I dove right in. "What about the police? Think they had anything to do with it?"

I watched their faces. They didn't look at me or at each other. In fact, they seemed to be staring at the air in front of their eyes.

"There's good and bad," somebody offered.

Silence.

Behind us, construction workers started jackhammering in a way that set me shaking. I wasn't going to be able to stay here much longer. My whole body was starting to revolt. In a minute, it was going to refuse to take the abuse of being cold, hunkered down, cramped and doing something that was rapidly proving useless.

I stood up and so did three of the four men. I got the feeling the noise was bothering them as much as it was bothering me. We started down the alley toward the street, but just as I took a step to avoid the man who was still sitting against the building, I felt him tug on my pant leg. He gestured and I leaned down again.

"Listen," he said, "Queenie thought those cops killed him somehow. You know how many crazy people they killed in the last little while?"

I nodded. There had been three in the very recent past, including one unfortunate young man, armed with a small knife, who had been alone in an empty streetcar surrounded by a cloud of officers, one of whom just let loose and shot him dead on the spot for no reason that anyone was convinced of.

"Seems like the cops are damn scared of the crazies...." I offered, in what I felt was a language not my own. "What's their game, anyway?"

From the rotten teeth and unwashed body rose an odor that I recognized, a certain smell of the street, a combination of long-dried perspiration, rotted food, unwashed everything. I hadn't smelled it in years, but I knew it. It was the smell of desperation, of defeat, of the freedom of never having to worry about being clean again. It made me sad and it made me sick. I pulled away, but I believed he had something to tell me, and I leaned down again toward his garbage-can mouth.

Too late. His eye caught what mine did. At the entrance to the alley slumped another male homeless person—not one of the ones who'd been there earlier. This man was dressed in even scuzzier rags than the four, but the minute he showed up, my man shut up.

Because he knew, as I did, too, that this was no homeless person. This was a plain-clothes cop.

SIX

I left the alley, thinking I might as well just go home, but old habits die hard and I found myself wandering the alleys near Queen Street.

I was surprised how little had changed in some ways. I could still tell the spots that would be good for curling up for a night's sleep in a doorway if it came to that.

But for the most part, the city had been transformed in the ten or fifteen years in which I, myself, had been transformed.

Gone were the old wooden porches that a rat or a man could crawl under for shelter on a night when it was too rainy to sleep on the sidewalk. The porches were gone. The houses they had graced were gone. Whole streets where those houses had stood—sometimes for nearly a hundred years—were gone, too.

In their place stood what in another city would be called skyscrapers. Here they were just called condos. They rose from the sidewalks in crystal magnificence, as though ordinary concrete—let alone wood or even stone—were not good enough for them to be made of.

Their ground floors boasted—according to signs on the not-yet-completed buildings—that the "best in retail" was soon to arrive. Which meant that the little neighborhood shops, often run by families, the skip-out-at-any-hour-for-a-carton-of-milk stores, the newspaper vendors, the lottery-ticket sellers, were gone forever, replaced by slick international fashion outlets.

There were no doorways to huddle up in in these buildings, but even so, there were plenty of doormen standing around just in case....

As I walked, I could feel the cool wind of the coming autumn on my cheeks. It suddenly occurred to me that I had forgotten to shave for the past few days. I was stunned, embarrassed. But then I thought that not shaving now, when my beard was nothing but white fuzz, wasn't same as it had been when I'd had a good, dark beard. Who would even notice my face now?

And as I thought this, that awful feeling at the bottom of my stomach came back. The feeling that was starting to tell me a hundred times a day that Queenie would have noticed how I looked, that Queenie would have understood my consternation at seeing our old city of wood and brick, like the bricks my father laid, disappear.

Maybe I staggered. I don't know. But I caught myself, breathed deeply and walked on.

So, then, autumn. I remembered the preparations we used to make on the street and in the valley for the coming of winter. I had now lived in a proper apartment long enough to have forgotten a lot of the scrambling for cardboard and plastic and discarded cloth that had filled our October and early November days.

The thought reminded me, though, that I needed to see Jeffrey, my son, and to check on his plans for the winter in the Village in the Valley, the unique homeless shelter that he and I had built together.

As I meditated on these things, I began to lose track of where I was. Suddenly, I heard my name. I turned to see two men whom I recognized as volunteers at a downtown food bank, one of the many projects that Queenie supported and that gave jobs to her "graduates," as she liked to call former clients who had beat the street.

"Ellis," one of the men said, "I wanted to talk to you at Queenie's funeral but you were surrounded." I'd met this man before. He was about forty, strapping, handsome, but he had a mark that ran from the edge of his left eyebrow all the way to his chin. I knew it had to be from a long-ago knife battle, a constant reminder of his past. "She was wonderful and I'm so sorry we lost her so soon."

"Thanks, Sam," I said to him, taking his hand and noting the power of his handshake. "I miss her."

He nodded. After a moment's silence, he said, "What are you doing down here?"

"I'm just checking a few things out," I said. "You have time for a coffee?"

"Sure. Just got off shift." He nodded toward his companion. "Mind if he joins us?"

The other man fell into step beside us. I didn't know him, but I figured if he and Sam had known Queenie, the chances were that they had known the Juicer, too. As far as getting information about him, my little trip downtown had been an exercise in maximum futility. Maybe these two had something I could use. The thought made me a little nervous, as if I were falling back into my old mystery-solving mode. As I said, I didn't want to go there.

As it turned out, it only took a couple of coffees to get both these two to open up.

"A lot of people had the wrong idea about the Juicer," Sam offered without my even asking. "He was big—not muscles—fat big and," he smiled, "I'm sorry to say pretty ugly. A lot of guys think it's cool to be bald today. But the Juicer, he had been bald since he was a teenager. Something wrong with his head."

The other guy snorted, but he didn't say anything.

"Anyway," Sam went on, "he was mostly completely non-violent." He smiled, "Some of the women at the shelter used to call him 'Pussy Cat'. He'd pretend to be mad, but you could tell he liked the attention."

"I heard he was a favorite with Queenie," I said. "How did the other people who lived at the shelter take that? Do you think they were resentful?"

"Resentful? What do you mean?"

"Well," I answered. "Maybe they figured the Juicer was getting special treatment. Maybe they thought that Queenie was being unfair." The very thought of that made the words stick in my mouth, but if I was going through all this trouble to get information, I knew I'd just better keep trying to get it.

"No." Sam shook his head. "Nobody ever thought that Queenie was unfair. She just happened to bring out the best in the ugly old Juicer and other people caught on and treated him better because of it."

"What happened to change things?"

"Them damn homeless tickets," Sam's companion piped up.

"Homeless tickets?"

"Yes," Sam said. "Homeless tickets. What happens is the cops can give out tickets to people just for being on the street—just for having no place to live. I don't know how much each ticket is for. Thank God I never got one myself. But I do know they mount up. And some cops give a ticket every day, seeing as a person is homeless every day…"

"Damn lousy shit-eating bags of crap…" Sam's friend offered. Presumably his view of the Toronto police.

Sam smiled, "Something like that," he said.

I had never heard of homeless tickets. I decided to ask Jeffrey about them as soon as I got down to the valley.

"So," I asked, "what did the homeless tickets have to do with the Juicer?"

"The thing about the homeless tickets is, as I said, they mount up. When they get to a certain number, the cops hand them over to a collection agency, you know, people whose business is to put the screws to people who owe money. And those collection agents are pretty scary dudes."

"Damn assholes," his friend added.

"What happened with the Juicer is this. He lived in the shelter for a long time—maybe more than a year. Queenie helped him to fill out an application for what they call 'permanent housing'. Nothing special about that. It was something the shelter workers did for clients all the time. Only for the Juicer, Queenie filled it out herself. I know this because he bragged about it.

"And maybe that's the reason he found an apartment he could live in with government help and all that right away. The old guy was so excited we thought he'd piss himself."

"Probably did," came the chorus.

"He went down to see the place with Queenie and they came back to the shelter to start planning about when he could move there and how he could get some furniture and where he could buy groceries and things like that. You could just tell how excited the Juicer was."

"How do you know all this?" I asked. "I thought you worked at the food bank?"

"Right. I do. But I still did volunteer work at the shelter. You got to give back…."

"Of course. So what happened next?"

"Queenie and the Juicer went back to the new apartment one more time. When they got back to the shelter, the shit hit the fan. There was a man waiting for them. He was from the collection agency the cops had given the Juicer's homeless tickets to. They told the Juicer that if he didn't give them eight thousand dollars, they were going to turn him over to the police and that he was going to end up in jail."

I was stunned. "Can this be possible?"

"Check it out, dude," said the companion.

"Unfortunately yes," said Sam. "Actually, a lot of us figured the Juicer might have been in jail before. You never know. Somebody said he'd been held by the cops a couple of times in the not too distant past. Again, not a big surprise. You have to expect to meet a con or two in our line of business."

Both he and his friend laughed. They had a dark sense of humor as did everybody who beat the street in my experience.

"That's when the Juicer lost it," Sam said. "He went completely berserk. He was screaming and dancing around like a total nut bar. It got so bad they had to call 911. They showed up right away and hauled him off in an ambulance. And that's how he ended up in the hospital and a few days later tried to escape and went even wilder and got beaten to death by four cops."

"Damn buggers."

SEVEN

It was a sweet early autumn night, and as I walked from the garage to the door of my apartment building, I could feel a breeze that seemed to rise out of the valley behind the building as if the river down below were breathing.

I was totally exhausted from the first day of my investigation. My first real attempts at keeping my promise to my gone love. What had I learned? Nothing as far as I could see.

I took off my "work clothes" and threw them in the laundry, making sure the machine was set to the highest temperature. Then I took a scalding shower. At first I felt clean. Then he I felt guilty. I glanced around our lovely living room with its four walls of bookcases, its mahogany tables, its leather chairs. Who did I think I had become?

I didn't try to answer that question. Instead, I decided to check the messages on my phone and if there was nothing pressing, just to go to bed.

"Dad, you've got to return my messages. Either email me or phone, but I've got to know how you're doing and where you are. Call me as soon as you get this, or I'll worry all night long."

That was Ellen, my daughter. To tell the truth, I was afraid of her. She treated me like an ancient. She acted as though I were in my nineties instead of what I really was, which was seventy-one. And in full possession of my faculties. I had a horrid image of her storming my apartment, kidnapping me and placing me in some facility—or worse—in her house. The only consolation there was her wonderful son, Angelo, my namesake and heir.

The second message was from Jeffrey. Short and to the point. Jeffrey, unlike just about anybody else in our family, was no talker. "Call me, Dad , or come down."

Both of my children were constantly warning me that if I didn't carry my cell phone with me at all times, some dire happening was sure to do me in and they would have no way of knowing that I was in trouble.

But to tell the truth, I never felt comfortable having valuables close at hand when I was out. This meant that the pocket I felt compelled to use for the phone was so secure, so inaccessible that by the time I dug out the phone, whoever had been calling had long since given up and hung up, presumably in disgust.

There was a third call. Aliana Caterina. Wanting to talk to me for some reason. I erased the message before I'd made a note of her number.

I cooked a bit of pasta added tomato sauce from a can and sprinkled it with grated parmesan. I ate a few forkfuls but my mind started to wander and I more or less forgot about the food.

Queenie and I always ate simply. She didn't cook much and the few things she did make were basic Canadian dishes: hamburgers, macaroni and cheese, baked chicken pieces. Every once in a while, I made a good, big Italian meal for her, which she consumed with enthusiastic delight. I had learned to cook Italian food not from my mother but from my first wife who was by no means Italian but who had loved my mother and had dogged her steps in the kitchen—which made my mother inexpressibly happy.

When I was still spending a lot of time in court during my "restored" legal career, I often had to go back to the courthouse in the evening. And Queenie worked lots of nights, too. Sometimes overnight. But we had managed quite a number of suppers at home. How precious those plain ordinary meals had become in my recollection.

I had to remind myself to get back to the supper at hand, but my appetite had deserted me. I ended up putting most of it in the fridge, where, I noticed with chagrin, it joined other suppers that I had not been able to get through.

I thought again about how little I knew about this "case". I intended to go to bed, but instead found myself on the internet. I inadvertently ended up at Queenie's obituary when I tried to look up the shelter where she had worked. That drove me into a few rounds of Angry Birds. Of course I well realized that not only are there new games to play, but also internet challenges more in keeping with my age, my education, and my profound disgust with the idea of wasting time during these, my declining years!

While I was idly confronting the birds, a thought occurred to me. Whether or not they had actually killed the Juicer, there had been four officers involved in subduing him in front of the mental hospital. This I knew from the newspaper reports published the day after the incident, reports that I had just read on the net. As I said, the story had quickly moved off the front page, and as I had been led to suspect, subsequent stories gave scant information and always seemed to end with the remark that further details were unavailable due to the possible involvement of PIC.

So, four officers. If they were four honest officers, four people determined to do their job, then presumably, all four would have the same intent, that is, they would have made the same deliberate choice to do whatever they did, a choice based on their training, training designed to control their reaction to dangerous situations.

I well knew that officer safety was the first concern in any takedown. That made perfect sense. An injured officer can do no good. Besides, no one is *required* to give his life for his job. So, four officers in danger, four legitimate choices to stop an aggressor from seriously or fatally wounding a cop.

But suppose one or more of the four had his or her own agenda, their own reason for fatally taking down the Juicer?

The more I thought about this, the more my mind began to swing into the habit of legal thinking. Queenie wasn't a judge and she wasn't a lawyer, but she was no fool. I was certain that she knew that intent was the crux of homicide. You could, God forbid, kill a man by accident. But you couldn't murder him by accident. Of course, in an individual case, that fact might become a technicality, and many a day was spent in court arguing about such an issue. But Queenie had to have thought that one of those officers had intended to kill her patient. Hence her conviction that there was a killer. Hence her making me promise that I would find that killer.

Did one of the four intend to kill the homeless man?
Which one and why?

EIGHT

I finally found the Wholeness Spirit Centre on the internet. And yes, it had moved. I was surprised to find out where.

When I checked out the location on Google maps, I saw that it seemed to be in an office building much closer to the downtown core than the old shelter had been.

On the one hand, this seemed strange, since the new location was right on Bay Street in the heart of the business district, which meant it could only be a multi-story office building. Anyone using the clinic would run into well-dressed business types who might not look kindly on the street people who would frequent the service. On the other hand, the business district was empty at night—just when the denizens of the street were most active, and in winter, most in need of shelter.

There were two other reasons why the shelter might have relocated to the business district. It was now considered socially acceptable to show that you were helping those less fortunate, which, mercifully resulted in financial help from the fashionable. And it was also possible that the shelter had secured corporate funding from a charitable trust set up by a large company.

So the location was possibly less surprising than the next fact I learned, which was that the center now had an official "Executive Director," and that that person was none other than E. Jonathan Dirk, previously known as the obnoxious thorn in my side, the ubiquitous, recently cleaned-up Johnny Dirt!

I had to hand it to the man, he certainly had a lot of experience that would qualify him for the job.

He and I went way back and my memories of him were not happy ones. I couldn't exactly remember the day I met him, which is no surprise. Until I gave up drinking, there were lots of days I couldn't recall. But I did seem to remember that once, during a hurricane-like storm that had ravaged Toronto, I had helped pull Johnny out of the Don River. If, however, I had done Johnny any favors, there would be no use trying for payback, because one thing I knew for certain was that from the start, he and I had nearly come to blows every time we encountered each other. Johnny seemed to harbor the notion that I, because of my fine education and my previous "job", lacked the qualifications to be a real street person. "Street cred," as it's known. In a word, he looked down on me.

Unlike me, he apparently came from a long line of reprobates who had passed their legacy of presuming upon the kindness of strangers for a livelihood down to Johnny. He had always seemed proud of that. It was all he had to be proud of.

Until now...

I actually had to make an appointment with his secretary to see him!

I figured he had to know a great deal about the Juicer and maybe about those four cops and what involvement they may have had with the man before his untimely demise.

***

The next day, I made my way downtown to Bay Street. I had to pay $30 to park for two hours, of which I used up a goodly portion by having to search among the marble and glass skyscrapers to find the right building. Even having the address didn't help because of the complexity of numbering the buildings, not to mention the suites.

The idea that Queenie's shelter now occupied a suite made me dizzy.

About as dizzy as it made me to look up toward the gigantic cranes that lifted their steel arms above construction sites that seemed to sit on every corner. I tried to remember how Bay street had looked twenty years before when I had been a judge the first time, but I couldn't get past the image before my eyes, which was of a city reaching toward the sky with nothing presently at its feet but piles of rubble behind wooden hoardings that tried, but failed, to hide the destruction of the old city.

Finally, I found the office building that now housed Wholeness Spirit.

34

With some difficulty in using the building's directory and the multi-stage elevators, I finally located the shelter, designated a "clinic" on the electronic directory board. I found that it was in the basement, which reassured me for some obscure reason.

The place was very clean, very bright, painted in white and light yellow with posters on the wall showing, presumably, street people who had "made it". There were a few clients waiting to be served. Even they look clean and bright!

I gave my name to the receptionist, who recognized me. It took me a minute to realize that she had been one of Queenie's most desperate clients, a young woman who had never lived anywhere except in other people's homes, their basements, their garages, their backyards when it wasn't winter.

"Susanna," I said, "You look wonderful!"

"Yes, Your Honor." She smiled shyly, "Off the drugs. On the job." She pointed to one of the posters where that slogan was prominently displayed.

"Good for you!"

"Thanks. Take a seat…"

I was kept waiting a long time, imagining the parking police hovering about my vehicle, but eventually I was summoned into Johnny's office.

"Hello, Ellis. Come in. Have a seat."

As though his surroundings had greatly affected his manners and his manner toward me, Johnny was remarkably polite. "I don't think I told you that I'm real sorry for your loss. I miss Queenie a lot, myself, so I hope you're getting along okay…"

"Thanks, Johnny, uh John, uh Jonathan…"

Johnny Dirt laughed his old hoarse guffaw. "I'll always be Johnny to you, and you'll always be a river rat to me," he said. Then he adjusted his facial expression. "No hard feelings, eh?"

"I should think not," I offered stiffly, and we both laughed, finally breaking the ice.

"What can I do for you?"

I cleared my throat. "Johnny, I did something I've come to regret."

He looked shocked, but then he smiled as if he were used to my inflated way of talking.

"What?"

"I made a promise I don't think I can keep."

"Hey, man, we all do that. Who was it to—this promise?"

"Queenie."

"Shit."

"It gets worse. I made it to her only a few minutes before she died."

"A death-bed promise," Johnny said softly, as though he'd read books and seen films that I was sure he hadn't.

"Yes."

"What did you promise?"

I took a minute. I wanted to say just the right thing in the right way. I wanted information and I was sure that Johnny had it, but to be fair, I figured he was probably mourning Queenie, too, in his own way. I didn't want to press him, just as I didn't want people to press me.

"What I promised," I began slowly, "was to find out who murdered the Juicer."

"Murdered," Johnny said. It wasn't a question. "So she told you that the Juicer was murdered?"

"Yes."

"Look, man," Johnny said after a moment's silence. "Queenie had what I guess you'd call a different take on the Juicer." He smiled, "Anybody tell you why we all called him that?"

"Of course I thought it referred to drugs," I answered, "but I heard something about orange juice."

"Yeah, you got it. The thing is, living with people in a shelter, well sometimes it ain't—it's not—so different from living in a family or something like that."

"Yes."

"So people got their little habits and all. The Juicer, he started every morning with a glass of orange juice that came right from an orange—not from a carton or anything like that."

"He made orange juice from an orange?" I hadn't heard about that in a good long time.

"No," Johnny said carefully, "Queenie made it for him."

I felt a ridiculous pang of jealousy. Queenie had never made orange juice for me!

As if he could read my thoughts, Johnny smiled. "She wasn't no cook," he said. "She stayed out of the kitchen. Plus, we had lots of volunteers for that. But the Juicer, he was sure he couldn't start his day unless he had that juice." He paused, "I think it was just one more way that Queenie made him feel special, and that was real important because it calmed him right down."

"He needed calming down?"

"Yeah. Just about every day. See, he had this problem—" Johnny smiled again as if he couldn't help himself, "Actually, he had a lot of problems, but anyway, he had this one big problem which was that he couldn't stand anybody to touch him."

"Except Queenie?" I was getting that jealous feeling again.

"Oh no. Queenie was the best at never touching him, not on purpose, not by accident, never at all. That, and the fact she was always so nice to him, was probably what made him act so good whenever she was around."

"So what happened if somebody touched him?"

"Well," Johnny said, "it didn't happen that much. Because he had this weird way of, I don't know, staying away from people. Like if he talked to you, he stood really far away. And if you accidentally got too close, man, he let you have it."

"You mean he hit you or…"

"No. He didn't need to hit you. All he had to do was yell at you. The way he went at it was worse than being hit. He could think of things to say to you and about you that just made you sick."

"Like what?"

Johnny shook his head. "I don't really want to say," he answered.

I was stunned. I would never have expected such delicacy on the part of my old enemy.

"Johnny," I said, "I went down to where the shelter used to be the other day…"

He shook his head. "It's a mess down there."

"Yes. Anyway, I went down there and there were a couple of people hanging around—"

He interrupted, "Yeah, there's people that still go there even though there's nothing there anymore but a pile of ripped-up concrete. Strange!"

"Strange, yes. And sad. But, as I was saying, a few guys were hanging around and they told me that the Juicer went ballistic when somebody showed up from a collection agency. That's when he got hauled off to the mental hospital."

"Don't you mean the mental restoration sanctuary?" Johnny said, and we both laughed.

"There's nothing to laugh about, I guess," I finally said. "No matter what really happened, the Juicer ended up dead."

"Yes," Johnny said. "Yes he did. He definitely did."

We were both silent for a moment. Then I took a deep breath and got down to my real reason for the visit. Johnny must have figured I was there for more than a friendly chat.

"Listen," I began, "I've got to do something about that promise I made. I've at least got to find out as much as I can about what really happened to that guy. Maybe everybody hated him except Queenie. That's a lot of suspects…."

"Suspects? Man, you sound like a cop!"

"No. But I heard there were four cops involved, four cops who took the Juicer down outside the mental hospital the night he lost it."

"Yeah. I heard that, too. Four of 'em. I'm not sure what they were doin' at the hospital because three of them been on duty near the shelter lots of times, and that's in a different neighborhood."

"Does that mean you knew them?" I asked, a little too eagerly.

But Johnny didn't seem to notice. He was being surprisingly co-operative. As if he respected Queenie's request. "Yeah," he said. "The one I seen most often is a guy named Mark Hopequist.

About thirty-five. Probably only been a cop for five, ten, years. Might have been something else before. Seems like the kind of guy who always wants people to like him."

"Not your typical cop."

"Not by a long shot," Johnny said, "and I do mean shot!"

It was a bad joke.

"I think they been moving him back and forth between things," Johnny said.

"What does that mean?"

"Well, you know, he's not that scary. Not like most of the cops these days. So they put him on youth work and work with the homeless—that sort of thing. That's probably why I used to see him around the shelter. There was another thing about him, too, another thing you don't get in cops, at least as far as they show it."

"What's that?"

"He was religious."

"Religious? What do you mean?"

"Sometimes he said things that came from the Bible. Like quotes or something. And once I caught him and Queenie together. I'm pretty sure they were praying."

"Praying at work?"

"You got it."

Somehow the idea of two people getting caught praying at work was more shocking than other accusations that might be made against them.

"There was rumors, too."

Johnny was on a roll now. As if he'd been wanting to talk about these things for a long time and had finally found someone to tell them to, surprising though the thought was to me.

"Yeah. You know, like gossip. People said things about Hopequist."

"What, for instance?"

"They said that he had to take time off once to spend a few weeks in the looney bin."

"Why?"

"Who knows?" Johnny shrugged. "People would say that about any cop who's sensitive." He made a face that let me know what he personally thought about people who were sensitive.

"What about the others—the two other cops that you knew?"

"Know," Johnny said. "I still know them. And they're a lot easier to know than that Hopequist weirdo. I mean person." He smiled, "I gotta watch what I say about people now that I got this position."

"Sure. So the other two, who are they?"

"Ted Downs and Al Brownette. Typical pain-in-the-butt cop types. Ted's an old guy—but not as old as you." He smirked. In the good old Johnny Dirt way. "He's old and he's wanting to retire from his life-long job as a body-and-fender man."

"A cop not afraid to use the old billy-club when called upon to do so?"

"You got it. And the other guy, Al, he's Ted's suck-buddy."

"Uh, what exactly is that?" I asked. Of course I had a pretty good idea of what Johnny meant, but I wanted to keep him talking. This little interview was proving a lot more fruitful that the one with Matt at police Headquarters or the scattered conversation with the men at the construction site.

"A suck buddy? That's a guy that hangs around with a more important guy and spends all his time sucking up to him in order to impress him for some reason or other."

"So who was this, uh, buddy?"

"Al? He's like those cops they got on TV now. Always frowning—like a smile would break his ugly face or something." He shook his head. "Head shaved. A lot of muscles. Hand always at his side like he's just about ready to pull his baton—or his gun."

I nodded. "Yeah, I know the type. Pain in the butt." I was trying to sound tough, which was ridiculous. Even in my most dire days, the manner of speaking I had acquired in my education and my work on the bench had stayed with me. "What about the other one. There were four, right?"

"Right. But I don't know nothing about that last one. And I told you everything I got on the other three. So, if you're going to try to track them down and talk to them or something like that, well, I gotta tell you, you're on your own, your Honor."

He snickered. And the door to Johnny's willingness to help slammed shut.

NINE

I made my way home along Eglinton Avenue, a major thoroughfare that runs east and west across what used to be the top of the city but what is now practically the bottom. The usual eighteen-hour rush hour was starting to peak now that it was two in the afternoon.

I live in a renovated apartment building, what they call in this city, a "low-rise". I own the place and I've had it restored to what it was when it was built sometime in the late sixties. The best thing about it is that it sits right at the edge of Wigmore ravine.

Toronto is a city of ravines, river valleys really. There are three great rivers, the Humber, the Don, and the Rouge that run through the city. Though high-rise office buildings and thousands of giant glass condos have taken over the cityscape in recent years, the rivers retain a margin of wilderness around themselves. When I lived as a vagrant in the valley of the Don, there were days, a lot of days, when I avoided setting my eyes on any building whatsoever, though high above, the houses and apartment buildings that surround Wigmore, looked down on me, a fugitive and squatter at their feet.

Of course, being the owner of the building, I had the best apartment. It had been two and was now combined into one. It was on the top floor, the eighth, and it looked out over the river and the ravine the way a stately home of England looks out on its park. Only my park wasn't a huge garden. It was a wild place with vegetation untamed since the last lone farmer had given up trying to subdue it a hundred years before.

I owned not only my building, but also a bit of land down in the valley. How I came to have the money for my real estate ventures is another story for another day, but suffice it to say, that I took advantage of the fact that a few acres of Wigmore remained in private hands—now my hands—and the rest belonged to the city.

On my land, I and my son Jeffrey had, over the course of the past few years, built a modest retreat that we called The Village in the Valley. We—Jeffrey really—ran it as a refuge for homeless people who didn't want to live in shelters in downtown neighborhoods.

Despite actually being at the heart of the city, the village was isolated, cut off by the steep walls of the valley and inaccessible except to those who knew the way of the river and its meanderings.

The site consisted of about a dozen one-room wooden buildings surrounding a central structure that had showers and other washroom amenities as well as a kitchen and a large room intended as a gathering place, though the denizens of the valley never gathered there. The main reason many of them had taken to living in the valley in the first place was to get away from other people.

I scrambled down the path from Eglinton to the site.

"Dad, I've been worried about you!" Jeffrey ran his fingers through his long blonde hair. He looked nothing like my daughter Ellen, who had inherited the creamy coloring of her Italian ancestors. "Where's your cell phone?"

I shrugged. Jeffrey clicked his tongue in mild disgust.

"How are we doing down here?" I asked him, surveying the village with a glance. "Looks good...."

Jeffrey smiled slightly. Another thing he had not inherited was the propensity to display a lot of emotion. "It's good, Dad. No fights. Nobody's sick. Nobody nosing around." He hesitated.

"What?"

"I'm a little worried about our people having to spend another winter without proper insulation. And if there's a freeze-up, I'm not sure how our water supply is going to handle it."

Jeffrey was adept at dealing with the city, the province and the feds, the main sources of our funding, aside from the foundation I'd been able to set up. We'd had arguments about private funding from outside sources, but I never brought the issue up if I didn't have to.

"Have you heard anything about the municipal grant application?"

"No. Of course I'm hoping that the city will come through the way it has over the past three years…."

"Keep me posted."

"Sure."

I reached out and put my hand on his shoulder. Jeffrey smiled that small smile again. "You keep your phone where you can get at it. I need to know that you're okay, especially right now."

Of course he was referring to Queenie.

"And I'm right down here if you need me. Two minutes away."

"Right."

I turned and made my way through the trees toward a second path, one that led directly up out of the valley and into the parking lot at the rear of my building.

When I got to the top, I looked out over the expanse of the ravine. Sometimes I still had nightmares about my years of living rough down there. I would dream that it was winter but that I had no clothes—literally--and that I crouched naked in drifts of snow that blew from the river into the snow-laden branches of the trees. I always woke up from those dreams shivering and shaking, even if it was the middle of summer.

But in the real world, I had little to fear from the coming of winter anymore, except ice on the sidewalks and other old-man things. So I could enjoy the magnificent array before me—the autumn trees, just beginning to turn. No. I had nothing to fear. Except of course, failure to keep my promise.

When I got to my apartment, I found my cell phone sitting on a table by the door, a table on which I always put things that I was supposed to remember to take with me when I went out.

There were two calls. Ellen again. I'd have to call her later when I had time to listen to her complain about my not keeping in touch.

Aliana again. This time I listened to her message.

"Ellis, hope you're okay. I was expecting to hear from you. I've got some information I think you might find helpful."

She sounded professional. Her voice was smooth and the years had deepened it. She sounded like a woman who had wrangled a thousand interviews from recalcitrant strangers who had warmed in the end and given her the great story she was always after.

The message went on, "I heard you're asking around concerning the four officers who were involved in the apprehension of that homeless man who subsequently died. Well, you may be interested to know that I can give you quite a bit of information about one of the cops. Call me."

She didn't say which cop.

But this time, I was careful to write her number down.

TEN

She wasn't there when I called, which, I have to admit, gave me a feeling of relief. But I left her a message asking her to email me with a suggested time and place and she did and I emailed her back and agreed to meet her for coffee the following afternoon.

Perhaps for some sentimental reason, she chose a coffee shop that had been in Little Italy before Little Italy had disappeared altogether. The shop was run by a nice couple from Pakistan now. And all who wanted to preserve their Italian essence in the middle of our multicultural city had moved north to the suburb of Woodbridge.

The Toronto Italians weren't bricklayers anymore. They were property developers, among other impressive occupations. Woodbridge was a model of an Italy that their grandparents had remembered with the blind fondness of the dispossessed. It sported newly-constructed Italy-like buildings like the campanile— the bell-tower that was the signature of the enclave. I had heard that you had to prove that you were really Italian to live in Woodbridge, but I wasn't sure about that.

Anyway. Aliana. As I may have said, I had known her since she had been a little girl sometimes coming to work with her father, Vince, who was my father's right-hand-man on the bricklaying jobs that provided our livelihood. I was a young man then so I had no interest in little girls, especially pesky, smart ones like Aliana. Sometimes-- lucky times-- she ignored me altogether. But other times she followed me around, peppering me with questions. How had my father learned to make designs in the driveways and the garden patios with bricks? How come our trucks were old and ugly when other people had brand new ones? What did it mean that I was going to go to university? Did they have a lot of books there? Did they have any girls there?

I lost track of Aliana for a very long time. I became a lawyer, then a judge. I married and had my two children. During all those successful years, I never saw her, though I gradually became aware of her reputation as a journalist, eventually, an award-winning writer.

And then, during the time of my troubles, somehow she had come back. Granted I was a great story: Prominent judge hits the skids. During my days of shame, she was my constant chronicler, trying, I imagine now, to touch the hearts of her many readers with the story of a man who had once lived as decently as they did, but now lived as a homeless vagrant in the ravines. It could happen to anyone, Aliana seemed to be telling her readers. It could happen to you.

Aliana remained faithful to her old friend and sensitive to the desperation I faced. In a sense, in those years, she wrote my life.

But she had always seemed to want something from me, something I just couldn't give. And when, at last, I'd returned to respectability, restored in the practice of law and eventually invited to return to the bench, Aliana had taken off with no goodbye

***

Preparing for our meeting, I surprised myself by taking some care with my clothing. I had never returned to the sartorial splendor of my pre-fall days, the made-to-measure shirts, the silk ties, the suits that filled two whole closets. But as I looked at myself in the mirror I felt almost proud. I still looked like a man of consequence. My gray hair was now pretty much white, and my face etched by the finger of time, but considering what I'd been through over all the years since Aliana had first set eyes on me, I thought, *Not bad. Not bad at all.*

And then, without warning, an image of Queenie smiling up at me and telling me that I was darn handsome for a bum, took my breath away.

***

The years had not been unkind to Aliana: still slim, still bright-eyed, still possessed of an amazingly thick head of black hair—now a little streaked with silver but not much.

She rose from the small table at which she'd been waiting and extended her hand, which I took in mine for only a second.

"The last few weeks must have been unbearably difficult," she said, gesturing for me to take the chair opposite her. "I know that when Ed died, I drifted in and out for some time…."

"But," she said smiling and, with a graceful motion of her fingers, summoning the boy who was serving the tables, "you look quite wonderful."

I smiled, not knowing exactly what to say. It occurred to me that this was going to be going on for some time. People telling me I was taking Queenie's death like a trooper and fighting the urge to tell them I was glad they were fooled but I wish they would mind their own business.

"Thank you."

"It's been a long time," she said. "And I've been away most of it."

"In the Middle East, I understand." I hadn't really paid much attention, but I knew she'd become a foreign correspondent for the *Daily World*. I wondered how much chit-chat we'd have to go through before we got to the point.

"But I'm home now."

"Still looking for a story?" I tried to keep my voice light.

"Sure." She reached across the table but stopped short of actually touching me. "A couple of stories, actually. But don't worry, you're not one of them."

"Thank God," I answered, and we both laughed, which broke the ice a little.

"Look, Ellis, I don't have time to waste and I'm sure you don't either. I called you because I heard from one of my sources on the street that you've been asking about those four cops that are accused of somehow being involved in the death of that wild homeless man."

"Wild? Is that what you've heard? That he was wild?"

"Something like that. And I also heard that you're going back to solving murder cases."

"Listen, Aliana, I don't know where you get your information but…"

"Sure you know. I get it the same place you get your information—from people who have the facts." She glanced out the window. The street was busy with pedestrians. They certainly didn't look Italian, the way they would have when I was a boy. "I'm not trying to do you any favors, Ellis.…"

"Of course you are," I answered, trying to be nice, though Aliana was smart enough to read my mind. The rest of that sentence, the part I didn't say out loud was *and if you do me a favor, I'm going to have to do one for you in return.*

She didn't respond. She drew in her breath as if she were going to give me a little speech or something. I was alarmed, until I started to listen.

"I know you're trying to get information about those four cops. I've got quite a bit of source material on the topic of police getting out of control. You may recall that I did a series on the topic a few months ago."

"Oh, of course…" I answered as if I had read every word, which I had not. "But…"

"But what?"

"Is that ethical? I mean you got that information when you were under contract to the World. Sharing it with me might breach confidentiality—at the very least."

She stared at me in astonishment. "You really never change do you? Still the little Catholic boy afraid to commit a sin."

"I didn't know you kept track of my conscience along with keeping track of everything else about me, Aliana."

We were both silent for an embarrassing amount of time.

"Ellis," she finally said, "my sources and my research belong to me. All my career I've taken measures to safeguard the independence of my reporting. If I hadn't done that, I wouldn't have been able to cover the things I have written about. Including you. You may have forgotten it after all these years, but you and I had an agreement. We agreed that anything I learned about you would be available for my use without restriction? Do you remember that?"

Now she was talking to me as though I were a child, as though I were the destroyed man I'd been when she'd written those articles about me and published them in the *World*.

I pushed my doubts aside. "What can you tell me?" I asked her. "What did you bring me here to tell me? What have you got on those cops and how did you get it?"

"Whoa! Not so fast." She looked me straight in the eye, pinning me. I imagined it was a technique she used to calm down an interviewee. It worked. I took a breath and sat back.

"You were right about the favor," she said.

I felt the old alarm bells getting ready to go off.

But she sat back too, and I could see she was now all business. "I'm working on a new series for the *World*. It's about gang members and the effect of their involvement on their families."

"Sounds interesting," I commented. What I didn't say was, *why do you think this has anything to do with me?*

She nodded. "In the course of my research, I've come across a girl—a precocious twelve-year-old. She's got three brothers who are suspected of being deeply involved in gang activity. I feel that with the right approach, I can interview this girl and get information that nobody else will have, but to do so, I feel I need your help."

"My help?" I asked with surprise, but she didn't seem to hear me. She just kept on talking.

"If you'll help me, I'll help you."

"How? I don't understand why…"

"The thing is, one of the four cops you're interested in, Mark Hopequist, knows this girl. He worked with her when he was assigned to youth detail." She met my eyes again and I was sure she saw the spark of interest there. "You know about that, right? You know that Hopequist moved around quite a bit?"

"I've heard something like that."

"Well, it's true."

"But I'm not sure how you think I could…"

"When I left Canada a couple of years ago, I heard that you had been named as the Judge of Orphans. Now that's an assignment that would have put you front and center in legal issues having to do with the lives of children whose status before the law was uncertain."

The intensity of her conversation was increasing as though she were revving up. Instead of being put off, I started to find her almost charming. I started to see the little girl I'd once known. *"Where do they get the bricks? Do they make them in a factory? Where is it?"*

"Aliana," I said, "You're such an excellent researcher and always so on top of things that it cannot have escaped your attention, even if you left Canada, that I never accepted that position, that I turned it over to another judge, a very promising young female."

"Cabrini, Capelli… Something like that. Sure I remember. I think you said at the time that you felt you needed to get back into full familiarity with the law before you could accept such a difficult and demanding role. Commendable."

She looked at me with admiration. I cleared my throat and resumed the conversation. "So my experience dealing with young people may not be as extensive as you imagine."

"Nonsense. Why would you have been chosen in the first place if you didn't have special skills and experience with the young?"

A server brought us cappuccinos. Aliana stirred hers with some care, pushing aside the little biscotti that came with it. "Why do they call it biscotti?" she asked. "As though it were plural. Why isn't it biscotto?"

I had to laugh. "I don't know Aliana. You have always had the ability to ask me a question or two to which I have no way of ascertaining the answer."

"And you have always had the ability to talk to me as if I were your student or your client."

"How should I talk to you?" I said lightly.

"I have no way of ascertaining the answer," she said with what could only be described as a giggle.

But in a second, she was serious again. "It's simple, what I want. The young girl's name is Kezia. As I said, I believe that you have always had a special sensitivity to the needs of young offenders."

"She's an offender?"

"Not yet. That's the thing. As far as I have figured out, her whole family has been involved in one crime or another for a very long time. Her father is serving a long sentence for manslaughter. Her mother, who has a record for minor things like shoplifting and disorderly conduct, doesn't have time for much crime these days. She works three jobs and is the sole support of Kezia. As for the other family members—her three brothers—they're the main subject of my articles. It's their gang activity that I'm interested in."

"Aliana, that sounds dangerous."

She laughed a laugh that sounded more like a sigh, one of those laughs that has tears somewhere deep at the bottom of it. "Listen," she said, "after you spend time in the Middle East, the antics of a few bad brothers in Scarborough isn't as much to worry about as it might appear."

I wasn't sure she was right, but I wasn't going to argue.

Again I had to ask, "So what does all this have to do with me—aside from my living in the same section of Toronto as the recreants?"

"When you worked with the young offenders—even back when you were a judge the first time—people said you had the touch."

"The touch?"

"Yes. The ability to get the kids to relax, to open up. I heard that they used to say that you weren't the tough guy that you appeared to be in court."

"Aliana, as you well know, that was a long time ago."

"No. Not only then." She kept her eyes down as if she didn't want me looking into them, as though some kind of private dialogue was going on between what she was saying and what she was thinking. "Recently. Since you were reinstated. A lot of people said that living as a vagrant had taught you a thing or two about pride."

I didn't know how to take this exactly, but as far as being a bum having knocked me down a few pegs, there was no arguing against that fact.

"So you're looking for somebody humble? How's that going to work?"

Now she looked up.

"Don't mock me, Ellis. What I want is this: I want Kezia to open up, to tell me how she feels about having her entire family being criminals. About how she sees her future and whether she is in any way afraid that she, too, will fall into the pattern that everybody else in her household has fallen into."

"You expect a twelve-year-old to talk about things like that?"

"She's a very bright girl. I'd even go so far as to say that she's ambitious."

"How do you know so much about her if she fails to 'open up' as you put it?"

"What I've told you is pretty much all there is to tell. The schools she's gone to have records of her failing to attend, causing disruptions with 'unacceptable classroom habits,' as they so quaintly put it, and never passing an exam or handing in an assignment. So there's no helpful information there. Nothing my editor would be interested in, at any rate."

The more she talked, the less I could see how I could have a role in this "research".

"I've had one interview with Kezia myself," Aliana went on. "I liked her. I liked her a great deal. Even though everything about her was different from everything about me, I could see myself in her. The restless curiosity that won't let you stop until your questions are answered, the persistence, the determination to know the facts…"

I knew from my own experience that it took decades to learn true things about yourself. Not because the true things might be bad, or even exceptionally good, but because the more you knew about yourself, the more you realized just how tightly the good and bad were twisted together. I admired Aliana's self-knowledge.

"I want you to help this kid, Ellis. I just want you to talk to her. I know from that brief interview—and from my research, too—that a person like her doesn't respect someone that they see as having sold out to the people in charge. Remember, this is a child raised by people in conflict with the law. It would make sense to think that if you are some sort of officer of the law, like a cop or a judge, that she wouldn't trust you. But you're different."

"Because of my nefarious past? So you think that my being an ex-offender would be a good recommendation? That sounds a little bizarre, Aliana. Besides, how would she even know?"

"You would tell her. You would gain her confidence. And besides, you can never discount two important things…"

Now *she* was acting like the professor.

"Which are?" I asked.

"That intelligent, ambitious people realize the fastest way to success is to obey laws rather than attracting attention to yourself by breaking them."

"That sounds great, Aliana. If only it were really true! What's the second thing I can't ever discount?"

"Kindness," she said. "I'm sure in your long career as a lawyer and a judge and even as a homeless person, you've realized how powerful simple kindness, ordinary patience, can be."

"Aliana," I said, "Whatever makes you think that I am kind and patient?"

"I know for certain that you are," she said with a small smile. "Because if you weren't, how could you have put up with me bothering you all these years?"

I needed time to think. To diffuse the intensity of our conversation, I suggested that we go to dinner. We actually found an Italian restaurant in the old neighborhood. As we dipped bread into the herbed olive oil that the waiter presented, I noted again the wedding ring on Aliana's right hand.

"So you are a widow now."

"Yes. Which is one of the reasons that I know what you must be going through right now."

I didn't want to talk about death. I didn't want to talk to anybody about Queenie. I wanted to keep her all to myself—just for a little while longer, just until I could get used to how I felt every time somebody mentioned her name or even suggested a thought that brought back thoughts of her. So I changed the subject. Sort of.

"Aliana, if I agree to see this child, there is no way I can ever be with her alone. There will always have to be another adult present in the room."

"Yes."

"And who would that person be?"

"Me. Do you have a problem with that?"

"No. I guess not," I answered, not at all certain I was telling the truth. "But I do have a problem with the whole picture. What's to protect you or me or the child herself from violent repercussions if we get close to what's going on in her life?"

"Nothing," Aliana answered. "Nothing at all."

ELEVEN

As we ate, Aliana talked about her work. "I turned down a big story to work on this gang thing," she said between tiny bites of her lasagna. It always seemed to me that Italian women had to fight especially hard to remain thin as they aged. Aliana was doing a good job of it.

"What story is that?"

"The upcoming Global Partners summit. There hasn't been anything like it in Toronto since the G20 conference."

I remembered the police brutality that had accompanied that affair. The official report on the security issues surrounding the coming to Toronto of top world officials showed unprecedented violence against rabble-rousers but also against ordinary citizens who were just conducting their legitimate, private affairs. Diabetics held without charge and denied insulin. People held in facilities without washrooms...

"I don't know how you can pass up a story like that. If things happened like they did the last time."

"There'll be plenty of reporters covering the summit," Aliana said. "They don't need me. And besides, the police have promised to behave this time." Her tone was sarcastic, but not bitter. She couldn't afford to be negative about the Toronto police. I was sure they were one of her most valuable sources.

"How did you find out that I was looking into matters concerning the police?" I asked her, surprising myself. It should have been the first question I had asked her.

"Oh," she replied nonchalantly, "I had a couple of conversations with Matt West."

"And he told you that he had talked to me?" I was incensed. Not only had Matt not respected my confidentiality but he had freely given Aliana information when he had been reluctant to tell me a single thing that would have been of any help.

"Not exactly," she replied, and she smiled. "I pumped him. He didn't even know he was talking about you."

"But you did?"

"Of course. So what do you say? Do we have a deal?"

"What do you mean—what deal?"

"You help me with Kezia and I help you get info about the cops."

I thought about this for one more minute. Considering that right then I had no information and no contacts, the answer seemed pretty clear.

"Okay."

"Great. This calls for a toast."

Before I could even open my mouth to remind Aliana that I'm a "recovered" alcoholic, she had summoned the waiter and ordered a bottle of San Pellegrino mineral water.

TWELVE

We agreed to meet in my office in two days' time. Which was a good thing because I would need a couple of days to clean the place up. It was a small space above a store on College Street. Cozy and private and close to the street and the people, which I could not have been had I taken an office in some glass tower closer to the center of the downtown business district.

It was a mess because I had neglected the small legal practice I had conducted since my retirement. Queenie's needs had overtaken all other considerations for months before her death, and not only did I not have time for anything else, I didn't care about anything else.

Apparently, that was now about to change, and I knew from a lifetime's experience that a change of direction always means cleaning up the detritus left in the wake of the old direction.

As I began to dig into the boxes of files with the aim of throwing everything out, I came upon the files of my last big court case: Regina vs. Supreme Court Justice John Stoughton-Melville. Though I'd successfully defended Stow against a charge of murder, our mutual and long-standing animosity had in no way lessened. We hadn't spoken in years. I consigned the papers concerning him to the "to be shredded" pile.

The next pile I attacked were boxes of papers that belonged to Jeffrey and that pertained to the operation of the Village in the Valley. I glanced at a couple of files in this box. They were quite recent and I knew that I wasn't breaching my son's confidentiality by examining the files, since legally, we operated the village together.

Among the papers, I found financial documents that seemed to show that in addition to the usual donations for the running of the operation, there had recently been several very large amounts attributed only to "Anonymous".

I'd neglected Jeffrey lately, the way I had neglected everything except Queenie. I was aware that there were several new huts in the village, not wooden shacks but actual little houses made of some sort of sturdy plastic-type material. Now that I thought of it, Jeffrey had recently refurbished the washroom building and the kitchen. I also recalled that the last time I'd been down there, several of the inhabitants had joked about the food getting to be like that in a "fancy restaurant". Had Jeffrey hired a new cook? I made a mental note to ask him who these generous donors were and to remind him of our position on private funders.

Among the papers I also found an article—a very positive article—about the village in a magazine that always featured special pieces about the city. There was no byline, which I found strange. I made a second mental note to ask Jeffrey about this.

***

At the appointed time exactly, there was a knock on the door and I invited Aliana in. The freshness of the autumn morning seemed to have added a becoming rosiness to her cheeks. I was surprised, then embarrassed, then made guilty by the thought that she had remained pretty over the years.

She was all business and without even accepting my offer of a coffee, she got down to it.

"Mark Hopequist," she said, "He's the one I know most about. I've interviewed him a number of times. Thirty-six years old, Toronto born and middle-class bred." She glanced up from her notes. "In the old sense of the term," she said, "when we used to have a middle class. His father, John, and his uncle, Paul, are retired old-school Toronto cops."

She consulted her notes again. "Mark hasn't been a police officer for long—about ten years—but he says he's been with the service long enough to feel that it's changed drastically since the day he gave up his banking career to join. This is some of what he told me."

She read, 'In the old days—a brief while ago—a cop could be trusted to at least pay lip service to the idea of maintaining the peace and seeking justice. But in today's city, that's not true

59

anymore. I think some men are more in love with the idea of having power than with exercising it for the good of the people. A lot of cops are head-shaved and gun-ready, like on the U.S. TV shows. Sometimes I think they're the enemies of anybody who's not one of them.'"

"That's a pretty strong statement from a cop."

"Yes. So maybe that's why some insiders seem to want me to think Hopequist the prime instigator of the attack—if it can be called that—on The Juicer."

"Retaliation for breaking rank?"

"Something like that."

"How could they make a case against him? Weren't all four in it together?"

"Yes. But he admits to being the last person to be with the victim before the poor old guy lost it. Which means he was the first person on the scene during the incident".

"What are the police saying about this? I assume nothing since PIC is involved."

"I don't know if PIC is involved. I do know the chief of police has promised to get to the bottom of 'things.' That may be his way of avoiding a full PIC investigation, which would put yet another team of cops in the limelight. I'm sure that's the last thing the chief wants on the eve of a major international event."

"If PIC is involved, everybody will clam up. I won't be able to get any information from anybody."

She gave me a look I couldn't quite read. It seemed to imply something between "Leave it to me" and "Don't give up so easily."

"Did you say that this Hopequist man was on duty at the Youth Bureau? How come he left? Do you know?"

"I didn't talk to him about his personal career details," she answered. "But it's not at all unusual for a cop to ask to be removed from a particular type of work."

"Why?"

"For any number of reasons, as far as I know. But working with the kids is really tough, as I'm sure you realize. By all accounts, Mark was a well-liked and highly respected officer."

"Is that all you have for me?" I tried not to sound disappointed.

"Give me a little time," Aliana answered. She took a deep breath and did that look-me-straight-in-the-eyes thing.

"The time has come," she said, "to talk about your part of the deal. Let me tell you a bit more about Kezia."

I nodded and sat back, ready but not one hundred per cent willing to listen.

"Her name comes from the Bible," Aliana began. "Kezia was one of the daughters of Job. She's Afro-Canadian, twelve years old and lives with the family I told you about earlier. They occupy a three-bedroom apartment in assisted housing in Scarborough."

She glanced at her ever-present little notebook. "Not far from where you live, but in a different kind of neighborhood."

Toronto is a complex city with literally hundreds of different ethnic and economic groups. It's not unusual to go a couple of blocks in either direction in some neighborhoods, and have the socio-economic scene changed drastically. And as was true of any city, violence and crime could happen in any neighborhood.

"There's some urgency to all this," Aliana said, "because there's reason to believe that the girl's three brothers are all active in gangs to one degree or another, although when I spoke to her, Kezia insisted that she had a 'good' brother who wasn't like the other two. Be that as it may, two of the brothers are highly-placed members of rival gangs. It wouldn't be far-fetched to think that they might be ready to kill each other at the slightest provocation."

"Not a very happy family…"

"It gets worse. The two 'bad' brothers only come home once in a while, but when they do, according to Kezia, 'they mess things up bad.' I'm not sure exactly what this means, and she laughed when she said it. But I think she's scared—maybe all the time. Plus, the mother, their only parent, works three jobs. She only comes home to sleep for a few hours every night. You can imagine the tension living like this would cause on an adult, let alone a girl not yet a teenager."

"It sounds hopeless."

"No," Aliana said, "Hopeless is not a word in your vocabulary."

I shook my head, but I kept listening.

"Kezia does poorly at school except for one class: English, and she is interested mostly in writing. In fact, she has actually been working on a book—not a silly, childish thing, but a recipe book called *Fifty Recipes for Snow.*"

"Aliana, I can't help saying that you got a great deal of information from this girl in what you called a brief interview…"

"I'm a pro, Ellis. And so are you. Kezia told me about a quote from the Book of Job that inspired her. She said that she did a lot of research and has already written a good part of her manuscript, based on all the things she's learned about snow and ice. She told me that she's writing about 'real miracle-type things.'"

"How was she able to do all this, given her circumstances?" I was pretty sure this kid had spun a tall tale for Aliana, though the idea of the ace reporter being fooled was not an easy one to entertain.

"Kezia said that she found all this information on the internet. She said that her brothers stole a lot of iPads but they would never give her one, so she has to use the internet at the library."

I had to stop her. "Look, Aliana, this is all very touching, but what does it possibly have to do with me? If you got all this information from this girl in a single sitting, it seems pretty clear that she's willing to talk about her life without reservation. The idea that she would 'open up' to me more than to you just doesn't make any sense."

"Ellis, a life of crime is reaching out to this girl. She learned about her name and she found that quote from Job in a Bible she stole from the Baptist church her mother goes to."

"That's not exactly an indication of budding criminality. A lot of Baptists would be happy to think a teenager had 'stolen' a copy of the Bible." I couldn't bear to add that I myself had stolen a copy of the good book very recently. Without asking for it, I took home the one the pastor used to lead Queenie in her last prayer, her last words.

"Kezia has been caught stealing a number of times, including shoplifting cosmetics, swiping food from sidewalk markets, even tricking mobile food vendors out of food by running away without paying."

I recognized these small acts of criminality, this lively contempt for law, and knew that Aliana wasn't wrong. They might in fact be signs of greater crimes to come. I had once had to sentence a young man for a particularly violent murder. His lawyer had, in an attempt to achieve a lighter sentence, read a long history of crime that began when the boy was seven and had stolen a donut from an unforgiving vendor who had called the police and sent the young man on a long journey toward perdition.

"You can talk to her. You can show her that there are two ways she can go. You can tell her from your own experience..." she hesitated, "from your own heart, that one way leads to sorrow and the other way leads to happiness."

"Happiness, Aliana?"

"Yes."

"Okay," I said before I could give the matter another moment's thought. "Okay."

THIRTEEN

The minute I got home, the phone rang. I assumed it was Aliana calling to say she'd checked her calendar and was ready to set a date for our first meeting with Kezia.

But she was not the caller.

"Your Honor, how's it goin'?"

I'd certainly never had a phone call from Johnny Dirt before, but of course I immediately recognized his gravelly voice with its underlying note of contempt.

"I've got some info on that Ted Downs guy."

"Downs—that older cop?"

"Right."

"What? What have you got?" I didn't trust Johnny, but, as with Aliana and our so-called "deal," I wasn't in a position to turn down any possible lead.

"One of our clients—a guy who never minds his own business, by the way—said he heard that Downs is assigned to special duty at Queen's Park. Seems the cops are really keeping an eye on the provincial parliament building because of that Global Partners thing."

"Why would they be going that?"

"Don't you read the papers, man? And here I thought you were up on everything. Just shows you…"

"Cut the crap, Johnny. Just give me the information. I don't need the footnotes."

Johnny laughed—his annoying cross between a chitter and a growl. "Yeah. So Downs would be on guard down there because of all the rioters. Looks like this summit thing is going to be just like the last one. Lots of yahoos all over the city rippin' things up."

"I know about the summit," I said, not trying to hide my irritation. "What's that got to do with me?"

"Get your butt down there, that's what," Johnny answered. "You're lookin' for info and if you can see Downs in action, you might learn something. Now I know that you think you got nothing left to learn in this world, but..."

"I've never seen the man. How will I recognize him?"

"You've got a good description of the guy, plus they all have to wear really visible name tags this time, seeing as they all forgot to wear them the last time the foreign bigwigs showed up."

He was right about that. A number of officers had removed their name tags during the G20. The better to remain anonymous when they were beating somebody.

"Thanks, Johnny. I'll check it out." I hung up. And I went to bed.

But the next day, I got up early and I headed down to Queen's Park. If Johnny wasn't pulling a fast one—sending me on a wild goose chase—there might be a chance to observe the officer—maybe even talk to him.

**

The traffic was horrendous, and the parking ridiculous, as usual. I had to pay twenty dollars for an hour and a half, and even then, I ended up walking for six blocks along College Street before I could even catch sight of the red stone castle-like building, set in a lovely park, that serves as the seat of the government of Ontario.

As I got closer, I could see that Johnny's information was accurate. A crowd of protestors—hundreds it seemed--was gathered in front of the building, yelling slogans and waving signs.

As was the case in so many of these public demonstrations, each protestor seemed to have his or her own reason for demonstrating. The demands on the hand-lettered signs they carried ranged from "Keep our city Green. Keep conferences out," to "Justice for the people of Afghanistan," and everything in between.

The place was clogged with cops. A line of officers with bullet-proof shields and riot helmets stood shoulder to shoulder between the crowd and the building. The nearer I got to the front, the clearer it became that these men were all young, not middle-aged like the man I was looking for.

If I hadn't gone through so much trouble to get there, I would have just turned around and gone home. But instead, I wandered through the crowd. Before long, I was freezing. The trees of Queen's Park were ablaze now, and despite the sunshine, I could feel the breath of winter on the wind.

I was headed back toward the car when I caught sight of him.

Except for the name tag, which, as Johnny had suggested, was readable from quite a distance, there was absolutely nothing to distinguish this man from any other old-school Toronto cop. He was moving slowly through the crowd, his hands nowhere near his weapons, on his face a neutral expression as if he could respond negatively or positively to any action of any party depending on what the circumstances required.

I watched him for a while, but the exercise told me nothing.

As I reached College Street, I stopped and turned for one last look at Downs. As I did so, he noticed me, strode toward me and said, "Move along, old fella. This is no place for you."

Miffed at the insult and the waste of time—not to mention money—I did as the officer commanded.

FOURTEEN

Aliana called that night. She didn't waste any time on small talk. "We're meeting Kezia tomorrow at 2 p.m. at her apartment. It's on Kingston Road near Eglinton." I jotted down the address. "Sorry I can't talk now," she said. "Deadline."

I felt a strange mixture of relief and disappointment when she hung up, but the next day, as I set out through the autumn rain, I was almost happy to be doing something that, at least on the surface, seemed as though it might help somebody.

Which is not to say that I wasn't apprehensive about meeting the child.

The traffic, as usual, was slow across Eglinton. Scarborough, a section of the city running along the northern shore of Lake Ontario, is very spread out, and I passed countless shopping plazas, high-rise apartment buildings, service stations and little local strip malls made up of what we called "mom and pop" operations, tiny stores stuffed to bursting with merchandise that ranged from cigarettes to health-food supplements.

Autumn was taking over. The yellow and orange leaves would soon turn to red and brown. A few of the trees were already bare.

As I moved across the city, the waning of the year brought back a cluster of memories about something I hadn't thought about in a long time.

It had been on an early autumn day just like the present one that I had asked Queenie to marry me. We had been walking in the valley, discussing winter and the fact that her clients, people who had once lived in a tent city by the river, now had warm, safe places to sleep every night.

"Safety is the best thing you can give another person," Queenie said.

She was walking a little ahead of me on the narrow path through the fading trees. When she had been a street person,

Queenie had worn all the clothes she'd owned at the same time, even in summer.

But it had been years since she had had to live like that. Now, she wore simple clothes appropriate to the season, but with a touch of the fashion of Canadian natives. On that day, she had been wearing slim black slacks and a black sweater. And over that she was sporting a beautiful wool shawl decorated with stylized designs that, she told me, represented myths about the seasons that were a legacy of her people. She also wore a silver cross on a chain around her neck. I never asked Queenie who had given her that cross and she never volunteered the information.

Once she had abandoned dressing like a pile of Goodwill rejects, Queenie had revealed that under all that cloth, she had a tricky little figure, an attractive, graceful body that the years had not yet stolen.

On that autumn day, as I watched her walk deftly ahead of me on the river path, I saw, in a flash of insight lasting less than a second that Queenie and I had been meant to be together from the start. I reached out and put my hand on her shoulder, slowing her and drawing her close. "Queenie," I said, "I love you. I want you to marry me."

She turned. There was shock in her eyes, then the wariness of a person who's been tricked a lot of times, then a softening that I had never seen before. She reached up and stroked my face. "Okay, Your Honor," was all she said.

I smiled at the memory. Instead of hurting, as all the memories had hurt in recent weeks, this one made me feel peaceful. It made me feel that I had been right in making that promise to Queenie and that I was right in doing whatever was necessary to fulfill it.

***

Aliana was waiting for me. As I pulled into the small "visitors only" parking lot in front of the Middle Scarborough Community Center, I saw her standing by the window in the lobby.

But when I actually entered, she was gone.

Seeing my confusion, the receptionist, a young black woman with a very cheerful face, nodded in the direction of a nearby hallway from which I could hear the melodious laughter of a young woman.

I followed the trail of the laughter.

And I found Aliana looking very efficient in a dark gray business suit that fit her slim figure as though made to measure and her thick dark hair drawn into a chignon at the back of her neck.

They were laughing, as if they'd just shared some hilarious joke. This I took as a good sign.

I stood in the door for a few seconds before Aliana jumped up and drew me into the room.

"Ellis, she said, "this is Kezia."

The girl looked up at me, but her wide-eyed stare was the only acknowledgement of my presence. No greeting. No smile. Not even a small change in the expression on her dark-skinned, lovely face.

There are, unfortunately, a lot of obese teenagers in Toronto, but this girl was not one of them. Like Aliana, she was slim. But unlike Aliana she didn't seem to feel that our interview merited any kind of special care in dressing. Kezia wore a pair of tight, faded jeans and a Maple Leafs hockey sweater that she must have borrowed—or even stolen--from a child because it was tiny and didn't make it all the way to her waist. Over it, she wore a tight little leather jacket, a scuffed and battered object with a couple of burn marks that I didn't want to analyze.

She had, however, taken some care with other aspects of her appearance. Her curly black hair fell in a shining tumble from her smooth brow and her cheeks were rosy, something I had never noticed on a black female before. And her wide, well-shaped mouth was quite beautiful even if she didn't smile.

The light, easy manner she had displayed with Aliana seemed to have instantly disappeared. She made a sassy remark that I didn't get, except to realize that it was personally derogatory and directed at my age, my gender, or both. Then she slouched in an attitude of bored contempt. She didn't move in any way to greet me, so I took a seat on an uncomfortable wooden chair opposite the couch on which she and then Aliana sat, not far from each other but not touching.

"Hi. I'm Ellis," I said, reaching out my hand.

The girl shook it with limp indifference and without a word.

"How is everybody today?" I sounded like an idiot.

"We're great," Aliana cheerfully answered. "And we're really looking forward to talking to you…."

The girl looked up. "Heard you been in jail. Is that true?"

"Yes," I answered. Remarkably, it wasn't the first time I'd begun a conversation by having to answer that question. The fact that it came from a teenager in danger of coming into conflict with the law was rather reassuring. It was easier than answering it in front of other judges at a social occasion or having to answer it for my grandchildren. "What was it like? Was it really scary?"

"Yes. It was really scary. Especially at first."

"Did they, like, torture you or anything?"

"No. But it was frightening to know that you were living with other people who'd done something seriously wrong—wrong enough for them to be sentenced. Frightening to be separated from your friends and family. Frightening to know that somebody was probably watching you every minute of the day….."

"Do you get to take your phone with you? Do you get to text anybody?"

I had to smile. It had been the better part of twenty years since the day I'd wakened in the Don Jail and realized where I was and who I was then, compared to who I had always thought of myself as being. "I can't say that I know the answer to that one, Kezia, because when I went to jail, there were no such things as I-phones, no such thing as texting."

For the first time, I got a genuine reaction from the girl. I think "shocked disbelief" would be the term Aliana would have used.

"OMG. How did you talk to anybody outside the jail?"

I didn't want to tell her that shame prevented me from wanting to talk to anybody. Not my former fellow judges. Not my then wife. Not my children.

"You didn't. You didn't talk to anybody on the outside."

"Holy shit!" She shook her curls, which bounced back exactly where they'd been before. "What about eating?"

"I don't know how it is now," I answered truthfully. I suspected that the food served to the detained and the incarcerated today followed the same rules as the food served in other institutions. Gone the French fries, the hot dogs, the tough little pieces of meat smothered in salty gravy. Gone the watery soft pasta swimming in gooey sauces that always tasted like they'd come out of a soup can.

Now, I imagined, the jail kitchen was full of fruits and vegetables and multi-grained bread and yoghurt and skim milk. I imagined visitors smuggling in bags of potato chips with the same concentrated stealth that they snuck in guns and drugs.

She shrugged, glanced at Aliana and shrugged again. "If you gotta eat it, you gotta eat it," she said. I figured she was talking about more than food.

She had a lot of other questions. Naturally I wondered why she was so curious, but I was very careful only to answer exactly what she asked and to tell her honestly if I didn't know the answer. Of course, I had to tailor my descriptions of my own adventure outside the law to suit the comprehension of a young teen.

"Wow!" she commented a couple of times, and I realized that I'd better avoid making my past life in the valley as a "hopeless" homeless person sound like a grand adventure.

With that caveat in mind, I tried to steer the conversation toward what I had learned from my life inside and outside jail, and of course I said that it had led me to the conviction that people always need to obey the law.

This was of no interest to Kezia. I could tell by her posture, which returned to slumping and the look on her face, which returned to its fine imitation of a statue.

"Ellis," Aliana piped up, "I'm sure you've given Kezia a lot to think about. Maybe we can..."

Suddenly, Kezia sat forward, as if some new thought had hit her. Some other angle, some other way of making me tell her what she really wanted to know.

"You have kids? Like grandchildren and that?"

Aliana reached across and put her hand on top of Kezia's. The girl quickly pulled away, but Aliana showed no reaction to this rejection. "I don't think we need to ask Ellis personal..."

"It's all right," I said quickly. "No problem. Yes. I have a son and a daughter and each of them has a child. So, two children, two grandchildren."

"How about a woman?"

"A woman?"

"Yeah, like are you married or do you have a girlfriend?"

"Kezia," I said, "I had a very wonderful wife named Queenie but she got sick and not long ago, she died."

The girl nodded. "So you'll never see her again?"

"No." Sometimes I wondered about heaven and about the things Queenie had told me that her people and also her church believed about the afterlife, but this was not the time or place to bring up that. "No."

The girl was quiet. Aliana opened her mouth as though to speak, then thought better of it.

"I had a grandmother one time," Kezia said. "She was real good, too. She could tell stories and make baking and everything. And a grandfather, too. He told me about slaves and how they got stolen from Africa." She shook her curls again. "I really liked them. I liked when they came to visit. But they went back to Jamaica and I never saw them again. Like maybe they died, I don't know. Anyway, one time my mother went to Jamaica, too. I was real scared that she wouldn't come back either. But she did."

As if this touching revelation had tired her out, the girl sank back on the couch and by her posture, seemed to indicate that she'd had enough talking.

Into the silence came the sounds of the community center: young people laughing and talking, in the distance rap music and the sound of a basketball being bounced against a wooden floor.

Aliana waited. I admired her skill as an interviewer, which, like everything else in the world, depended on a sense of timing. After what seemed a very long interval, she gently said, "Kezia, remember what you promised?"

The girl nodded.

"You promised Ellis that you would tell him about Mark— about the time you and your friends spent with him."

The girl pouted. Then, her face softened and she smiled. "I like him. He's cute and he's cool. He's not mean and ugly like some cops. He used to show us how to do them puzzles with the numbers—sudsoko—or something like that."

"Sudoku?" Aliana offered.

"Yeah. That's the one. He brought in a book with all them puzzles and other kinds of puzzles, too, and we took turns figuring them out. I was the best. I was better than all the other kids!"

"So he was smart and nice and you all liked him?" I asked.

"Not was, *is*. He's not dead, is he? That's not why you're asking me all these questions, is it?"

"Oh, no!" Aliana hastened to reassure her. "We're just talking to some people who know Mark to find out what he's like and how he gets along with other people."

"He gets along perfect." She drew in a breath. "He told me a secret once. And he told me that I was the only one who knew the secret and never to tell anybody else."

I froze at this remark, and I could feel Aliana stiffen, too. The idea of an adult male telling secrets to a pre-pubescent female sent off warning signals in both of us.

But, without consulting, we seemed to agree that this might be better handled on another day.

"Kezia," Aliana said, "you've been very helpful today, and very interesting, too."

The girl nodded and smiled at Aliana but not at me.

"I'm wondering if you would let us visit you again soon. Maybe you could tell us some more then. You could tell Ellis a little bit about your brothers and about your unusual hobby."

I wasn't sure about any of this, but I could tell that remaining silent was the best way to get the girl to agree to meet us again. I wasn't sure what it would accomplish, but she had told us several things about this Mark Hopequist. If PIC was really involved in investigating the death of the Juicer, I'd have to rely on unusual sources like this young girl to gather whatever facts I could.

"Okay. I will. I'll see you again."

"I'll give you my business card, Kezia," I said. "That way you'll know who you're talking to."

"Sure."

I reached into the pocket of my jacket to get my wallet. It was gone.

Laughing, Kezia reached into her own pocket, pulled out my wallet and handed it to me.

"Don't worry," she said. "That's just a trick. I heard what you said about following the law. I always do."

She laughed again and without quite meaning to, I laughed too.

FIFTEEN

"Let's have a coffee!"

I agreed. Aliana had come by TTC, by transit. As she slid into the front seat of my car, it occurred to me that nobody else had sat there since Queenie. I felt that rush of sorrow that now seemed to be my constant companion, and I wondered whether I would have to go through every single mundane experience of my daily life before I got to the point where I could stop thinking *The last time I did this I was with my beloved wife.*

We choose Tim Hortons. Of course we did. The ubiquitous donut shop was a Toronto fixture. We sat by the window, which here in the suburban part of our massive city, looked out only on traffic, low-rise apartment buildings and other stores in the strip mall.

I suppose we chose to sit by the window out of habit. Downtown there was lots to observe. Well-dressed business people, students, even beggars offered opportunity for observation and reflection. Out here, there was no one on the sidewalks.

As we drank, Aliana asked, "How's the detecting going?"

I thought she probably meant it as a joke because her tone was teasing, but, to tell the truth, I had nobody else to talk to about my so-called "case" and to my surprise, and I think to hers, too, I started to lay out all that I knew so far about the death of the homeless man. I glanced at her from time to time and she seemed to be paying rapt attention, so I just spilled it all out.

"The way it looks is this: Four cops are suspected of homicide because they took down a homeless man who was acting out on the street—brandishing two pieces of metal, one in each hand, that appeared at first to be knives but turned out to really be pieces of a metal towel rack.

"All four claimed the man died from a heart attack and that they didn't have anything to do with killing him. They claimed it was a tragic accident and that they were in the vicinity because of another emergency call. They insisted that they were summoned to the front of the hospital where the man had been a patient for a couple of days and that all they had done was to calm the man down before he was returned to his room.

"This much was in the news," I continued. "But almost immediately it was announced that PIC had been called in to investigate. I don't need to tell you that this means that anyone involved in the case has been rendered incommunicado until the PIC has completed its investigation."

Aliana nodded. "It's a real problem," she began. "As a reporter I've had to…"

Before she could complete her thought, the glass in the window beside us shattered, spraying us with fragments.

Too shocked to think, I instinctively grabbed Aliana and pulled her under the table. She was bleeding and so was I, but I could tell at once that we weren't seriously hurt.

"My God, Ellis, what the hell…?

"Shots. We've been shot at!"

"Us?"

"Somebody."

Behind and above us we heard wild screaming, swearing, crying. And the sound of people fleeing the scene.

Within minutes, there was dead silence. I took Aliana's hand. Her fingers were wet with blood but she kept her hand in mine as we carefully crawled out from our hiding place.

The shop was totally empty. Everyone was gone. There flashed through my mind all the news reports in which witnesses were called on to provide the police with information about a shooting. Witnesses that never came forward. Shooters that were never apprehended. Cases that were never solved…

Aliana pulled out her phone and dialed 911.

***

First the medics attended to our "wounds", which, by some miracle turned out to be minor.

Then the police got a hold of us. I had to leave my car in the parking lot of what was now a crime scene, and Aliana and I had to climb into a cruiser for a nice little ride locked in the back seat until we got to 41 division station where we finally convinced the officers that we knew nothing.

We had to take a cab, at a cost of thirty dollars, back to my car, which, I was relieved to see, was unharmed.

I regret to say that drive-by shootings are common now in our city. So we could have been simply been caught in the crossfire between two rival gang members, or have been the mistaken target of someone who took us for somebody else, or we might even have been a miscalculated target of someone who'd just gotten a gun and wasn't used to using it yet.

Or maybe someone knew I was questioning the police and didn't think I should proceed...

SIXTEEN

As I made my way home through the congested rush-hour streets, I was still shaky but I calmed down, though I wasn't sure why. I couldn't help but think about the increasing danger in the city, the careless—and sometimes intentional—use of firearms that had taken the lives of so many teenagers, the fatal fights at bars and parties, the increased domestic violence, especially in times of tough economic downturns, and the violence related to the activities of gangs in so many neighborhoods like some of the ones I was driving through to get home. For a moment I wondered whether little Kezia's interest in my time inside might be connected to the gang violence where she lived.

On my way to my apartment, I decided to go down to the Village. Here in a sheltered bend of the Don, the trees were alive with color and the persistent wind abated.

The slope down to the site was slick from autumn rain. And darkness had begun to fall early.

I made it down without too much trouble, reaching out to steady myself on the branches of bushes and low-growing trees.

"Dad! What are you doing down here at this time of night?"

"Son…" I reached out and touched his shoulder. Jeffrey was not what you would call a physical person, but I couldn't help that small sign of affection. "It's not night."

"Come into the lounge." He gestured toward the one-story building, a modest structure made of chipboard and looking as if it had been constructed by amateurs, perhaps with the volunteer guidance of helpful professional builders.

It was warm and bright inside with shelves of books and tables with games and a computer for the valley residents. I took one of the worn wooden chairs that surrounded the tables—donations, no doubt—and Jeffrey sat on another. Over his shoulder, I could see that there was a desk in the corner, which probably served as his office. And on the desk was his computer opened to the screensaver that showed his wife Tootie and his children, two of my four grandchildren.

"How are you doing?" he asked with genuine concern. "Tootie and I want you to come over, but you're hard to get on the phone and you don't answer your emails...."

I shrugged. There were about two hundred emails lined up on my inbox list. I just couldn't bring myself to read any more after I'd read the first few. They were all about people's memories of Queenie. All about how wonderful she'd been.

"I'm fine, Son. I'm okay."

Jeffrey was a tall, strong-looking man. I remembered the day he was born, the day my Italian mother cried with joy over the fact that the baby was a boy. Ellen had been born first, and her grandparents had always been wonderful to her. But a son! A son was different.

He was different from me for sure, fair, muscular. And steady in his thoughts, his speech and his actions.

"What's going on down here?" I asked. "You've got some new huts, I see."

Jeffrey looked down, his long blond hair shading his face. "I would have told you about them, Dad. But I didn't want to bother you when I knew you..."

"You have to 'bother' me Jeffrey. We're in this together, remember?"

I wanted to reach out and touch his shoulder again, but he was sitting too far away.

He looked up. "There's something else," he said. "Something that happened just today." He hesitated. "Two City Councilors were down here."

"Down here?"

"Yes. Even with this lousy weather. I don't think they hiked all the way down. One of the residents who was on his way up to the street said he saw a limo parked in the parking lot of your building right at the entrance to the path."

"How would they have found access to the site?"

"I have no idea."

I couldn't help it. This answer filled me with anger. "Jeffrey, what have I said about security? We've discussed this. I…"

I fought to control myself. "What did they want?"

"They said they were on a 'fact-finding mission', that the city is looking to save taxpayer dollars by cutting funding to unnecessary and/or improperly approved projects."

I began to feel my temper rising toward the danger level. In the old days, before my downfall, before age mellowed me, I was famous for spurts of anger that put fear into the hearts of my opponents on the bench and on the skids.

"This is private property! Did you tell them they were trespassing? Did you demand that they leave at once?"

"No. I…"

"How in heaven's name do they figure that the tiny grants we get from the city to shelter the homeless are a waste of the taxpayers' money? Did you tell them that our major expenses are completely covered by the investments in the foundation that we set up at the beginning? "

"No, Dad. I couldn't do that."

"And just why not?" I was shouting now.

"Because," Jeffrey said calmly. "It isn't true."

"What? What do you mean it isn't true? What isn't true?'

"It's not true that we have no other public funding. For the past two years, we've accepted an additional grant from the city, a grant that was a proportion of our overall expenses. We've used the money to improve housing."

He hesitated. "And we've also accepted a grant from the province."

"We? What do you mean, we? You mean you." I was so mad I had begun to pace.

"Dad, sit down. Calm down. It's a very small grant. All I had to do was fill out a simple form to apply. You weren't available. It was right around the time that Queenie started to get sick. I remember that I tried to reach you, but I had no luck. The deadline was approaching, so I just submitted the application."

"Without my knowledge? Without my signature?"

"My signature was all they needed."

"So you signed! Without even telling me! Well that's just fine! Maybe you'd like to cut me out of this operation all together!"

"Dad, please…"

"Maybe I'm of no use to you. Maybe your pals on City Council know more about what goes on down here, than I do. Maybe you told them how to park in my parking lot and get down by our private path."

"Dad, don't be ridiculous. I never saw those two before in my life."

"Well you're going to see them again. You can count on that. You're going to have them down here on a regular basis. Just watch…"

I strode toward the door. I tried to slam it, but the flimsy board just swung in the breeze of my departure.

SEVENTEEN

By the time I got out of the valley and into my apartment, I was a total wreck. Not only had I had a fight with the person I realized I now loved most in the world, my clothes and shoes were covered with mud.

My first thought was that Queenie would kill me when she saw the mess I was tracking into the apartment. My second, piercing, thought was that I could track anything into the place at any time without anybody caring at all.

I was so distraught that I actually thought of having a drink, the first time that had occurred to me in so many years that I couldn't even remember the last time. But that was a weakness I knew I would never give into again.

As I cleaned up, the burden of guilt and embarrassment over how I had acted with my son began to ease. It had by no means been the first time we had argued. I knew I would apologize to Jeffrey and that he would apologize to me and that together we'd work out the problem with the city, whatever it really was.

But I had no such confidence when it came to the fact that I had not yet talked to even one of the four suspects in the murder of the Juicer.

What was I supposed to do? What or who came next? What if none of the cops ever agreed to talk to me? It was all very well that some kid had talked to Mark Hopequist, but where did that leave me?

As the hot water of my shower washed away the cold of the day's rain, instead of feeling relaxed I started to feel angry again. I remembered the last time I'd gotten mad enough to embarrass myself. It was the day several years before when I had come to fisticuffs with John Stoughton-Melville. The last day of the court battle that he had coerced me into as his defense. The day I had saved him. The last day I had ever seen him.

And suddenly I realized what my anger had always really been about. It had been about people who put me in situations that threatened my sense of self-worth. People who made me feel unable to do what they so clearly required me to do. It had once been about Stoughton-Melville. But now it was about somebody else. It was about Queenie. Queenie who deserted me, who left me alone, who gave me this stupid puzzle to solve. This case without a clue.

I decided to go back to the one place that had never failed to give me information, never failed to show me something I needed to be shown: the street.

First I went to the place where the Juicer was supposed to move before he ended up in the hospital.

It was a dilapidated rooming house in a neighborhood that had had its ups and downs but was now headed on the road toward gentrification. As a matter of fact, there were wooden fences surrounding this house on Howard Street not far from the center of the city, and at first I thought they might be police barricades marking off the scene of a crime. But I soon realized that the fences are were only slightly less dilapidated than the house, sliding down toward the cracked sidewalk beneath signs that bore the name of a real estate developer who perhaps had once had high hopes for this project but who had now clearly abandoned all hope of turning a profit from it.

I figured that this situation was temporary. Soon this developer—or another with more money—was going to tear this old slum down and build a towering, shining condo.

I also figured that the police had not closed off this site because PIC wasn't interested in it or else had finished whatever investigation they intended to do there.

I knew from my years in court, but also my years on the street, that despite the avowed vigilance of the force, it was almost impossible to convict a policeman of anything. As to convicting a police woman—well—you can forget that, too. In fact, you can forget it first!

As I checked out the site, seeing nothing that gave me the least clue about the Juicer, I ran into a couple of current inhabitants of the building. I tried to get away before they saw me, but I'm an old man and I've never been much of a runner. Besides, I was tripping and sliding on the uneven pavement in front of the building. When one of the miscreants grabbed my jacket and twisted it in his huge hand until the collar choked me, I was almost grateful. If he hadn't been hanging on to me, I would have fallen flat on my face.

"Looking for something, buddy?"

"No, I—"

"Hey, Danny," he called to another raggedy young man. "Check out the old dude!"

My captor was dark and big and truly mean-looking. I knew the next thing that was going to happen was that I was going to be frisked. It almost made me laugh. All I had in my pocket were two two-dollar coins and four senior TTC tickets.

"Okay, where is it?" he demanded. "Where's your damn wallet?"

To my surprise, I reached up and punched him. The second I did so, I realized just how stupid that was. I actually closed my eyes, hoping to protect them from the blows to my face that were sure to follow.

I waited for a second in the darkness.

"Hey," the other man said, "lay off. You know who this guy is? He's Queenie's old man."

"Queenie? The Juicer's Queenie?"

"Yeah. He paused. "She passed a few weeks ago."

"Is that so? My attacker turned, grabbed me again and spun me around until I was facing him, his fat hand pulling together the two sides of my jacket and holding them in his fist at my chin. "Sorry about your loss…"

If he was being sarcastic, I wasn't appreciating it. I tore loose and raised my own fist.

"Easy, old timer," the other man said. "Come over here and sit down. Sorry to give you trouble, but we got to be careful around here."

As if it were a fine couch in an elegant living room, the man gestured toward a collapsing front porch step and actually gave me his hand as I stooped to take the seat he offered. Then he sat beside me.

I caught my breath. "Why?" I finally managed to ask. "Why do you have to be careful?"

The other man stared at me and sneered, as if my question were pretty stupid.

"Cops," he said. "They're crawling around here like cockroaches." He shook his head and I tried to move away a little. He had long, matted hair and I didn't want him to shake anything onto me. My days of living comfortably among the insects of our city were long over.

"Yes," I said, beginning to understand that these shabby outcasts could probably be brought over to my side if I were diplomatic. "You see, you're right about the Juicer being Queenie's man."

"You said it," the other man offered. Unlike his pal, he had no hair at all. No real hair that is. On his shaved head was a ridiculous tattoo made to look like hair. "I heard the last thing she said was that he was murdered and somebody had to find the killer."

I didn't bother asking him how he could possibly have known the last words that my beloved had said to me. The street had its own system of communication.

"Right again," I said, trying to keep my voice emotionless. "And I'm the one who's supposed to do it."

"You? Because you were a judge or something like that?" He made a fist and swung his hand toward my face. I flinched and drew back. "You're not a cop, are you?"

"No. Not a cop. Not a judge anymore. I'm Queenie's widower. I'm her husband. She used to help me in my work because she knew so much about the street, and I used to help her in her work because I knew about the law."

Both men nodded, which I almost found touching. I was sure respect for the law was not among their skill sets.

"So I have to help Queenie now, even though she's gone. I have to find out what really happened to a man that she cared about."

"Even though she was the only one in the world who could stand the bastard?" one of the men said, and the other chuckled.

"Right yet again. Because I promised. I promised Queenie I'd find out what really happened."

"There were four of them bastards," the bald man said. "Guess you know that much?"

"Yes. But I'm having a hard time finding anything much about them. Let alone actually talking to them."

"You're not going to get much info talking to a cop," he said. "And you better make sure they don't get much talking to you." He smiled at his own joke. "But, yeah, I think we could tell you a thing or two about a couple of those cops anyway. What do you want to know?"

I decided to start slowly and build my way up. "The female—I think her name is Feeance or something like that. Know anything about her?"

Both men shook their heads. "Bitch. A perfect black bitch. Stay away from her and she'll stay away from you. That's all you need to know about that piece of cop garbage."

"No love lost, eh?" I said with a weak smile.

They both stared at me like they didn't know what I was talking about. I cleared my throat and proceeded. "Ted Downs. What do you know about him?"

The bald man looked down. The other answered right away with a litany of what sounded like familiar phrases, as if he'd known Downs for a long time and the cop had never changed. "Old guy. Tough-looking but basically okay. Wouldn't bother to get on your back if he didn't need to. Wouldn't bring you in for nothing unless you were waving a gun or something."

"Or looking like you're waving a couple of knives?"

"Yeah, yeah, I guess so."

His companion nodded at this remark and my friend went on, "Downs is what we used to call a body-and-fender man. Which means that you cross him and you learn that he's as tough as he looks and he don't hesitate to rough you up some to get what he's after. He ain't bald but he's got lots of muscles—must work out, I guess. The word on the street is that no living person has ever seen him smile. Smart people steer clear of him because he isn't afraid to use his baton."

"And his Taser…." the other man added.

But my friend hastened to correct him. "No. That's a rumor. Only supervisors have Tasers…."

"Sometimes they sign out somebody else's," his companion insisted. "I seen it myself."

"You saw someone Tasered by a police officer?"

"Yeah," the man answered with jumpy enthusiasm. "It was actually some old lady. She was screamin' and swinging a couple of them things with yarn or whatever you call it…"

"Knitting needles?" I suggested.

"Yeah. That's right! I seen a cop Taser her and pull her down and take her away. A fucking ancient old lady!"

The other man added calmly, "I'm not sure what he really saw, but I can tell you I heard more than one guy say he was Tasered by somebody who looked and acted like Downs only it was real dark, so there weren't going to be any witnesses or anything."

I let that sink in. Then I said, "What about a guy, a cop, named Al Brownette?"

They both snickered at mention of the name. "Yeah," the bald man said, "Al Brown Nose. We know him, alright. Where the big guy goes the little guy follows."

"What? What does that mean?"

"Look," the hirsute informer offered, "we're only telling you how we see things."

"Sure," I answered. "So--?"

"So this Al Brown Nose cop, he follows Ted Downs around like a sick puppy. I don't know nothing about how the police assign duties or anything like that, but I do wonder how Al and Ted always get stuck together like peanut butter and bread or something."

"Why do you think that might be the case?" I asked.

"Because he's a brown nose pure and simple. Why else?" Baldy offered.

The other man shot him a look. "The reason is," he said with exaggerated slowness, "Al's always trying to impress the old guy—show him he's brave or whatever. He tries to act so tough that nothing can touch him. Even old Ted isn't as tough as that all the time."

"What do you mean?"

My cooperative informant sighed. "I don't know. I only know what I heard."

"You mean about the kid?" his pal piped up.

"Yeah."

"What kid?" I had to be careful. I was getting somewhere here. I couldn't blow it by being too eager.

Both men shook their heads. It was touching, really, such sympathy among the downtrodden. I knew that whatever they were about to offer me now was going to be the tidbit that made the whole trip worthwhile—and also the cash item—the bit that would make me cough up all I had. Two twonies. Four tickets. Sorry, guys. But they didn't know that yet.

"Ted had a kid," the bald one began.

"Yeah. The only time he ever sounds human is when he talks about his son. The kid killed himself about a year ago and the rumor was that Ted took it real hard. People even said that Al helped him out, like gave him comfort or something like that. Other people said it was a deal. Al helps Ted get over his son's death and Ted helps Al get out of some kind of trouble with the police force—"

"Trouble? What kind of trouble?"

They both shrugged. "Who knows?"

I took a chance and asked the big question. "Did either of you personally see anybody using force on The Juicer?"

The two scruffy men looked at each other and I saw a nearly-imperceptible signal pass between them, as though they were giving each other permission to answer.

"You mean guns or something anything like that?"

"Guns, fists, Tasers…"

Again a look passed from one man to the other.

"Look," the hairy man said, "we don't know any more than anybody else about this stuff. The Juicer was a problem. A lot of people on the street think he got what was coming to him. Queenie was an angel. Anybody who could help her, helped her. All I can say is the Juicer wasn't one of them. Wasn't one of the people who made Queenie's life easier. She used to say if you only help good people, what good are you?"

I had to smile and it didn't even hurt this time. "Yeah," I said, "that sounds like Queenie all right!"

The man beside me stood up and I knew that was it. That was all I was going to get here. I gave it one last shot. "What about Mark Hopequist? What did he do during the takedown?"

The men look at each other, their faces screwed up in puzzlement.

"Who?" they ask. "Who the hell is he?"

EIGHTEEN

That night, I got a phone call from Aliana, not a message, but an actual call. To my surprise, I was glad to hear from her.

"I've made progress," I told her with a little too much enthusiasm for an old judge, "I found a couple of reprobates who made me right at home and told me a number of things about three of the four cops!"

I filled her in, eager to share the details of my "interviews".

When I stopped for a breath, I could hear her breathing on the other end of the line, as if she were hanging on my every word.

"But nothing about Hopequist," I said at last. "Not a word about him…"

"That's why I called, Ellis," she answered, finally able to get a word in. "I've got a lead."

"On Hopequist?"

"Right."

"Through your police contacts?"

"No. I got to him through our mutual acquaintances at Child Services."

I was surprised at this information. Over the years, I'd often worked with them, and I couldn't think of an organization more dedicated to keeping information secret than the workers at the agency in charge of the welfare of young people.

"How can we get anything from them, Aliana? They're tighter than…

"I identified you and me as volunteers on the Kezia file. Apparently they checked our credentials."

"And I passed? That's good to know."

"Don't be ridiculous, Ellis. Of course you 'passed'. Anyway, they gave me some background on the case. Nothing we don't already know…"

"Of course." I imagined that it was a pretty regular occurrence for Aliana to be handed information she already knew—ace investigator that she clearly was.

"The upshot is this: we can make an appointment with Mark to talk to him directly. I had to swear on my mother's blood that we would not mention one word—not a single syllable--to Mark about any actual police work. We have to stick to matters immediately concerning Kezia's welfare."

"Aliana, that's wonderful! When did you have in mind for us to meet Mark?"

"Whoa! Not so fast. Before we meet with him, we have to thoroughly familiarize ourselves with the girl and her circumstances, which will necessitate at least one home visit, possibly more than one."

I knew better than to bother asking whether this meant that Aliana and I would soon be working more closely together.

***

Two days later, I found myself sitting behind the wheel of my BMW reluctant to leave the car—I almost thought *abandon* the car--anywhere near Kezia's building, not that her building looked very different from my own. In fact, Kezia's home was only a few miles east on Eglinton beyond my apartment building. I was totally familiar with Kezia's neighborhood and I knew that a few blocks in either direction in Scarborough could make a big difference in the quality of the so-called "community".

As Aliana approached, I couldn't help but notice that she was all business today. She wore a slim black wool coat and boots with higher heels than I would have previously imagined on a woman her age. Her long hair was loose but very tidy and its blackness was set off by the fine streaks of gray near her animated face.

"Ellis! A bit early. That's great. I've got a few notes here…"

She took off her black leather gloves, flipped a few pages in a small notebook and pretty much shoved it in my face, too close for me to read what she'd written there without my other glasses.

"Fine, Aliana. I'll just follow your lead."

She nodded and turned smartly toward the front door

Through the window, I could see that the lobby was completely empty. Nothing. No furniture. No curtains. No rugs. No pictures on the wall, not even the ubiquitous cheaply framed prints of long-ago rural scenes that graced the lobby walls of many an apartment building lobby in this town.

"Doesn't look bad from the outside," Aliana observed. "But I don't like this sterile lobby. It can only mean one thing!"

"No furniture is safe here," I said with a smile. "Mailboxes aren't doing so well either."

Just visible against the back wall, stood rows of steel cubbyholes, some clearly suffering from having been broken into. In one corner a vending machine covered with graffiti leaned toward the elevators. Even through the plate-glass lobby door I could see that one of the elevator doors had an out-of-service sign that was singed on the bottom edge and browned from age.

Aliana reached toward a metal panel displaying apartment numbers. I tried to suppress my skepticism as to whether anyone would answer any of those buzzers—that is assuming that they worked.

Before Kezia—or anyone else in her apartment—had a chance to answer, the door swung open and two people sauntered out. One was a tall, lean young black man in full street regalia: falling-down jeans, big bright running shoes, gigantic mass of dreads.

The other was an old Muslim woman. Her hijab covered only a part of what I could tell had once been a very pretty face. She reminded me so strongly of my beloved long-gone Italian grandmother that I got that pang of grief again, a pang I realized was beginning to lessen.

As we got closer to the bank of elevators, it became quite obvious that people were getting into and coming out of only one—and it was the one with the old out-of-service notice on it.

As if she could read my mind, Aliana leaned close to me and whispered. "Bite the bullet."

I slid into the elevator beside her, trying to convince myself that whatever shape it was in, it was safer than trying our luck on the stairs….

As we ascended to the tenth floor, various people got on and off. Every time the door opened, the cooking smells of a different cuisine seem to rush in: curry, cabbage, barbecue, odd indescribable, undecipherable mixtures that instantly turned my always overly-sensitive stomach.

I soon realized that the presence of Aliana and me was no more reassuring to the other inhabitants of the elevator than ours was to them. They shot us glances of distrust, nicely peppered with disgust.

We slowly negotiated the dark hallway and searched for the right number on the apartment doors we passed. Several bore spray-painted inscriptions in a script that I couldn't read. I was not exactly reassured about our safety when I noticed two bullet holes in the door of the unit we were looking for.

Distracted by the sight, I wasn't paying attention when Aliana knocked on Kezia's door. I was unprepared to see it swing open immediately and to find myself face-to-face with a dark, snarling young man in leather, chains, tattoos, dreads, complexly knotted scarves, rings—the lot.

Despite all my years' experience, or maybe because of them, my first reaction was the intense desire to turn on my heels and run. Or at least to expect to have the door slammed in my face. I glanced at Aliana. She wore a look I had seen many times before. The look of a reporter who has sniffed a good story.

But, instead of the hostile—even violent--reaction that I feared, the young man smiled rather winningly and said, "You here for my little sister?"

I wasn't sure he really meant his little sister or whether that was some kind of gang parlance. I just nodded, but Aliana smiled widely and held out her hand, which the young man stared at but didn't touch as he gestured toward us to enter.

NINETEEN

The youth breezed by and away, leaving us standing in the doorway. I glanced in and saw that the apartment was very tidy and comfortable-looking with the sort of furniture that could be bought at the local stores: Leon's, Bad Boy, The Brick.

We stood there for what seemed quite a long time.

"Should we call out for Kezia's mother?" I asked.

Aliana shook her head. "She's not likely to be here. The woman works pretty much twenty-four/seven. Apparently she only comes home to sleep."

Before I could comment on that difficult fact, the door was yanked wide open and a familiar young voice demanded, "What you doin' here?"

Aliana took a very tiny step forward. "We came to see how you're getting on…."

The girl's face was unreadable as she said, "I'm getting on fine. How come you have to check on me or whatever?"

"We were just thinking about our conversation of the other day and we decided to drop by…."

I had to laugh at the expression on the girl's face at that announcement. She was no fool. She'd heard lines like that before, that was for sure. However, she just bowed her head and said, "Okay."

"Do you mind if we come in?"

I kept silent. Though I had interviewed and counselled many young people, I strongly felt that females responded more naturally and easily to other females. I seldom articulated this idea, however. Or, for that matter, any ideas that might be seen as gender prejudice.

The girl glanced around as if there were someone else there, perhaps someone whose permission she sought. But there was apparently no one else in the apartment.

"Okay. I guess it's okay if you come in. You could sit on the couch if you want."

Aliana sat at one end of the long sofa, I sat on the other end, and Kezia took a chair opposite. Not surprisingly, the conversation got off to a slow start. Questions about school elicited the remark, "I don't always get there." Questions about hobbies, about reading, about helping to keep the apartment in such a nice state, met with pretty close to dead silence interrupted by the occasionally uttered monosyllable.

When I finally found my tongue and ventured to ask a question, I got a surprising and encouraging reaction. "The young man we saw at the door seemed quite friendly," I began, "is he a friend of yours?"

The girl could only be described as bursting into smiles, smiles that seemed to enliven her whole body. She straightened from the slouch that she'd sat in and bolted upright.

"Yeah, he's my friend all right. That's Cano. Old Cano is my best friend. He's my brother. I mean he's my *real* brother. So I knowed him since we was born. And in all the time, he never did nothin' bad to me. He be my *good* brother."

"I understand you have two other brothers?" Aliana asked carefully.

Kezia's fists closed on her knees but she still sat forward as though she really wanted us to hear what she had to say.

"They are not so good," she said. All the warmth, the spontaneity was gone from her voice, and the intensity of her posture fled as quickly as it had come. "They against each other and us."

"What do you mean, Kezia?" I asked gently.

She looked up at me and I could see her trying to make up her mind as to whether she should trust me.

"You the old guy that used to live by the river?" she asked.

I had to smile. "One of 'em," I answered.

"Did you live down there in the winter? Like when the ice was there?"

"Yes, Kezia. I lived there all year long."

"In the snow and that?"

I had no idea what this was all about. I glanced at Aliana who smiled and nodded and looked so reassuring that I felt I'd tell her anything she wanted to know myself.

"To tell the truth, Kezia, in a lot of ways, I liked winter down by the river more than any other season."

The girl's dark eyes seemed to light up. "Yeah? Like what do you mean? You musta been pretty cold down there, sleeping near the river in the snow."

"Well, the thing I liked best was how quiet it always was. Lots of days there were no loud sounds at all. No people. No animals. No birds. Not even the sound of the river under the ice…"

"Didn't you get lonely or scared or anything like that?"

Something about the innocence of the question touched a deep chord in me. "Kezia," I said, "I've been more scared and lonely in the presence of other people than I've ever been when I've been alone."

"See," the girl said after a moment's thought, "that's one of the things that's bad about my two brothers. They just so damn noisy! Always swearin' and yellin' and rappin'. Plus they tease me and my good brother until we feel like smashing them, but we never touch them. Otherwise, we be hurt bad! You see, those two brothers are enemies. They belong to gangs that hate each other. Sometimes they kill each other. And I get afraid that my brothers might…."

As if she realized she had said too much, the girl cut the conversation. "What are you doin' here?" she asked again.

Aliana came to the rescue, carefully asking "Is it true, Kezia, that you haven't been in school in quite a while?"

"Boring. School is too boring."

At the mention of school, my eye settled on a desk against one wall, a desk littered with books and papers, as if someone studying there had been suddenly interrupted. I fought the urge to ask the girl whether her "good" brother was studying and going to school. But I kept my peace. For two people to be questioning the girl would be too much like an interrogation.

"Are you afraid to go to school?" Aliana gently asked.

"Hell, no!" the girl answered so emphatically that I knew she was lying. "Anyway, I can learn more here by myself than at any dumb, stupid school." She looked over toward the books and papers. "My mother, she got to work three jobs, so me and my brother are alone here most always. We study together. Sometimes the other two come here and tear up our papers. Once they even set fire to our books, but mostly, they don't come around. So me and my brother, we can work on our own projects.

"My brother, he got an iPad that some rich guy in the church give him." She lowered her voice. "It's hid so nobody can get it. But I don't need no iPad. I got a libary card and I can get all the books I want and even use the computer there if I stand in line. And they didn't even make me pay when my brother burned one of the libary books, and when he cuts up my libary card, they just give me another one. And she—the libarian—even lets me keep the card right there where it's safe in her desk instead of taking it home."

I stood and moved toward the table, not sure what I expected to see, but not expecting what I did see. Instead of juvenile and graphic novels or books about movies or music, all the books seem to be about the weather. "Are you studying about climate change?"

"No," Kezia said, "Snow and ice. A person can read them, just like you read a book. Ice and snow, they can tell you things you couldn't learn in other ways. They can answer questions. They can even tell the future."

I hid a smile. "Is that so?"

"Your future?" Aliana asks quietly.

"Yes. My future. My future as an author. The future of my book, *Fifty Recipes Made With Snow*."

"You are working on your book?" Aliana and I said simultaneously, not even trying to act unsurprised.

"Yes. I sure am. And I've even done research on it. I went on a field trip put on by a youth group thing and the man running it was Mark."

"Mark Hopequist?" Aliana asked.

"Yes. He was the leader. They said he leads a lot of groups and he knows a lot about the city. He told us all sorts of things about what winter is like in the valley."

She looked at me. "I bet you know those things, too. Anyway, I learned a lot on that field trip. I even learned that secret from Mark. He told me a secret that he didn't tell anybody else."

I smiled at this child-like revelation. Again I worried about what it might mean. But I forgot about it when Aliana gave me a phone number for Mark and he agreed to a meeting.

TWENTY

We met at a Tim Hortons down the street from police Headquarters, though I had been diligent in remembering that I wasn't supposed to utter a word about current police business.

"I'm happy to learn that you and Aliana are willing to help Kezia," Mark began, shaking my hand and offering me a seat in the crowded coffee shop before he disappeared.

He returned with two large coffees, which I took to be a good sign. By the time we finished those, we'd have had plenty of time to talk.

He slid his lanky body into the seat across from me. The place was buzzing with conversation. It was almost hard to hear his voice, which seemed soft for so large a man. "I'm really sorry to hear that she isn't going to school," he began. "That's one of the things we worked on. She's a clever girl, but she has a hard time settling down and concentrating on one thing at a time."

"Aliana has the same concern," I said. "She did question the girl a little on that matter."

Mark nodded. "I have a great deal of respect for Aliana. And if she's doing a story on how gang membership affects families, I'm happy to help. In the time that I spent working with youth, it was one of the major issues I had to deal with."

"One of the things Aliana is interested in," I commented, trying to find an angle that would be helpful to me, "is how police officers who might be otherwise engaged in more uh—dramatic— work find helping children and teens exciting enough."

Mark's handsome features softened at this question, which gave me a sense of relief. I didn't know whether I'd overstepped any bounds in asking it, but he seemed eager to answer.

"It's an old cliché, you know," he said. "The idea that helping people is the most exciting thing a cop can do."

I thought about the officers I'd seen at Queen's Park the other day. Their black face masks. Their helmets. The broad shields that covered all of their bodies, except their hands, which bore their raised batons.

"I don't think it's much of a cliché anymore," I said. "I mean I don't think people feel that way. I think most people feel that fighting criminals is what the police are supposed to be doing…."

"Sure. But helping kids is a good way to fight criminals. Especially when you're talking about kids in danger of falling prey to gangs."

"And that's the case with Kezia, isn't it?" I asked. It wasn't a trick question. Like Mark, I had quickly seen what a clever girl Kezia was.

"She's in a bad position," Mark answered. "Has been for a long time. I don't know how much she opened up to you, and I wouldn't discuss her like this except that Aliana convinced me that it was okay, since you're going to keep an eye on the kid." He glanced out the window where crowds of people rushed by the corner of College and Yonge, an intersection packed with stores, coffee shops and directly across the street, a branch of the criminal courts. "She's got three brothers. One's as straight as a rod. A real good kid. But the other two…" He shook his head.

"She did tell me a little about them," I said. "Something about them being in rival gangs."

Mark looked sharply up. "I'm surprised," he said after a moment's thought. "I'm surprised she told you about them. It's a good sign, actually. If she trusted you that much right away maybe you can give her a boost. Get her to go back to school."

I felt guilty. My real interest wasn't Kezia at all, much as I wished the kid all the best. My real interest was Mark, and I could already see that he wasn't your average Toronto cop. I really wondered how he mustered the toughness needed to do the job. Even to give somebody a traffic ticket would require more negative authority than this man seemed capable of marshalling. Unless he had another personality beneath his very pleasant manner.

"Anyway," Mark went on, "helping kids like Kezia was the most exciting police work I ever did." He glanced down and seemed to study the coffee cup he held between his large hands. "I know how that sounds. But I never been a body-and-fender man, myself."

"Unlike some people?" I ventured.

Mark glanced up as though he knew I meant someone in particular. His gaze hardened and the smile left his face. I saw in that moment, that he was all cop after all.

"I'm sure you realize I'm not at liberty to discuss any other officer."

"Of course," I said, trying to sound as if that were the last thing I would ever imagine doing. I cleared my throat and changed the subject. "If you found working with the young people so rewarding, why did you leave?"

"I left because of the wife," he said. "She was terrified that working with young people put me in a position of vulnerability. She's a social worker and she knows how a lot of these kids—especially the girls—act out. She kept telling me that all it would take to ruin our lives would be for some girl—or even a boy—to accuse me of misbehavior."

I knew what kind of misbehavior he was talking about.

"Yeah, the wife accepts that my being a cop entails a lot of risks. But to be falsely accused by a young person—that's a risk she won't take."

"But as a social worker, doesn't she face the same sort of risk?" I asked.

Mark finished his coffee with a gigantic gulp before he answered. "Heck no. She only deals with old people."

I didn't see fit to comment on that observation. I almost mentioned Kezia's remark about the secret. But I thought better of it. It seemed nothing but a casual aside that probably had no real meaning. I was sure that someone as clearly competent and aware as this man would not have made an inappropriate disclosure to Kezia.

I tried to recall the few things that Aliana was able to share about Mark. "I understand that you come from a long line of cops and that you had a career in banking before joining the force.

Mark laughed. "That's correct. And let me tell you, compared to being a banker, being a cop is a walk in the park."

There was a moment of silence then and, embarrassed, I couldn't think of what to ask about aside from what I was longing to ask about which was, of course, the Juicer.

"You know," Mark finally said, "helping the homeless was just as satisfying as helping children, but it turned out to be even riskier."

"You mean The Juicer?" I dared say.

"Can't say anything about him," Mark replied. "Except that he was a sorry man with a future that contained nothing but further suffering."

I realized that this might have been something Queenie had known too, though it didn't stop her from helping the man.

Mark stood and held out his hand for me to shake. His grip was powerful. I could easily imagine how much it would hurt if a man with his obvious strength were to wield a baton against fragile bones. But his demeanor, his whole way of carrying himself, his way of speaking—all of it was so gentle, so controlled, so basically benign—that I couldn't imagine him harming—let alone killing--anybody. The very thought embarrassed me and I hoped my face showed nothing of my feelings as he said goodbye and headed off on College Street toward Headquarters.

TWENTY-ONE

When I got back to my car, which I'd parked in the public lot underneath a nearby hotel, I found a note on the windshield.

At first I thought it was some sort of ticket, though I couldn't imagine why I would get one. But as I got closer to the car, I saw that it was a folded piece of white paper that turned out to be a small sheet of the hotel's stationery.

My fingers shook a little as I unfolded the note. In handwriting that was firm and clear, it said, "If you're as smart as you think you are, you'll stay out of things that are none of your damn business."

My mind sped back to the moment in which Aliana and I had jumped out of the way of the flying glass from the window shattered by gunfire. We'd heard nothing more about that, and I was fairly sure that we wouldn't hear anything. Unfortunately, random gunfire in the downtown core was not such a rare occurrence that it would elicit a great deal of investigation.

But the note was a different kind of threat. It was personal. I glanced around. The parking lot was huge with several levels reaching down deep beneath the building. For someone to know which car was mine and where exactly I had put it could only mean that someone had followed me. Perhaps they had known that I'd met with Mark, maybe even overheard our conversation. Not that they would have learned much from it, I was sorry to reflect.

I refolded the note and put it in the glove box. The thought of going to the police occurred to me. Of course it did. But I didn't want to complicate matters. And I wanted to think about the note for a while. The tone didn't seem familiar, but it did seem distinctive, as if I could almost picture the type of person who would use those words.

In the end, I decided to leave the car where it was and to walk back up onto the street and over to police Headquarters to try and see Matt West

I wasn't sure Matt would even talk to me. I imagined he was extremely busy these days as Deputy Chief, supervising the vast security detail that would be necessary with world leaders about to descend on the city in preparation for the world affairs summit.

I had to deal with the front desk, and the men on duty there were pretty sure Matt wasn't available without an appointment made well in advance.

The more difficult it began to seem to get to him, the more determined I became. As I had sat in my car in the parking lot of the hotel, I had come to the conclusion that it was probably a good idea to run things by Matt. To ask him whether the police had made any progress in finding out who shot at me and Aliana the day we were having coffee. And I wanted to show him the note. Above all, I wanted to ask Matt if there were any way I could talk to the other three cops.

I was almost about to give up on Matt when I looked up and saw an officer I knew had been a special friend of Queenie's. Over the years, her relationship with the police had climbed all the way up the scale from being shooed away from the doorways in which she had once slept to having lunch with the chief at a special function at which she'd been given a medal for her work among the city's disempowered.

"So sorry to hear about Queenie," the officer said. "You here to see Matt?"

"Yes, but I'm having a little trouble…."

"I'll call him for you."

I waited a few minutes longer before Matt showed up. I had expected to be asked up to his office but what happened instead was that he came striding down the massive central steps of the Headquarters lobby, charged toward me and asked me what he could do for me.

It was clear that my old pal didn't really want to see me. Matt and I been good friends for years, working together on a number of cases. But now Matt was cold and distant and formal, as if I were just some pesky citizen demanding something from the police that an ordinary citizen had no right to demand.

I could tell that he wanted to conduct our conversation right there in the lobby. "What is it, Ellis? What can I do for you?"

"Matt," I began, "I'll only take a minute of your time, but there are a couple of things I want to run by you and…"

He glanced at his watch. "I'm pressed for time. What exactly is it?"

"Can we go upstairs? I'm uncomfortable talking about these things here…." I gestured broadly toward the lobby into which another group of school children on another sort of tour had just marched.

He let out a sigh, a gesture I'd not associated with Matt before, and nodded toward the stairs, which we managed to negotiate before the crowd of kids beat us to it.

I sat in the hard chair in front of the sterile desk and got right down to it. "I have a couple of things on my mind, Matt. For starters, I'm sure you're aware that Aliana Caterina and I were sitting near the window of a Tim Hortons when somebody shot at…"

He didn't even let me finish. "Ellis, I'm sure you understand that we are investigating that incident, just as we would investigate any shooting. However, I know you can appreciate the fact that since no one was hurt, we are handling it as a misuse of firearms issue rather than attempted murder or anything like that."

"But…"

"Look, Ellis. I'm sorry you were involved in such an incident. But the fact is that there are so many occurrences of gunshots these days, that you'd have to line up with everybody else who claims to have heard, seen, or even been threatened by a gun."

I was shocked at Matt's attitude. But it got worse. When I showed him the note I'd found on the car, he laughed and said, "Sounds like good advice to me."

I got up and turned toward the door. I'd had enough. I felt as though someone had kidnapped the Matt I'd always known and left this officious imposter in his place.

But as I reached the door, I felt Matt's hand on my shoulder.

"Look, Ellis," he said. "I'm so very sorry about Queenie. I can't begin to understand what you must be going through right now, but I think the best thing you can do is to forget about police work at the moment. Leave all this to us. Don't be trying to solve mysteries right now when, I'm sure, everything must seem like a mystery to you. Don't worry about the gunshots. We've got squads of people working on things like that. And as far as the note goes, it was probably just a coincidence. Some nutbar in the parking lot. Happens all the time. If you really want to hear my advice, it's this: Go home. Take it easy. Wait until your life gets normal again. I'm sure that if you do that, you'll forget all about your detective work."

Before I had a chance to respond, he went on, "Listen, buddy, I know you're trying to find out what happened to Queenie's friend. I wish I could help you, but you have to understand my position. There's an ongoing investigation regarding the death of that man and we can't have any tampering with witnesses."

To accuse a former judge of attempting to influence a witness was a grave insult, and I knew that Matt knew it. But I also knew that Matt would never have said such a cruel thing carelessly. I figured somebody must be on Matt's back bigtime.

"I can tell you this much, Ellis. I have a feeling that PIC is going to come to a quick decision on this one." He hesitated and lowered his voice, "And in the past, quick decisions have almost always been in the favor of the accused." He went back to his desk, jotted something on a slip of paper, stood up. "Look, give this guy a call. He's over at forensics. He's the examiner in the case." He handed me the number. "Sorry, man. I'm out of here. I've got a meeting."

As I made my way back to my car, I realized that I'd learned something very valuable from the interview with Matt after all. That Matt suspected the PIC investigation would soon be over. And that that meant I would get a chance to talk to the four accused about the case. They would no longer be accused. They would just be four good cops who did their job with unfortunate results that no one could foresee.

TWENTY-TWO

As was becoming my habit, I stopped at the village on the way home. As I approached on the path down, I could hear the raised voices of two men arguing, the crushed voices of the down and out, but not of the drunk or drugged because the village had strict rules about sobriety.

As I got closer, I realized the men were arguing about some small point—who said what, who showed someone disrespect—the inconsequential subjects of the arguments of the bored or otherwise discontented. But I knew that among the clients who lived there, even mundane arguments could escalate into deadly conflicts.

I carefully avoided the two, seeking among the village buildings to find Jeffrey. When I found him in the main building, he was deep in conversation with a client. Not wanting to breach the confidentiality with which they were obviously speaking, I turned around immediately. But Jeffrey saw me, excused himself from his work and called out, "Dad! Don't go. We have to talk."

He disengaged himself from the man with whom he'd been speaking and came toward me with both hands outstretched.

"Son, I…" I knew I had to apologize for the way I'd acted the last time we'd been together, but Jeffrey stopped me with a smile and a nod.

"I'm really glad you came down, Dad. I've been meaning to call you." He waved toward the client as the man walked out the door.

"What's up?"

Jeffrey drew in a breath. "There were some people down here again the other day, a man and two women. They said they were from a committee struck by the city to examine possible problems with below-standard housing."

"Below-standard housing? What the heck is that supposed to mean?"

"They said they're concerned with wooden structures—that there are buildings in our compound that are constructed of inferior materials." He hesitated as if he were afraid to say what was coming next. "They said there's a new ruling. It's called 'condemn and confiscate'. It would give the city the go-ahead to expropriate property in sensitive areas, property that doesn't meet standards. It's intended to protect environmentally-endangered areas—like the whole valley of the Don.

"What does that have to do with us?" I could feel my ire beginning to rise, but I watched it. I didn't want to display any anger in Jeffrey's presence, even anger directed at somebody else.

"Well," Jeffrey said, taking his time as if he wanted to be sure to say exactly the right thing, "apparently there are councilors who are preparing to argue that all buildings of whatever nature should be removed from this section of the valley."

I made a broad gesture intended to take in the entire village—the main building, the building that housed the kitchen, the fifteen small wooden huts where the men—and sometimes women—slept, the washrooms. "This is not City-owned land. It is private property."

"Dad, zoning laws apply to private property, and I don't need to remind you that governments can expropriate land whenever they see fit."

"They actually talked about expropriation?" I had a hard time keeping my voice steady.

Jeffrey reached out and touched my hand for a second. "No. No, Dad. Calm down. They didn't threaten. Like the others who came down, they said they were on a fact-finding mission."

"Typical government double-speak! What other nonsense did they spout?"

"They said that private citizens are invited to appear at an upcoming meeting of City Council—date to be announced--in order to give their views on the issue."

"Yeah? And exactly which private citizens do you suppose they have in mind?"

Jeffrey shrugged.

"There's no way I can do it, Jeffrey," I told him. "There are still people down at city hall who haven't forgotten my days of disgrace—and there are enemies of Queenie's, too, people who thought it was absurd that the city should support a woman who had once been among the most raggedy of the street people and was now asking for funding in order to run a shelter."

"We have a friend at city hall."

"Is that some sort of a catch phrase: a friend at city hall? I wouldn't joke about it. If one or two of those councilors got on their high horse, we could be looking at a lot of trouble."

"No, Dad. It's not a joke. We really do have a friend there, someone who'll take our side if there is a real debate. Somebody with a lot of clout."

"Who?"

"Look," he answered. "Let's leave this for now. They haven't even set a date for a council meeting. And you're right. Our holdings are private and our buildings are sound—no matter how modest." He looked me in the eye. "You said I had to keep you posted on everything. Well, I'm just letting you know they came down here."

"Okay, Son," I said, "that's fine. Be sure to let me know if you see them again."

"Will do."

I turned to leave, but Jeffrey stopped me with an offer of coffee and I couldn't refuse. I took a seat while he manned the coffee machine.

Beside the chair in which I sat was a small table and on the table were arrayed the day's newspapers with Aliana's paper, the *Toronto Daily World* on top.

I picked it up intending to leaf through to see if I could find her byline, but before I even got past the first page, I saw a headline "below the fold" as they say. It read, "Investigation of four Toronto Cops Halted."

I read the article as fast as I could get my brain to work. For the first time, there were real details about what had happened that night. The four had been called not to a possible crime scene but to a "medical emergency" in front of the mental hospital. They had turned up because two of the four were regularly assigned to that beat and the other two were nearby in their cruisers. It was true, the article stated, that the four police officers had found it necessary to physically subdue the homeless man and that they had spent the better part of half an hour restraining him.

But it was also apparently true that aside from minor scrapes and bruises and the spraining of two of his fingers, the patient had suffered no injuries from this encounter. In fact, the reporter stated, the police officers had not apprehended the homeless man but had instead turned him over to three duty nurses who had led him under his own power back into the hospital.

The article continued, "At some time during the night, the elderly patient succumbed to a heart attack. PIC, the Police Investigative Commission that examines allegations of police misconduct, concluded that the officers had had no direct connection with the death. However, the coroner's office is reported to still be investigating the case."

At first I felt an immense sense of relief at this news. It meant that I could now interview the four cops. But then it occurred to me that there was no longer any reason why I should want to. No murder. No killer to find. No case.

As I sipped the coffee my son gave me, I felt as if I were relaxing for the first time in many weeks. We chatted. I asked him how my daughter-in-law Tootie and my grandchildren were doing. "Fine, Dad," he said. "Everybody is just doing great."

I asked him if he saw his sister, Ellen. He frowned a little and said she seemed always to be too busy to come over for dinner but that her husband and her son, Angelo, kept him informed of her duties as a crown attorney. He said that there were rumors going around that Ellen might follow in her father's footsteps.

"What does that mean?" I asked, genuinely puzzled.

Jeffrey laughed. "The bench, Dad. The bench."

The very thought of my little girl possibly be named to the bench in the near future filled me with concern. It was not an easy calling, as my shadowed life had proved. But, I had to admit, pride soon replaced concern.

I would have left the valley a happy man that night, had I not overheard yet another altercation among a few of the valley inhabitants on my way out.

Listening in for only a few minutes, I learned at once that the village was divided into two camps—those who believed that the four cops really didn't have anything to do with the Juicer's death, and those who thought the cops were "saving their own," that is, that some kind of cover-up was going on.

I made my presence known and took the risk of asking the men what the general consensus was. A couple of them clearly considered me an intruder, but I had a few friends among them, too, men with whom I'd often discussed matters having to do with the news and the city and even their lives.

"Well," said one man, "I think you could say we're six of one, half dozen of the other on this thing. Half of the guys down here think the cops are liars…"

"Which would make them killers," someone interrupted.

"No news there," came another voice.

"Take it easy, Dude," the first man said. "One of them cops is Mark Hopequist."

"Yeah? So? He's a fag. A useless sissy."

"Which means he ain't likely to kill anybody. Especially the Juicer."

"Another useless bag of shit," his opponent answered.

"What about this Mark Hopequist?" I asked. "What kind of a guy is he?"

"Not so bad, especially for a cop. He's tough on people who are mean to the homeless, like teenagers and tourists and rich ladies. He never gave nobody a homeless ticket, that's for sure. And also, he ain't no liar like some cops I know."

A few others joined the discussion. They didn't hesitate to say that most of the people in the village hated cops. As far as they were concerned, the Juicer was murdered by somebody. He never had any heart condition, and the way Queenie kept at him about eating the right food and exercising "all the time," he hadn't been likely to.

As we stood around talking, a cold wind suddenly rose. "Hey, someone said, "that's winter blowing in."

And it was. Not only the winter of cruel weather, but the winter of my return to the realization that despite what the newspaper had revealed, I was not in any way excused from the obligation of my promise to Queenie.

TWENTY-THREE

As I climbed out of the valley that afternoon, I had the uncomfortable sensation that someone was watching me.

In the old days, I could climb into and out of the valley at any time of the day or night in the light or in the dark without thinking twice about it.

But now I was over seventy, and although my time living rough meant that my life had been more physical than the lives of others my age, it also had also taken its toll.

So now I navigated the rough path with some difficulty in the gathering dark. I stopped a couple of times, and each time, I thought I heard someone else stopping just a second or two after I did. If whoever or whatever was making this sound was behind me, then I knew I'd reach the top of the ravine before my pursuer. This idea gave me some comfort, but not much.

When I did reach the top, I heard a sudden rapid scurrying. A little rabbit, mostly brown but with a bit of white here and there, rushed up to meet me, rustling through the dry autumn leaves.

I smiled at the little thing and marveled that it could make so much noise. But not enough noise to hide the fact that something—or someone—else was also scurrying away.

***

Alone at the kitchen window of my spacious apartment, a window that looked out over the valley, I thought about the people in the village at their supper.

Though I had never been what anyone would consider a gourmet cook, I had had to be quite creative in feeding myself when I was homeless in the valley. I remembered some of the awful things I'd had to eat in those days: squirrels, snakes--and some of the meals Queenie and I had enjoyed in very much more recent days: steaks, broiled fish, Italian delicacies.

It suddenly occurred to me that, despite frequent invitations from friends and family, I hadn't tasted a decent home-cooked meal in a long time. My fridge was empty because I'd thrown out the remains of meals I'd fixed but hadn't had the appetite to eat.

So I headed for the grocery store, checking the parking lot of my building for any intruders, since I couldn't seem to get the idea of a possible pursuer out of my mind.

I was home within twenty minutes and I managed to recreate a viable facsimile of one of Queenie's best dishes, a vegetarian chili made with four different kinds of beans and three kinds of tomatoes.

I set the table, served the food, picked up my fork...

At first, a pang of grief gripped me, but I pulled myself together and I ate. It wasn't the same as it used to be. But it was good. It was damn good.

***

After dinner, I got an unexpected phone call. Mark Hopequist.

"Ellis, I enjoyed our conversation," he began. "I'm really happy that you've taken an interest in Kezia."

"Yes," I said. I still wasn't sure why people thought I could do something to help this child, though Kezia herself seemed eager to pick my brain, and I was certainly willing to share my adventures in the valley with an eager young person. It was beginning to occur to me that one of the things I might consider doing now that I was pretty much fully retired from the law was to write my memoirs. When I thought about that idea, I had to laugh. But then, I always came back to thinking about it

"I have someone else you might like to talk to about teens and gangs," Mark said. "Her name is Feeance Blake, and she's willing to give you a call if you're interested."

He said nothing about who this person was, but I knew. And I wondered whether he had some reason to draw me into the matters he had refused to talk about in our meeting. Of course, with PIC off the case, everything had changed. But that still didn't explain why these two cops were suddenly willing to talk. Once again I got the feeling that I wasn't getting out of dealing with a murder—I was getting deeper in.

"I can give her your phone number," Mark said.

"Sure."

Only a few seconds after I hung up the phone rang again. A low, smooth, cultured voice told me she was ready to meet me and she set the time and the place.

Tim Hortons again. The next day at eight a.m. I thought maybe she was meeting me after a night shift or before a day shift, though I couldn't pretend to know how the cops at Headquarters were assigned their work times.

She was beautiful. Dark, smooth skin, wide eyes, high cheekbones and a lovely wide mouth. But oh, the attitude! I was afraid to look at her. Afraid that she wasn't a keen fan of old white guys.

Her greeting of me was neutral. Officious. No smile. No handshake. No coffee offered, until I asked her to wait and that I'd get her whatever she wanted, which, to my immense surprise turned out to be some big-cup thing with a lot of froth and a skinny piece of chocolate sticking out of it.

"Thanks."

She took a sip and for a moment, the white of the cream on top of the coffee sat in a line over her mouth until she reached up with her tongue and licked it off. The gesture made her seem human and I felt less apprehensive about dealing with her.

"So," she said, "you're the man who lived in the valley all those years."

"One of them."

She gave me a look that seemed to say, "If you're going to be a smart ass, this conversation is over right now."

"Unfortunately," I added, "there are quite a number of people who find it necessary to live rough in Toronto."

She nodded. "I always wanted to meet you. Your story is not unknown around the city. I've considered the fact that you are a sort of model."

I grinned uncomfortably.

"It's a story that young people can relate to—if it's told in the right way," she went on. "And I'm sure you're the right person to tell it."

Oh no! I could see it coming. An invitation to address countless bored students to tell them how I rose and fell and rose again. This was not the first time I'd been asked to "share my story" with the masses, and it wouldn't be the last time that I would steadfastly refuse.

There was a moment's awkward silence, during which I studied her. You could tell just by looking that she was the no-nonsense type of modern cop. She was dressed in civilian clothes, but everything about her screamed police, her neat hair, her almost stiff posture, and her clipped way of speaking. I figured that the fact that she was female, black and beautiful probably had no bearing on how she carried out her job—which was, I suspected, with conscientious thoroughness.

I sensed that being straightforward would probably net the best results with a person like her, so I got right to the point. "Why did you agree to meet me? What's in it for you?"

She smiled as if she appreciated the question. "Kezia," she answered. "And kids like her." She took another swig of her latte supremo, sat back a little and said, "I've been aware of Mark Hopequist's work with kids for some time now. I understand that family matters got in the way of his continuing. So I help out now when I can. As you can imagine, I haven't got a lot of time to engage in off-duty volunteer work...."

I couldn't really imagine anything about her off-duty life, but I didn't have the nerve to ask. I didn't quite have the nerve yet to ask her about her on-duty life either, specifically whether it included physically subduing the mentally ill.

"When I heard that you had taken an interest in the girl, I thought it would be good to meet with you. The thing about Kezia is that her problem is a gang problem and the sooner gang problems are solved in Toronto, the longer people like Kezia will live."

I was alarmed at this information. I wasn't trying to solve a gang case, I was trying to find out who killed the Juicer.

But Feeance suddenly seemed obsessed. Without my asking, she started to spout facts and figures about teens—mostly black—who had been killed in Toronto in the recent past. Their names were a sad litany and I recognized a lot of them from the news. Targeted shootings, mistaken identity shots fired from fast-passing cars, young men—it was usually men—shot outside of clubs, in shopping malls, and even outside their own homes, which were as often as not in fine suburban neighborhoods.

I expressed my genuine concern over these horrible facts, but I had to gently steer our conversation toward what I really wanted to know, which was Feeance's view of what had happened the night of the Juicer's death.

"Nothing. Nothing happened that night that doesn't happen somewhere in the city every night of the week—more than that. Time after time, night after night. Somebody loses it. Somebody gets to the point where they can't take it anymore." She shrugged. "Anyway, there were no charges, no misconduct at all. Just a sad case of an old guy losing control and ending up giving himself a heart attack. It's nothing. There's no need to even think about it anymore."

She didn't sound hard. She sounded tired.

"Have you ever worked with the homeless?" I asked her.

She looked at me like I was an idiot. "How could I work downtown—or anywhere in Toronto—without working with the homeless?"

"I'm sorry, I…"

"To tell the truth, though," she went on, "before the night of the incident, I was never in the presence of a homeless person who was in any way apprehended except in a completely peaceful manner. Now I think I was lucky all these years—I mean never to see anything like what that old guy was doing…."

"What? What exactly was he doing?"

She didn't answer. She started quoting again: use-of-force policies, police-treatment-of-the-mentally-ill regulations, use of less-than-lethal devices…

"Less-than-lethal devices? What's that—Tasers?"

"Yeah. But only supervisors have them. Never touched one myself."

"Had you ever seen the man they called the Juicer before?" I asked, trying once again to get back on track.

Feeance shook her head. "Before that night, I never met him, didn't know a thing about him."

"What do you know about him now?"

TWENTY-FOUR

At first, Feeance just stared at me, as if she had no intention of answering that question.

Then slowly and thoughtfully, she began to talk, sounding more like a person than a cop. "I had heard about the good work that Queenie did with the homeless, and when I was radioed to attend an incident that I soon learned involved one of Queenie's clients, I was a little surprised. I was starting to feel that even the safer shelters and hostels in the city were becoming increasingly violent.

"Al Brownette..." She glanced up to see whether I recognized the name and when I nodded, she continued. "Al and I were walking the beat that night, not far from the hospital. We ran over as fast as we could to answer the call."

She hesitated before she went on. As if she had decided to open up to someone who might really understand what she was talking about, she got personal. "To tell the truth, I sometimes feel a little uncomfortable working with Brownette. He's just so damn tough. Working with him makes me feel like a pussy."

I was shocked at the word. In our politically-correct city that word was never spoken in public. But I said nothing, not wanting to interrupt her.

"When I first joined up a few years ago, I felt nothing but pride. There were—still are—few young black women in the police service here. I really believed I could help people by keeping the peace and maintaining order."

She lifted her coffee cup to her lips, but put it down again as though she had discovered that it was empty. I resisted the urge to offer her a fresh one.

"My people came to Canada more than a hundred years ago. I grew up on a quiet street in Scarborough. All the families except mine were white. But that was no problem. Sure, I was teased in school, but I was smart and strong even as a little girl.

"Three families on the street had fathers who were police officers, and from the time I was small, I wanted to be a cop, too.

"As a kid, I never saw a gun, but I knew the cops had them, and I knew, even then that having a weapon meant that you could go places and do things in the city that other people could never do.

"My own neighborhood was perfectly peaceful—always. But sometimes my family went downtown and I saw a city different from the street we lived on.

"I knew from talking to the kids whose fathers were cops, that was where the action was, and I wanted a piece of it."

"A piece of what? What action?" I asked.

"You tell me," she answered sharply. "You tell me that there weren't days—and nights—lots of them, when you'd rather have been out there—she gestured toward the window and the street—than anywhere else?"

She'd opened up to me and I felt I could safely return the favor.

"Listen, I've had a very long time to think about how my life has worked out. Yes, I've had freedom and yes, I've had adventure, but my life would have been much more peaceful and productive if I had lived it square and straight."

"Oh, yeah? How about your village with all those people you're giving a home? How about your wife? Would you have had Queenie if you'd played it straight?"

"No. No I wouldn't." I had to gather myself. "But what does all of this have to do with the death of that man?"

"The Juicer? Everything. Nothing. Except I've seen dozens like him over my time as a cop, and they all have one thing in common as far as I can see."

"And that would be?"

"That they're asking for it. Oh, don't get me wrong. I feel sorry that the guy bought it. But sooner or later, it would have happened with him one way or another. I'm not exactly saying he had it coming. I'm not the kind who believes that crazy people are bad. But they are dangerous—very dangerous. And anybody who doesn't believe that just isn't being honest."

"He must have been dangerous if it took four of you guys to subdue somebody as old as him…."

"Listen," she said, "the main reason the investigation into our actions was dropped was because the man didn't die on the scene. You gotta get your facts straight. He died the next day of a heart attack. Natural causes. No big deal."

"But the news reports say the coroner is still investigating…"

She laughed. "Come on, don't tell me you believe that crap. I guess in the absence of facts they initially figured we did the old guy in. But, like I said, he did himself in. If he hadn't put up such a fight, we wouldn't have had to subdue him."

"Why did he have to put up a fight?"

"Beats me. So to speak." She crushed the empty coffee cup in her long fingers. "Listen, nice talking to you but I've got to go on shift. Good luck with Kezia. You're going to need it."

TWENTY-FIVE

As I drove across the entire huge city to get to the brand-new facility housing the coroner's office and the centre for forensic sciences, my mind sped back to the old days. There had been a time when my long-dead friend, Gleason Adams, and I had solved a sad and mysterious death that we had become interested in as students. I remembered the old morgue on Lombard Street and how what had begun as what I had believed was nothing more than a law-school assignment became a tangled tale of shame and violence.

The new facility, far in the west end of Toronto was, like the thousands of new buildings rising all over town, a fortress made of glass. By a freak of the time of day, the sun glinted off the front of the structure and blinded me for an instant as I pulled into the parking lot. I assumed there must be a secure parking area for the professionals who worked in the building, but for me, I had to pay a considerable amount to park and walk a long way before I got to the door.

At the reception desk, I used Matt's name as a reference, and to my immense surprise, was told that he had called and told them I was coming!

I was given instructions as to how to reach the office of Dr. M.M. Singh, and all I needed to do to get to him was to walk down a startlingly clean, well-lit corridor. I wasn't even sure whether there was a morgue in the building, but as I walked down that hallway, I thought I could catch the lingering smell of death. Or maybe that, too, was a memory of the night that Gleason and I had spent among the deceased.

Dr. M.M. Singh turned out to be a chipper young man with an obvious love of his odd work and a high regard for brief, fact-filled sentences.

"The man's name was William Collins. He was a 49-year old male, in fairly good physical condition, considering his life-style, which was one of intermittent poverty and homelessness."

He glanced at his notes. "There was no indication of an overdose of any kind of drug, nor was there any involvement with alcohol. There was indication of a past addiction to nicotine, but the lungs were in an acceptable condition for a man of the deceased's age."

"And the cause of death?" I asked.

"The man in question died of heart failure. The post-mortem showed a heart relatively undamaged considering years of living a difficult and unhealthy lifestyle."

"Then why...?"

"The records show that this man had a long history of mental illness of one sort or another. He was highly excitable. The night of his death, he was subject to what is commonly referred to as a 'take-down' by the police." He glanced at me again. "I don't think it's commonly known how powerful a person can become while in a psychotic state. It's perfectly within reason to expect that even a man of the age and physical condition of William Collins could threaten and possibly seriously harm four police officers at least three of whom were younger than himself."

"Would being in such a state harm his heart?" I asked.

"Mr. Portal, I'm a coroner, not a physician. What I can tell you is that his heart was harmed."

"Could that have been the result of some sort of shock—perhaps the shock of being treated roughly by the officers?"

"I can't say. Theoretically, a great shock can cause harm to the heart. Whether physical or psychological shock..."

I thought about what I had been told about "body-and-fender" men.

"Where there marks on the body—bruises, for example?"

Again he consulted his notes. "Yes. There were a lot of bruises—but none serious enough to cause lasting damage. There were no fractures and only a few lacerations."

"Were those bruises consistent with being assaulted with police batons?"

He smiled. "I can't say 'assaulted' Mr. Portal, I can only say the bruises were clearly the result of the repeated application of pressure."

"Anything else? Any other marks on the body?"

"Yes, there were two small marks on the inside of his left arm. They were obscured by bruises perhaps caused when he raised his arm to defend himself against the batons. Examination of them was inconclusive."

An idea that had been forming for a while, I now realized, struck me. "Were these marks consistent with Taser burns?"

The coroner smiled like a man who thinks he is being tricked and isn't going to fall for it.

"Yes. And also consistent with careless smoking, with a cooking accident, with a fight involving a cigarette lighter. In short," he said, "consistent with the life of a sometime vagrant and a person whose life has probably been cursed by violence from birth."

TWENTY-SIX

When I got home, Aliana called. "How are you making out, Ellis? How did things go with Mark Hopequist?"

I was happy to unload some of what I'd done and learned in the few days since I'd last spoken to her.

"Mark was very pleasant and cooperative—especially for a police officer--but as far as offering any real clues as to what is going on, that just didn't happen."

"Nothing?"

I thought back on our talk. "He did mention one thing that I'd more or less forgotten about."

"What's that?"

"The gang angle."

There was silence on the other end of the line. As if Aliana had stopped breathing.

"Aliana?"

"I thought that was fairly clear," she said with an edge to her voice. "I mean Kezia was very forthcoming about her brothers."

"True, and I suppose I shouldn't have lost track of the fact that you're writing about gangs in the city, it's just that…"

"What?"

"Aliana, I'm no police officer. I can't get involved in something that so clearly has nothing to do with me. I'm only interested in finding out what happened to Queenie's client. That's all."

"Look, Ellis, a deal is a deal, and the deal is that you help me with Kezia in exchange for my helping you with your inquiry. I've done that, haven't I?"

Of course she had. Without her I wouldn't have been able to talk to Mark and without Mark, to talk to Feeance.

"Yes, Aliana. Yes you have."

"Well unfortunately, at the moment, Kezia and the gang issue go together. Anything else?"

"I talked to Feeance Blake."

"The female member of the Fearsome Four?"

I had to smile. Aliana was back to being her friendly self.

"Yes. A very impressive lady."

"Woman."

"Woman. I also had an interview with a Dr. M.M. Singh."

"At the coroner's office?"

Did she know everybody? "Yes. He told me that there were two small marks on the Juicer's body that he wasn't able to identify conclusively. I can't get my mind off the idea that Tasers might be involved here."

"There's been no mention of that," she answered, "but if you think there's the least chance, I can do some to research on the subject. Give me a couple of days."

I was about to end the conversation when Aliana got to what it was that she really called to say. "Ellis, I've got a couple of things for you. The first is that Mark was apparently the first on the scene the night of the incident. I got this from one of the duty nurses at the hospital. She recognized Mark from the night before when the Juicer had also wandered outside. She said that a few of the hospital workers saw Mark struggling with the Juicer. Everybody agreed that he was just trying to get him inside, especially since it had started to rain. The Juicer must have been unusually cooperative that night, because he eventually went inside without much trouble."

"I have to think about this, Aliana. What can it mean?"

"I'm not sure. On the surface it just means that the night the four accosted the patient, he was just being exceptionally difficult." She stopped for a long moment. I could almost hear her thinking over the phone. "You know," she said, this whole thing depends on motive."

"Doesn't any murder depend on motive?"

"Yes. That's the trouble. If there's no motive, doesn't that mean there's no murder?"

"What it means is that I have to find the motive."

She had no answer for that. "There's more, Ellis, there's something else I have to tell you."

"Yes?"

"I'm afraid I have some bad news about Kezia. She's apparently gone missing. She's been absent from school pretty much since the day we visited her. She hasn't shown up for her after-school corrections program, and when I tried to visit her at home, I encountered somebody who could only have been one of the 'bad brothers'."

"Oh, no."

"Yes. I checked the Scarborough juvenile detention facility and also a couple of the ones downtown—a few hospitals, too, but no luck. I even attempted—unsuccessfully--to talk to her mother."

"What about the police?"

"That's the first thing I tried. The officer in juvenile told me that they had so many reports of Kezia disappearing in the past that they no longer took them seriously."

"I find that hard to believe, Aliana."

"Believe it. Do you know how many children and teenagers there are in this city who spend a great deal of their time unsupervised?"

I didn't want to try to answer that. "Leave these things with me. I'll give them some thought and get back to you."

She hesitated for an instant. "Want to discuss them over coffee?"

"Let's wait and see whether I come up with any ideas. In the meantime, I still need to chase down the other two cops I want to talk to."

"Brownette and Downs?"

"Right. Do you know them?"

"Not yet," Aliana answered.

I could tell by the tone of her voice that she'd be getting back to me on them soon if only to have an excuse for that coffee. As this thought hit me, another one did, too. *Who the hell do you think you are?*

The thought that Kezia was roaming the city on her own was deeply disturbing. That night, as I lay awake in my usual struggle to stop thinking about everything, I recalled the day that I had met Kezia and how interested she had been in my life beside the river. I had promised her that I would tell her more about it, and I had intended to, but the opportunity to speak with her again hadn't presented itself. The thought that she might be gone was certainly not one that encouraged me to go to sleep.

I remembered that she had been particularly interested in the fact that the river froze. It had not always been capable of doing so. In the past, contamination from factories in the valley as well as pollution from the cars that sped in an unrelenting stream along the Don Valley Parkway that ran beside it, had raised its temperature so that it had never got below the freezing point.

But things were different now due to the dedicated work of volunteers and the commitment of City Council to clean up the Don. It was capable of freezing again, though never as completely as it had once done.

I remembered Kezia's astonishing ambition to write a book about ice and snow, and that thought brought to mind the cold wind that had assaulted us the day I'd visited Jeffrey and talked to some of his clients.

If there were ever a time of year when a person interested in the freezing of the river would be likely to be down in the valley, it was now at the fragile line between autumn and early winter.

I recalled the recent sensation of being followed as I had ascended from the village in the valley to my apartment. Could it possibly have been the girl—working on her so-called project or maybe even up to something else?

It was a far-fetched idea. Besides, Kezia lived distant enough to the east of my neighborhood to be near a different river altogether, the Rouge, which, like the Don, ran south toward the beaches of the lake.

Perhaps, I thought, the idea of her exploring the Rouge was less unlikely than of her being in my own neck of the woods.

I decided to venture out into a couple of the ravines to the east just to check as to whether by some stretch, Kezia might have a reason to be exploring out there.

***

The valley of the Rouge was nowhere near as familiar to me as the valley of the Don. Though I had managed to find spots in the Don valley so isolated that I might have stayed there for months without my presence being detected, for the most part, the further south you went along that river, the more developed it was until, at its mouth, it was pretty much an urban jungle.

Where once old factories had smoked and clanked on the banks of the Don's mouth, there were now towers of condos so dense that it was impossible to see past them to the waters of the harbor beyond. But you knew the harbor was there because of the traffic: boats and cranes and delivery trucks and thousands of cars. There were huge stores down there selling food and liquor. There were entertainment complexes and clubs and offices.

But not at the bottom of the Rouge. Here a wide wild bay lined with woods led the eye smoothly to miles of sandy beach. It was possible to stand near the mouth of this river, to stare straight ahead and to think you were in a wilderness undiscovered by the people of the city of four million that you could see in the distance if you looked the other way.

Not knowing the valley, I couldn't take a chance of venturing too far away from the path that led along the river.

Once I was down there amid the thick trees beside the wide stream, I realized the folly of my idea that wandering in this place would lead me to any information about the fate of the young girl I sought.

It was cold, and I was tired. Since I'd lost Queenie, I seemed to have lost a lot of other things, too. And chief among them was energy. When I thought of the days—of the years, really--that I had spent wandering beside a river like this, it appalled me that now I became exhausted after only an hour or so. I turned to walk back the way I had come, back to the parking spaces and my car.

It wasn't until I was nearly on the animal in my path that I realized it wasn't a dog.

Of course, in my time in the valley, I was fully familiar with the wildlife down there. A number of times I'd seen deer, but I suspected they were gone from the valley now. And of course I'd seen rabbits and squirrels and snakes and rats. I'd seen feral cats and dogs and even a couple of guinea pigs. But I had never seen a coyote.

I was aware of their presence in the city, aware that people were afraid of them and made no attempt to befriend, tame or adopt them. I was as frightened of the idea of confronting a coyote as anyone was.

But clearly the coyote was not afraid of me. He stood directly in my way, in the middle of the path. In the autumn light, the shadows of the surrounding trees played on his coat, which was thick and shiny and though similar to a dog's, fuller and more variegated than that.

He seemed to look right into my eyes, and his own were a shade of green that reflected the green of the surrounding fir trees, of the river, of the lake beyond the path where we stood confronting one another. His wide, bushy tail swayed in a narrow arc between his slender, balanced legs. He had the snout of a wolf, only shorter and the facial expression of a creature afraid of nothing—especially not afraid of me.

I, on the other hand, was terrified. Like a lot of people in Toronto, I had heard stories of coyote attacks—of cats and small dogs killed in an instant in the snap of powerful jaws, of babies snatched by mothers seconds before being carried away, of old people swinging out with useless canes to chase the beasts away.

I was frozen. If I turned and ran, surely it would run after me. Maybe I was supposed to walk slowly toward it, but I lacked the courage. My heart began to pound and I wondered, wildly, whether he could hear it and realize that I was afraid enough to be dragged away despite the fact that I was so much larger than his usual prey.

I don't know how long we stood like that. Long enough for me to note the smooth sound of the river rushing toward the lake. Long enough for me to hear the honking above me of a vee of Canada geese heading south. Long enough for me to think for one brief moment of how Queenie would have laughed at me for being such a coward.

As if the thought of her had somehow broken the spell, the coyote's head shifted a fraction of an inch, and I realized that he had suddenly lost interest in me as a target. I heard a barely-audible rustle in the bushes behind my back. Then the coyote darted forward with such speed and strength that the wind of his running rifled my clothing. I turned and saw him dashing away from me. In his mouth was a tiny rabbit exactly the same brown and white shades of the rabbit I'd seen in my own valley.

***

In the end I decided that my adventures in the valley of the Rouge had told me nothing except that I loved the valley of the Don, even with its surrounding buildings, its highway, its crowded mouth, more than I could ever love another river—another landscape.

Though it was quite cold, when I got home, I decided to walk in the valley for a while.

In places not far from my building, the river was quite shallow, and I could see where people had thrown things in—shoes, even shopping carts, but the further up I got, the cleaner the river was and I was soon walking along clear, sparkling waters only interrupted now and then by early ice that had formed close to the shore.

I was studying that when I was suddenly confronted by a pair of fellow wanderers on my familiar path.

Directly ahead of me I saw a homeless man that I recognized. He was a harmless old soul possessed with a certain amount of naive charm. And helping him walk along the path, as if he couldn't do it alone—though I knew he could—was Kezia.

I had no idea how she had found my valley, but she was a clever girl who knew how to research, based on what she had told us about the computers and the library. There were detailed maps of the valley online and there was also, of course, a people-finder app that could tell her exactly where I lived. She could have even seen a picture of the place on Google earth.

I considered confronting her, telling her that she should be in school rather than roaming around the city in the company of questionable old men.

Instead I slipped behind some shrubbery that had not lost all its foliage and observed the two, ready to break in on them if I saw the least sign of any impending impropriety.

But as I watched, I saw that it was not just Kezia who was helping the old man. He seemed to be helping her. She was asking him questions about the river and the weather and the temperature and she was actually taking notes in a little book!

I figured she must be working on the project she had told us about, her book about ice and snow. The sight of her intensity was downright inspiring. I remembered then what she had said about her brothers being in the habit of destroying her work, and I wished I could offer her a safe place to work and to keep her materials.

But that, of course, was out of the question. The best I could do at the moment was to leave her alone.

But I wasn't comfortable with this decision and I got back up to the apartment as quickly as I could.

I called Aliana.

"I think we need to get in touch with Child Services," she concluded.

"They have a file on Kezia already," I answered.

"Quite a thick one," she replied. "But whatever they've got on her, they haven't taken her into custody."

"Into care,' I corrected.

"I'm afraid if we contact them, we might never see Kezia again," Aliana said.

"I know. But I don't think we have a choice.

"And," I added, "we'll never find out what the secret was that Mark Hopequist told her."

We both laughed gently at that. If a cop had told a kid a secret, it was bound to be some harmless thing, some tidbit of advice like "Only cross the street at the lights and you'll never get run over."

***

Child Services politely thanked us for the information about Kezia. "That was it?"

"Yes," Aliana answered. She paused for a second. "Ellis, let's get together. I've got a lot to tell you. How about our Tim Hortons?"

"Where we almost got shot? Are you sure we should?" I didn't know what made me more afraid, the thought of being gunned down or the thought that Aliana thought there was an "our" coffee shop.

"I talked to Matt West about that, and I'm sure you did, too. There's nothing to connect the incident to us. And besides, lightning never strikes twice...."

"Unless you're still standing under the same tree in the same storm."

She looked much younger than her years in her red coat and her white "eternity" scarf, an unending circle of white wool that wound around her long neck and set off the darkness of her thick hair. Her wearing a red coat and sitting near the window, which she insisted that we do, made me pray that Matt was right about our not being the intended object of gun-wielding Torontonians.

"So, what's up?" I set a large latte in front of her and took the seat across from where she sat.

"I'm working on a series of articles about the world affairs summit. The full twenty member nations have given final confirmation of attendance, and we're getting close. It's in a couple of weeks."

"Right." I had no idea what this had to do with me.

"This isn't a freelance deal I'm working on. It's an assignment. That means I'll have full media credentials. I can interview anybody that I can get near at any time. Including any police officers who are assigned to the event itself, to the preparations that are taking place all over the city, and even those guarding dignitaries and their staffs.

"Congratulations, Aliana. I'm happy for you. But I don't see why you brought me here to tell me this."

"Didn't you tell me that you ran into Ted Downs at a demonstration about the impending conference?"

"Yes, but that wasn't an official event. It was just some keeners getting ready for their big day…."

She actually rolled her eyes. "Ellis, there is not one thing that is going on in this city that is in any way connected to the world conference that isn't subject to the same police attention. Part of the reason that our friend Matt West is so upright most of the time is that he's second-in-command of the biggest police team ever put together involving our police. And it's not just Toronto police. They've got an amalgamated force from around the province, from neighboring jurisdictions, from the Ontario Provincial Police and even the RCMP."

"They've got the Mounties involved?"

"They've got everybody involved. From the top guns, so to speak, to the little guy in the trenches."

"Which would be our Ted Downs?"

"Which would be our Ted Downs."

TWENTY-SEVEN

The next afternoon, I picked Aliana up at her downtown condo, a glass tower overlooking the harbor, and we set out for 52 Division, a police station in the north central section of the city on Eglinton not far from Yonge. We had to park several blocks south of the station on a side street lined with typical old Toronto homes, two- and three-story brick buildings that had once spelled middle-class respectability with their orderly dormers and their stately porches. Where once had lived prosperous but ordinary families, there now lived people who had a million dollars to spend on a three-story brick house.

Aliana was in reporter mode. She talked in clipped sentences and seemed to think that it was appropriate to give me orders. "There will be no recording of the interview, so we'll have to keep cell phones out of sight."

"Do you mean we're going to sneak a recording?" I asked. I felt like some sort of junior and the feeling made me angry, which I made sure I kept hidden. I wanted to talk to this cop and I didn't want anything to stand in the way, including—especially—pride.

"Of course not!" Aliana snapped. "We are going to take notes. You take yours and I'll take mine. Later, if you want to, we can compare, though a lot of what I want to discuss with Ted Downs concerns the security measures being taken for the conference and won't involve you or your issues."

"I just want to get a feel for the man, to see what kind of a person he is, and to judge whether he's capable of violence."

"If he's not capable of violence, he's not going to be much of a cop then, is he?"

"No, Aliana," I said, trying to sound completely neutral, "he's not."

"You can sit in on the whole interview. I've informed Downs' supervisor that I'll be accompanied by my lawyer for security reasons."

I wasn't sure why a person would need to worry about security in a police station, but then the irony stuck me. I was here to find out whether a cop had killed Queenie's client. Maybe being concerned about security wasn't so ridiculous after all. As far as the lawyer bit went, that was certainly legit, though I'd never thought I'd be Aliana's lawyer.

Of more concern to me was the possibility that Downs would recognize me as someone he'd encouraged to move on during the demonstration at which I'd seen him.

But when Aliana introduced me as her "assistant" and the three of us sat together in a cramped little office without a window, Downs showed no sign of recognizing me—or if he did recognize me, showed no signs of caring.

The talk was mainly about the world conference.

"I understand you have more than a thousand officers assigned to the event," Aliana began.

Downs thought about her question for a moment and in the silence, I took a good look at him. He was a sturdy-looking character, a man in his fifties, maybe late fifties. He was wearing his uniform and he certainly filled it out. His arms were muscular with the look of limbs that would run to fat if he didn't keep up his workouts and maybe his weight-lifting. He had, of course, removed his cap, which sat on his knee, and I saw that his hair was close-cropped but not absent the way it was in his younger colleagues. Close up like this, he looked handsome with a strong profile and a well-defined mouth.

But the mouth looked mean.

I glanced at his hands. They were curled into fists. I couldn't tell whether that was because he was nervous at being interviewed by a reporter whose work he had surely read at one time or another.

As though he realized I was staring at him, he flexed his fingers. They were short and as powerful-looking as the rest of him.

"We've got a combined force," Downs began, in a deep, even voice. "Several local forces are helping out, along with the Ontario Provincial Police and the RCMP."

"I assume the Mounties will be handling foreign dignitaries…." Aliana said.

"Yes. But we already have details set in place everywhere in the downtown core. We anticipate the sort of street violence that other cities have experienced when the conference was in their jurisdiction."

"Store windows being smashed, cars being burned?" Aliana inquired.

"Yes. Of course, crowd control will be a major initiative for the duration, but we have special facilities set up for detaining troublemakers."

I didn't really listen as he went into detail about the holding pens that had been set up in buildings commandeered near the sight of the conference, which was taking place at the Royal York, a hotel conveniently across Front Street from Union Station, where a number of the attendees would be brought in by train from Pearson airport.

I was more interested in observing his manner, which was so purely cop, that I could hardly get a sense of the man. He sat straight in the hard chair that had been provided. His heavy belt rested on his hip. There were so many gadgets on it—every one of them black—that the belt itself could have been a lethal weapon had he chosen to take it off and swing it at somebody.

As if she were reading my mind, Aliana asked, "Will you have special tools and techniques—perhaps special training—to deal with the crowd? I understand that protestors are expected from many different groups and…"

"The Service is always at the ready with regard to crowd control," he answered defensively, and I felt as though I were back at Queen's Park standing in front him and hearing him tell me to get lost. I imagined he had a thousand phrases at the ready and he was using one now. It was a way of giving Aliana information without giving her information.

Of course she wasn't going to stand for that.

"I've been told by reliable sources," she began, "that a whole arsenal of special weapons is being made ready for possible deployment: heavily reinforced shields that cover the whole body, bullet-proof boots and gloves…"

"These items are standard issue for crowd control," he answered. "As I've indicated, we don't wait for special occasions to be completely prepared to handle out-of-control members of the public."

"I understand," Aliana said, bowing her head in admiration—completely fake of course--of their sterling preparedness. She consulted her notes. From where I sat next to her and opposite the cop, I could see that the page she was studying was blank.

"What about Tasers?" she finally said.

"Tasers?" Downs repeated with a surprised look on his face as though he had never heard of the things before.

"Stun guns," Aliana said with mock patience. "Non-lethal control methods."

Much as he tried to hide it, I could see Downs' posture change minutely, stiffen.

"I am not aware that the combined forces have been issued with any such thing," Downs said, "but I can state unequivocally that no Toronto police officer will be armed with a Taser during the world conference. Only supervisors on our force are authorized to use Tasers and they will not be using them at this event.

"Have you ever used a Taser?" I dared to ask.

Downs glared at me, as though the paperweight on his desk had deigned to address him. "When I have been assigned as acting supervisor on two occasions," he said, his voice as emotionless as a talking textbook, "I have carried a non-lethal weapon. I have never discharged one, nor do I expect to discharge one at this event nor at any event in the future."

The old line from Shakespeare found its way into my consciousness. *The lady doth protest too much methinks*. I didn't know whether he was being defensive or merely professional. I figured he had answered my question—whether truthfully or not—and I didn't feel brave enough to venture another.

Into the silence left by the end of this little exchange, Aliana dropped a personal question. We had not agreed to it ahead of time, but there couldn't have been a better way of trying to find out the sort of things I needed to know.

"Tell me, officer, how does your family feel about your working on what could potentially be a very dangerous assignment? I mean police cars being burned, glass shattering all over the street, not to mention trained assassins who might be following world leaders. How will your children feel to know that you are protecting their city against violent men and women who may have come from far away to wreak havoc here in our streets?"

Despite her professional phrasing and the cool that she maintained as an objective seeker of truth for the public through the media, Aliana had clearly stepped over the mark with this question. What business was it of hers or of her readers what this man's family felt about his work? I was almost embarrassed at the question, even though I knew that an answer to it would give me more information about Ted Downs than anything I'd managed so far.

But I expected him to freeze at this question, if he didn't get furious that is.

To my amazement, he did neither. He sighed and said, "I have no family, and if I did, they would not factor into this equation." He sounded sad, almost defeated.

This disclosure was news to me. Both Aliana and I were under the impression that he had a wife and a teen-aged son. We'd gotten this information from a file that Aliana had assured me was up-to-date. Whatever had changed about Ted Downs' life had changed very recently.

***

After the interview, Aliana and I walked over to Yonge Street to grab a quick lunch at a Mexican place. When I had been a judge the first time, I had hated the little restaurants that lined

Yonge Street for miles—every cuisine imaginable. I had, in those days, preferred lunch at the Royal York, or at private clubs that I entered as a member or as a guest of some distinguished member or other. When I had lived in the valley, I had eaten a windfall apple or a discarded loaf of stale bread for lunch. Queenie and I had had healthy lunches made with her own hands.

I wished I could stop thinking about such things all the time. I picked up my burrito and prepared to take a bite when a thick blob of sour cream slipped out of it and landed in my lap.

Aliana stared at me, and I felt a moment's intense embarrassment.

Then she burst out laughing and handed me a fistful of napkins to clean up the mess.

"I wonder what happened to Ted Downs' family," I said.

Aliana delicately placed her burrito on her plate, wiped her long fingers and said, "I do, too. He definitely had a wife and son up until recently. I hope they haven't met with some sort of tragedy."

"Or deserted him for some reason."

"I'm sure information about this angle would have a bearing on your investigation, Ellis. It's a clue as to the state of Downs' mind at the time of the incident. I'll see if I can find out anything else...."

Talk turned to Kezia.

"We've made no headway there," I had to admit. "No news from Child Services?"

"No. But..."

"But what?"

"Ellis, I've gotten some scary phone calls recently. It's not at all unusual for this to happen when I'm working on something controversial or something the public considers a threat to their safety."

"What? What kind of calls?"

"Calls warning me to lay off gang business." She paused. "I keep thinking about Kezia. I keep wondering whether her inaccessibility, her failure to get in touch with us after so strong a beginning, has to do with her brothers and the gangs they belong to."

"But you're working on the affairs summit now…"

She shook her head. "That's a temporary thing. In two weeks it'll all be over and anything I've written on it will be forgotten by most of the readers of the *World*. But the gang series of articles is different. I've been working on that for months, and when the series runs, there's going to be a lot of response to it, I'm sure."

"What concerns you? What are you worried about?"

"I'm afraid that our offer to help this girl has focused the attention of one or the other—or both—of the gangs on us. I know that Matt West is sure the shooting we witnessed had nothing to do with us, and he's probably right about that one, but I don't want to think that my work is putting you and me in danger."

At this point, I could have told her about the threatening note I'd received, but I was totally convinced that it wasn't connected to my interest in Kezia. Besides, it wouldn't have been very reassuring to Aliana to learn about it.

"I can't allow myself to be intimidated," Aliana declared. "I'm going to visit Kezia's home again. "I want to talk to her about those brothers. If they are going to shoot at me, let them shoot…"

I admired her bravery but had to be quite frank. "Aliana I don't think we should play with fire, here. These are dangerous people—Kezia as well as her relatives."

"Look, Ellis, we have a deal. I've helped you get to the cops and you've promised to help me with Kezia. Don't you see that you're my cover? With you along, it doesn't look like I'm nothing but a ruthless media type sticking my nose where it doesn't belong."

"Aliana, I admit I'm curious about this girl and sympathetic to her plight. But I still can't see what we can do for her. When I saw her down in the valley with that old man, I realized that she's a totally loose cannon. She's going to do whatever she wants. I don't see how we can even influence her."

"Just come with me on one more home visit," Aliana insisted, as if my objections counted for nothing. "Hopefully, she's back there by now. But even if she isn't, maybe we can do something to help her mother and her other brother."

"Okay," I said. "Okay."

It wasn't until I was on my way home that I thought again about those gunshots Aliana and I had witnessed.

Maybe those shots were not random.

Maybe they were meant for me.

But why? Why would they be?

TWENTY-EIGHT

As had happened the first time, our visit with Kezia began with negotiating the busy lobby of her building. People were coming and going in all directions, and among them were more decent-looking ordinary citizens than suspicious characters. But, given our current frame of mind, we were bound to feel suspicious of the large number of big, young, black men that I couldn't help thinking looked like the archetypical gang members that the city saw on the news night after night.

We waited so long for our attempt at entry to be answered that we actually gave up and had turned to leave when the door buzzed open and I heard Kezia saying what she had said the last time, "What you doin' here?"

Cowardly though it was, I had to admit relief that the only other occupants in the elevator were two darling little girls and their well-dressed mother.

My paranoia didn't end when the elevator doors closed behind us on Kezia's floor. I followed Aliana's sure steps with a hesitation I tried hard to hide. When we got to Kezia's door, I suppressed the urge to mention that I was glad that there were no new bullet holes since our last visit.

Kezia opened the door before we knocked, which, since she was smiling widely, we took to be a good sign.

"Hey, Kezia," Aliana said, "thanks for letting us up. I'm really happy to see you because I heard you haven't been in school and I was afraid you might be sick."

The girl looked good. Her thick, black hair had obviously been carefully curled and the jeans and sweatshirt she wore were clean and fashionable. I figured that despite the girl's unwillingness to cooperate with those who might help her, her mother was taking good care of her—and had trained her to take good care of herself.

Kezia just shrugged, a gesture that segued into a different gesture—one ushering us into the apartment.

As it had been before, the place was clean and as tidy as one could expect for a home where teens lived.

"Are you alone today?" Aliana asked, glancing around.

"Yeah. Like most every day. My mom comes home after work at 11. When she gets here, I give her something to eat and then I go to bed. Sometimes JoJo comes over...."

"JoJo?" I asked.

"Yeah. He's my good brother. But he ain't been around in the last while because he got locked out."

"What does that mean?" Aliana asked.

Kezia sat down and we did too. Without missing a beat, she went on. "He's no longer allowed on the premises because a couple of weeks ago, some friends of his busted the lobby up. They tore down a picture and banged up a lot of the mailboxes."

I really couldn't imagine how any level of violence could "bust up" that lobby. There was nothing in there the first time we saw it and nothing in there the last time we'd seen it.

I noticed the small desk in the corner was still covered with books and papers. That seemed like a positive sign. "So, have you gone back to school? Looks like you're doing your homework."

"Yeah, I guess you could say I went back. But I ain't doing homework. There's no such thing. I heard they used to have it in the old days, but it's not allowed anymore."

"What do you mean it's not allowed?"

She looked at me in a way that made me feel I had just emerged from the Middle Ages, not that I thought she'd been taught what they were.

"I go to a non-judgmental school." The phrase tripped off her tongue as if she had a knack for buzzwords. "We got no homework, no essays, no tests and no marks. Everybody gets to pass. Even if they can't make it there every day. That way nobody can feel bad about theirselves because of failing."

"What do you think about that, Kezia?" Aliana asked. "Does it make you feel successful?"

The girl yawned. "Nah. It makes me feel bored. Everything about school is boring. Plus it takes too much time. I got other things to do."

I couldn't help smiling. "Like what?" Before she could answer, it occurred to me that I hoped the answer wasn't "doing housework for my mom."

"Well," she said, drawing in her breath as though she needed it for a long explanation. "I got my own studies and I need to have time to go to the libary and that-- because I have to work on writing my book."

"Your book?"

She gave me that look again. "Yeah. You know, I need time to work on the book I'm writing. It's a really neat book that people will want to buy and even to read. It's called *Fifty Recipes For Snow*. My whole life, my mother had to work at night. My grandmother used to cook for us, but she went away. So I learned how to do it and I been doin' it for a real long time. I had to do more before than I do now, though. In the old days my five brothers lived with me and my mom here in this apartment, but two of them are in jail and the two who come back don't come here to eat. Only JoJo. He's the only one who eats here, but now he's locked out.

"Anyway, for most of my life, I been making all the suppers. And I'm a really good cook. I watch cooks on television and the internet, and I know they write books so people can try the recipes theirselves and not forget them like they would if they just saw them for a few minutes on TV."

I was astonished. How could I not be? But she wasn't finished.

"There's a lot of money to be made writing books," she said as if she'd memorized the line. "So I'm writing one myself."

She sprang up and headed for the cluttered little desk. "Look," she said, shoving a handful of papers toward me. "This is what I'm working on now."

I glanced down at the pages. I expected to see the pretend writing of a child, scribbled sentences, amateurish drawings.

What I saw was nothing like that. I took one of the sheets from her hand and studied it for a moment. A neatly printed headline in rather large letters spread across the top of the page. It said, "Desserts Made With Fruit and Flowers for Special Parties". And beneath the title was a tidy list of ingredients that, yes, included both ice and snow. For an instant, a long-ago memory worked its way into my consciousness. It was of my mother who was a very good ordinary cook but who, every once in a while jumped into some sort of culinary disaster that was clearly beyond her skills.

"Aliana" I said. "Look at this."

She studied the page as I had, and her reaction was the same. "Kezia, this is amazing!"

"How long have you been working on this?" I asked.

"A real long time. I was almost finished with it once but one of my brothers came over and he got mad at JoJo for something and then he started tearing the place up and he just grabbed all my papers and he burned them in the sink. JoJo and me, we were afraid to stop him, so I lost everything I wrote." She stopped to draw a breath.

"But that was the old days when I had to write it all by hand. Now I only got to write notes by hand because I go to the libary down the street and I type all my writing in on the computer. Then I put it on the cloud." She looked at me. "You know what that means, right?"

"Right."

"Kezia," Aliana said, "this is wonderful—I mean about you going to the library and working on your book. Does the librarian help you?"

"Sometimes."

"How do you feel about adults helping you?"

"Okay, I guess."

"Did Officer Hopequist ever help you?"

"Who?"

"Mark Hopequist. You told us before that you knew him from the Youth Bureau."

The girl smiled. "Oh, yeah. Officer Mark." She thought for a minute. "Yeah, he helped me a lot. We used to read books together. They were like mystery stories and that. I really liked it when we read because he explained all kinds of things about the police, about how they catch criminals from clues and like that. He told me how cops have special powers."

"Powers?" I asked.

"Yeah. Like how they can arrest people and that. Course I knew that already because of my brothers being in jail and all, but they got other powers, too. Like they can ask people questions and make them answer. And they can read your email if they have permission from their boss. And they can take your car away, too. Except none of us here got any cars."

"Kezia, the last time we talked to you, you said that Officer Mark told you a secret. Do you remember that?" I asked.

She looked puzzled for a second, then she seemed to remember. "Oh, yeah," she said. "I did. He was real nice. He told me that he's a preacher."

"A preacher?" Aliana failed to hide her surprise.

"Yeah, like in a church. Only they call it a 'prayer palace'. He told me lots of people go there on Sunday. Maybe even hundreds of people. And he stands up in front of them and gives sermons about being good and helping the unfortunate and them and not belonging to gangs or shoplifting."

"Is this the secret?" Aliana asked sounding disappointed. She seemed to have abandoned her usual reporter's cool.

"No."

There was a long silence then. Neither Aliana nor I seemed to know what to say. It wasn't an easy thing to get a person to divulge a secret. I knew that as a lawyer and a judge and even as a father. Of course it was Aliana's job to get at things people didn't want to say. And from what I understood about her, she'd won a lot of awards for doing so successfully. But her reputed skill seemed to fail her now. The two of us just sat there.

"No," Kezia said again. Then she shrugged. "I promised not to tell anybody this secret, but you're a judge, right?"

"A retired judge."

"That's the same thing isn't it? I mean a retired guy is the same as a real guy?"

"I guess you could say that."

"And people say things to judges all the time, don't they? I know that because I went to court once and I heard them—the lawyers and the witnesses and everybody. The judge, he just sat there and everybody said everything in front of him so he could hear the whole case. Right?"

"Right." I could see where this was going.

"So I s'pose I could tell a judge the secret."

Aliana sat perfectly still and quiet during this exchange. I think the two of us were afraid of what we might hear.

"Okay. Here's the secret. One time we were reading a story and there was something in it about weapons. There was guns and that stick the cops can hit people with—"

"The baton?" I asked.

"Yeah. Something like that. So anyway, I asked Mark if they had weapons like in the movies, with guns that killed people with a big ray of red light and things like that. He said that they did have something. He said it was called a Taser." She hesitated.

I could hear Aliana breathing. But she said nothing. And Kezia went on.

"I asked him what that was and he said it was a 'non-lethal weapon.' I remember these things—I mean about the Taser and what it was called—because I keep a notebook and I write everything down when I hear it."

Out of the corner of my eye, I saw Aliana smile faintly at this. I had never seen her without a notebook tucked away somewhere on her person, though they had eventually been replaced by her Blackberry and her phone.

"Yeah," Kezia continued, "The secret is: Mark told me that maybe someday he could show me a Taser, maybe even show me how it worked. He said that right now only the police bosses had them, but that sometimes ordinary policemen like him got to have one for a little while and that if that happened to him, he would show me."

Then Kezia sighed. "Course that'll never happen because now he doesn't work with kids anymore and I'll never see him again."

TWENTY-NINE

"It's not much of a secret, is it?" Aliana said. "And a preacher? What can that mean?"

"That he's not a murderer?" Of course I knew it was an absurd thing to say, and Aliana laughed pleasantly. I had invited her back to my place for a coffee. I realized that having her in my home was a more personal gesture than I'd engaged in with her, but since it was pretty much halfway between Kezia's place and hers, it seemed the logical thing to do.

The place was spotless and in good order, with nothing lying around except a pile of books that I'd been reading. In the first weeks after Queenie's death, I had let things go until my daughter, Ellen, had insisted on coming over. I couldn't stand the thought of Ellen seeing my home—or me—in disarray, so I had hurriedly cleaned up before she'd arrived. After that, I got back to the usual standard of neatness and cleanliness that Queenie and I had always maintained.

"I think we should go and hear him. I'm sure it'll tell us something about the man."

"How are we going to find out where this so-called 'prayer palace' is?"

"There aren't very many of them around town," Aliana answered. "Leave it to me. I'll call them all and ask them when Mark Hopequist is appearing."

"Not appearing, Aliana. He's not a rock star or anything!"

"Wanna bet?"

Of course she was a good as her word, and a couple of nights later, we found ourselves in the huge parking lot of a west-end church. It was a massive building whose architecture was something between a cathedral and a hockey arena.

At first I was concerned that Hopequist might see us and figure out why we were there, but it was such a big hall with a so large a number of people! We slid in at the very back and tried, unsuccessfully, to blend into the crowd. Within seconds we began to be greeted by members of the congregation who immediately considered us as possible new participants. We politely declined invitations to Bible Study and the Welcome Club. Most of the people in the congregation were racial minorities, another reason why we failed to disappear.

"Mark seems to be the featured speaker of the evening," Aliana said, studying the program we'd been handed. "I don't think this is a service. I think it's some sort of a lecture...."

I didn't want to admit my relief at this news. I had fallen away from the religion of my childhood, a fact that still made me feel guilty sometimes. Guilty enough to be uncomfortable in any church or church-like atmosphere that wasn't Roman Catholic. Better to be damned for not going to church at all than to be damned for going to the wrong one!

I felt a tug at my sleeve. "Earth to Ellis. What are you thinking? You seem to have gone away there for a minute."

I was spared having to answer by a sudden extremely loud slam of the huge organ at the front on what looked more like a stage than an altar, followed by about a thousand people singing a hymn that sounded typically Protestant to me. I noticed Aliana did not join in. She had been raised the same way as I had been, give or take the slight changes in the Church during the thirteen or so years between us in age.

Hopequist's topic was the evil of guns and how the congregation should continue to work as hard as they could to remove them from Toronto streets. He also spent quite a bit of time explaining that each of us is responsible for alleviating the suffering of others. I felt he could alleviate my suffering by cutting his sermon short.

During the obligatory Q & A following his talk, someone in the audience mentioned the use of non-lethal weapons used during police work.

Hopequist seemed to go a little wild at the question. His talk had been calm, reasoned, more like that delivered by a professor than a preacher. But on this topic, he was clearly emotionally involved in some way.

"There is no such thing as a non-lethal or less-lethal weapon!" he declared, his voice rising both in tone and volume. "When a weapon is used, a police officer intends one thing and one thing only: TO KILL. We must stop this. We must stop the police killing of our citizens. Whether guilty or not guilty, no man woman or child deserves to be shot dead on any street in our city—in any home or business—in any park or place of recreation!"

The congregation went wild, too. Their shouted amens echoed all the way into the parking lot.

I couldn't image how such a person could be a police officer.

"Do you think his supervisors know about his feelings on this?"

"I can't imagine that they don't," Aliana answered.

"Then how can they keep him on the force?"

"By assigning him to deal with the young people?"

"But he doesn't do that anymore," I responded. "The night that the Juicer died, Hopequist was on the beat. That's how he got to the scene. And remember, he had had a confrontation of some sort with the Juicer the day before. None of that would suggest that he's been relieved of regular duties."

"There's no way of getting around the fact that the Juicer didn't die on the scene," Aliana said. "There's also no way of knowing why PIC initially got involved then refused to lay charges and cancelled the investigation into the incident. But everything points in the same direction, which is toward ordinary police action. The evidence of wrong-doing against Mark is slight. Confrontations like the one you mention are part of life on the street."

I nodded. "And as for Feeance and Ted Downs. They're just regular cops as far as I can see. That leaves Al Brownette. I know we haven't talked to him, but the people we have talked to seemed to suggest that aside from his being an obnoxious person and a lackey to Ted, there's no evidence against him, either."

Aliana opened her mouth to speak, but before she got a word in, I went on. "Aliana, I don't think you and I need to work together anymore. If you want to keep helping Kezia, that's fine. But as far as I'm concerned, I'm finished."

She kept her face perfectly still, her fine reporter's face. "What about your promise to Queenie?"

I didn't meet her eyes. "Queenie was dying. I don't think she knew what she was saying. There's been no murder here. Just a tragic death brought on by severe stress."

I wasn't sure who I was being disloyal to here and whether it was the oddness of having another woman in Queenie's and my home, but I suddenly felt done. I just couldn't handle this thing any longer.

THIRTY

My abrupt "dismissal" of Aliana and my sense of relief that I no longer had to worry about solving a murder case lasted about twelve hours.

Then the doubts began to assail me, as they used to say.

Why would PIC have been involved at all unless they had had at least a suspicion in the early stages of their investigation that the cops had been involved in the killing of the Juicer? Why would there be such conflicting evidence about whether or not the Juicer was violent? And if he were violent, what had set him off the day of the incident?

And then there was the fact that it was quite possible that Aliana and I had been deliberately shot at, either to wound us or to scare us. Try as I might, I couldn't convince myself that the shooting was a coincidence. There are only two sets of people who regularly roam the streets of Toronto with loaded guns. Cops and gang members. It was certainly true that my recent adventures had put in touch one way or another with each of those groups.

Plus, when I thought about it, there was clearly something mysterious going on in the village in the valley. I thought about Jeffrey's recent behavior, his neglecting to fill me in on important information. I couldn't recall his ever doing that before. Was he acting in a secretive manner—one not usual with him?

And what about the day that I was convinced that someone was following me? And, oh yeah, the note warning me to mind my own business. About what? The Juicer? The village?

I needed a rest. I needed to think about these things. I needed to figure out whether all these threads were connected to each other or to nothing or, as Queenie had believed, to murder.

Of course, I was fooling myself if I thought Aliana was going to stay away. She didn't phone. She didn't email. But after a week of nothing, I got a forwarded invitation to a very swish banquet. There was a nice paragraph announcing that Aliana

Caterina was to be a guest of honor because she had written so many fine articles about the city. The banquet, the invitation explained, was being held in honor of women and men who had furthered the cause of Toronto in the world view.

That sounded rather grandiose to me, and I nearly erased the thing, but something stayed my finger at the last moment and instead, I phoned Aliana to ask her what it was all about.

"Oh, hi, Ellis," she said with a breeziness I'd never noticed her use before, "It'll be a fun occasion. It's going to be held in a restored building down at the Brick Factory, in the valley. The speakers will all be people who have worked to develop the city in a way that respects its history and the environment. The tickets are five hundred dollars each, but that as a celebrity guest, I've got two complimentary ones." I could hear her draw in her breath on the other end of the line. "It would be a shame to waste them."

"Congratulations."

"Thanks." I heard her breathe again. Pause. "Would you like to attend?"

"I…"

"I think you'd really enjoy this. A number of the speakers will be dealing with the Don River valley and the impact on the city of the development of land surrounding it. I mean since you're a stakeholder—being a landowner, I can't see how you could fail to be interested in this topic."

I was interested. I gave it a few minutes thought, for the sake of propriety if nothing else.

"Thank you, Aliana," I said with a bit more formality than I'd really intended. "I'd be honored. I would very much like to accompany you to this affair."

At the word "affair" she actually giggled. "Great," she said. "I'll email you the details."

***

It turned out to be a black-tie event. I hadn't worn a suit since Queenie's funeral, and I was surprised that I couldn't help feeling good about myself when I looked in the mirror. *Not bad for an old guy.* The sight of myself in a tux lifted my spirits, in fact, they soared.

I could tell that Aliana was mightily impressed when she set eyes on me!

The banquet was wonderful with several courses, each prepared by one of the city's top chefs. There were exotic cheeses wrapped in crisp phyllo for appetizers and a salad made of greens I'd not seen since summer. There was a fish course, a lovely smoked salmon, accompanied by plenty of comments about the fact that wild salmon had returned to the Humber River in the west of the city, and even perhaps to the Don, which I knew they had once inhabited.

There was a beautiful beef tenderloin done to just the shade of pink that I preferred, accompanied by asparagus cooked with olives and fennel. At the end of it all: an amazing chocolate cheesecake.

I had always been a man who enjoyed his food, and I was really having a good time. It didn't even put a damper on things that I couldn't share the fine wines that went with each course. There were a number of teetotalers at our table, men and women who felt that drinking alcohol was somehow bad for the environment. I privately remembered how bad for the environment it was in the old days when Queenie and I went on benders and tore up various elements of Queen Street—even sometimes including our fellow denizens!

All went well until the speeches started. Then I came to my senses about where I was and what was going on. Not only was this recently-built, multi-story building an intrusion on the pristine setting of the valley, but many of the speakers—and quite a number of the sponsors of the banquet--were real estate investors determined, as they would have it, to up the monetary value of the valley lands. Since this could only mean development, it meant that these people were determined to ruin the valley by building on its banks and even, I was horrified to learn, on its floodplain, since at least three of the speakers were contractors who boasted of having developed new methods of flood control that would allow buildings to be built right up to the water's edge.

I was appalled. To make matters worse, one of the men at our table began to talk about the Village in the Valley as if he knew all about it. "I'm aware," he said, "that you are a significant private landowner of property adjoining the floodplain. I'm in a position to give you the opportunity to be in the forefront of the environmentally sound reclamation of valley lands. "If you'll give me your card," he said with a slick smile, "I'd be happy to send you some information to show you how you can help the city and gain very high returns for yourself at the same time. There are several kinds of land deals that are possible for a man in your position."

"What about a deal that developers get out of the valley and stay out?"

He chuckled as though I were joking. "Many of the city's most prominent citizens," he went on, "—and agencies, as well— are working together to develop the river lands in the most profitable and environmentally sound way possible."

I was dumbstruck. Everything this man was telling me ran completely contrary to my devotion to the preservation of the valley, my determination to keep high-rollers from having a stake in Jeffrey's and my project. I was about to tell him so when I was distracted by a sight I found hard to believe.

A man that I was sure was Officer Ted Downs, looking very business-like and totally un-cop like, dressed in a tuxedo, was holding an animated conversation with none other than the mayor of Toronto!

Of course I had no idea of what they were discussing. But one thing was certain. Ted Downs was a complex and somehow bothersome man that I had thus far been totally unable to figure out.

"Just because a man is a developer," Aliana whispered, "doesn't mean he's a killer."

I studied the crowd. "I'm not so sure," I answered.

THIRTY-ONE

I had to talk to Jeffrey. I had to know whether he was aware of the things I'd heard at the banquet. I was still leery of opening any sensitive issues with him because of the last argument that we'd had, but I needed to know if my son had noticed any more unusual activity in the valley or the village.

I found him hard at work leading a workshop for the villagers on personal safety in the city streets. He was perched, sitting with casual ease, on a wooden packing crate that made a serviceable bench. He was talking about how to walk down the street, staying far enough from the buildings to avoid being sprung upon and far enough from the street to avoid being thrown into traffic. The basic implication of his talk was that a person who appeared to be destitute was in danger from all manner of other citizens of the city.

He interrupted his talk when he saw me standing in the doorway of the main building of the village. "Dad!" he said. "Great to see you. Maybe you can help us out here...."

I obliged by handling the Q & A. There was lots of discussion about practical matters: when pursued, should you run or is there something else you can do? Is it safe to stow valuables on your person or does that invite a more intimate and physical attack than if somebody just grabs your bag?

This chat with the villagers went on for half an hour or so, and as I spoke to them, I had the opportunity to observe the audience. I thought most of the people were looking well. Clean and sober and alert.

So I congratulated Jeffrey on his work.

"It's a daily struggle, Dad," he said, "for me and for them. It seems every time we turn around there's some new hurtle."

"What do you mean?"

"Everything seems to get harder every day. More complicated. There have been some men down here from the city again. Nothing major, just some forms to fill out."

"Forms?"

"Yes. It seems there's a new city committee that's looking into land utilization around the river."

"Jeffrey, that's what I came down to talk to you about. I want you to watch out for anybody you think is interested in developing our land."

"Developing?"

"Yes. I think there is a move on to build condos and perhaps private houses down here."

"How can that be? Isn't everything protected? I mean we couldn't get a permit to build a permanent building, even though this land is ours and it's not directly situated on the floodplain."

"Right. Which is why I want you to let me know the minute you find out that anybody from the city is down here. You got that?"

He frowned at my treating him as if he were still a boy. "Dad, you have to understand that I have never held anything of importance back from you. I know that you've had a lot to deal with lately. The whole point of my running the village is so that you're left free to handle other things. I don't want you to ever think that I'm holding out on you or withholding information that you should have."

I reached out and put my hand on his shoulder. He touched my fingers for an instant and then we both sat back a little farther apart then we'd been.

"So, Dad," he said, "there is something I have to tell you. Not only have things down here become more complicated, they've also become more expensive. I know that you've wanted us to run solely from the Trust, but lately, I've had the offer of some small donations, and I've accepted."

This was an unwelcome surprise. "Jeffrey, I thought we were definite on that. Nobody has a financial interest in this enterprise but me and you."

"But Dad—"

"It's not a matter of finances. It's a matter of control. We don't want anybody telling us what to do or how to run things down here. Once we get donors, the pressure is going to start. They'll begin to demand things, like a Board of Directors. They'll start to ask questions about whether we have a philosophy, even whether we foster any particular religion...."

"Take it easy, Dad. I'm not talking about millionaires here. I'm talking about people in the neighborhood who've learned about us and want to help. It's no big deal."

"So we're talking about small amounts of money?"

"For the most part."

"What's that supposed to mean?"

Jeffrey looked away as if afraid to meet my eye. It reminded me of how he had acted as a boy—usually an impeccably obedient boy—when something had happened to cause him to disobey. "There have been a couple of large donations in the past three years. I actually talked to you about accepting them, but you were distracted by the situation with Queenie and you were at the stage where you were still working and trying to take care of her at the same time."

"So you took money without telling me?"

"I accepted three grants sponsored by corporations. These donations have been carefully recorded and proper tax receipts have been issued. I can show you the books."

I had to avoid confronting him. If I trusted him to run the village on a daily basis, I really had to trust him all the way. "Son, I appreciate what you're doing down here. I don't want you ever to think that I don't. You're right. You're in charge and you're taking a great burden off my shoulders. You just go ahead and do whatever you think is right."

Jeffrey smiled more warmly and more widely than usual. "So what brought you down here today in particular?"

"I was at a banquet last night," I answered. "One of those awards ceremony things. There were a number of developers and other investors there, and one or two of them seemed awfully interested in our work. A couple of City Councilors were sniffing around, too. So, as I said, I'd like to know if you see any of these people down in the valley again or—most importantly—expressing undue interest in the village or the land on which it sits."

Jeffrey nodded.

"There's something else I think I better tell you. One day when I was down here, I had the strong impression that somebody was following me—dogging my steps on the way back to the apartment."

"Who? Did you get a look at him—or her?"

There was alarm in Jeffrey's voice. I didn't mean to scare him or to cause him concern, but I thought he should know. Especially since nobody else knew.

"That's not all, son. I also received a threatening note. It told me to mind my own business."

Jeffrey thought for a minute. "Listen, Dad, you've reminded me that I have to keep you posted. You've got to do the same thing. And I'm telling you right now that if either of these things happen again: you're being followed or you're getting threats, I want you to go to the police immediately. Have you got that?"

Now I was the one being treated like a child, but to tell the truth, I felt touched at Jeffrey's clear concern for his old man.

I decided not to tell him that I suspected I'd also been shot at.

"You know, Dad, if I had kept track of every visitor and curious person who has visited the village in the years I've worked down here, the list would be as long as the river itself. Remember a couple of years ago when that reporter, a man, came down for a few days and then wrote that quite nice article about the village?"

"To tell the truth, I don't remember. It may have been published during a time when Queenie was sick and I was in over my head."

"That reminds me," Jeffrey said. "One day recently a young woman showed up, saying she was working on some sort of writing project. She was just a teenager, and I told her it wasn't safe for her to be down here by herself. I gave her TTC fare and told her to go home, which I hope she did.

I had to smile. I knew who the young woman was. "I'm sure she made it home safely, Son or I would have heard otherwise."

Jeffrey was clearly puzzled by this remark, but I had no intention of explaining it. Telling him that I had been helping a young girl whose family included rival gang leaders was not going to exactly put Jeffrey at ease any more than telling him about the gunshots.

"What do you mean?"

"A student. Probably just a student. Don't worry about it. Anything else?"

Jeffrey thought for a moment, then he said, "I don't think this is important, but the other day, a group of people showed up from some community group or other. They asked a lot of questions about ethnic diversity, which I'm always happy to answer because the inhabitants of this village come from everywhere. I told them it's a global village down here."

"Well, it's certainly a busy one. How do they find their way down here, anyway?"

"I'm not sure, Dad. I suppose it's a security issue. Up until a couple of months ago, there were only three paths—the one up to the parking lot behind your building, the one through the play area of the school up on the hill, and the one we built for villagers. Anybody who looks us up on Google now can see how to get down."

"Well I think you should consider checking this out. A lot of people who don't belong down here can only mean one thing: A lot of trouble….Anything else? Anybody else?

Again Jeffrey seemed to need a few minutes to inwardly check his recollections.

"The only other thing I can think of to tell you is that there were a couple of cops down here a day or two ago."

"Cops? Were they looking for one of the villagers? That can't be good."

"I'm not sure what they wanted. They just looked around. One was an older guy. I've seen his type before. They act pretty friendly but then they start doing things like handing out homeless tickets."

"They were handling out homeless tickets down here?"

"No. No, Dad, that was just an example. Our village is classified as a residence. Nobody can ticket the homeless down here—actively or retroactively."

"Then what were they after?"

"I never did find out. I tried talking to them at first, but they were the type who are likely to say that they talk and you listen. So I didn't bother. That older guy, he gave me the feeling that even if he was nice on the surface, he would be quite frightening if you crossed him."

"You say there were two?"

"Yeah. The other, a much younger cop, looked like he'd be frightening all the time. After they left, a few of the villagers admitted that they'd encountered these two before and that when they see them coming, they get out of the way. When they left, they said something that scared me. They said, 'Say hello to your father.' Do you know these guys? Do they sound familiar? It wasn't friendly—the way they mentioned you."

This was startling news, and I didn't know what to make of it. I didn't want my son to worry about my safety—or his own. Besides, to be worried about the police harming you when you were a law-abiding citizen was something I didn't even want to think about.

I changed the subject. "How's the food supply holding out?"

"Great. We've got a full supply of canned goods and the City Help Pantry has promised to keep an eye on us when it comes to fresh goods—fruit and meat and bakery products. They say all we have to do is ask."

"And everybody's been briefed about warm clothes and being careful about sleeping on below-freezing nights?"

"Sure, Dad. It's all under control." His voice was starting to show a bit of impatience and I decided our conversation had gone on about long enough.

"There's one great thing about winter," he said with a slight smile.

"And what's that?"

"As soon as it comes, all these nosey visitors to the valley will be gone."

I nodded, but I wished I could be as sure of that as he was. In fact, I was growing more and more concerned that that would not be the case.

THIRTY-TWO

Back up from the valley, I stepped out onto my magnificent balcony and surveyed the scene spread before me.

Like so much in Toronto, the valley had changed greatly since I had lived there as a vagrant, though here, beneath my feet, it had changed much less than in other places.

I felt a stab of deep concern when I thought about the brief conversation I'd just had with Jeffrey. My efforts to preserve my segment of the valley had, it seemed, resulted in the acceleration of its destruction. By drawing attention to its beauty, had I hastened the demise of its pristine wilderness? I thought again about that stupid banquet, about the travesty of "restoration", which was now, it seemed to me, just one more excuse for so-called environmentalists to self-celebrate. Lately it had seemed that anything anyone did to make the city better just turned out to make it worse.

As far as my village went, I had wanted to provide safe, simple and comfortable homes for men and women who otherwise might have had to live in dreadful shelters, not to mention doorways, subway grates and back alleys. I had wanted to give such people the chance to live in freedom unmarred by desperation.

And it had worked—until now. Now there was dissention and dissatisfaction among the residents; there were rich donors who sooner or later would make some claim on the running of the place; there were City Councilors opposed to my project and— most dangerous of all—there were greedy developers just waiting to get their hands on land that I had foolishly thought no one would ever want except me.

Across the wide expanse of the ravine, the late autumn wind was tormenting the trees, but the sound it made was a song to me, and the pale colors of the few remaining leaves shimmered and danced to it.

Without warning, I remembered the day I married Queenie. I remembered the ceremony—both Anglican and Cree. And I remembered our honeymoon—three days in a fancy downtown Toronto hotel—then back to work—I as a lawyer and she as a community nurse. I remembered the fun and the love and the plans and the hope.

But it was all gone now. Gone like the green of summer.

I glanced around the whole valley. To the west I saw high-rise rental buildings that had been there for a long time. To the east stood old suburban homes, many now being torn down for much grander houses on the streets that neighbored my own street, where my building—a low-rise apartment building from the 60's that I owned and had completely restored—sat among a few others like itself, though they were not in such pristine condition.

Toward the north, I saw rising glass towers of sweeping height and glowing transparent walls that reflected back the sun that was now heading relentlessly toward the southern hemisphere.

These were new buildings, some not even yet finished. Newcomers to the neighborhood that like all newcomers seemed so full of promise. But what were they promising? Their very presence threatened to destroy the wildness that was the main selling point of the buildings.

I felt anger overwhelm me. Anger at the way that everything I knew and loved— even the bad things in my old life—everything was being replaced by something big and shiny and new and foreign. I felt a dizzying surge of grief. Then anger again. I lifted my fist to pound it on the railing of my balcony.

But before my hand touched the metal, I heard the doorbell ring.

I had never seen the man at the door before, but I knew who he was. Al Brownette stood there in full uniform, including a bullet-proof vest, with his police cap in one hand and a sheaf of official-looking papers in the other. The soft light from the hallway played on the skin of his bald head, making it look like a billiard ball.

His clean-shaven and nearly lineless face bore an expression of non-specific, officious threat. It took only seconds for him to manage to get past me and into the apartment, like a worm gets past the holes of a sieve.

"What can I do for you?" I asked, hiding the combination of fear and contempt that I had for the man.

Brownette didn't answer at first. He glanced around the apartment as though he were about to search it for something. I tried to see whether one of the papers he held was a warrant, but I couldn't make any of them out even from the short distance I stood from him.

He turned toward me. "You can lay off Ted Downs. He's got trouble enough. You can just mind your own business, which, I'm here to tell you, you got plenty of…"

He shook his hand, rustling the papers he held.

"It was you, wasn't it?" I challenged him. "It was you who followed me in the valley and wrote that note… How dare you harass me? On what grounds can you…"

Al Brownette smiled an unpleasant smile. "I don't need grounds for anything having to do with the breaking of city ordinances, Portal. And I don't need them for these, either." He shoved the papers he was holding at my chest.

Before I could even look at them, Brownette shook his fingers in my face.

"I don't know what you're trying to prove," he hissed. "I know you've talked to Mark Milktoast and Feeance. But you're not going to get anything else. That dirty old geezer died of a heart attack. That's all. Happens all the time."

He looked around the apartment again and made a sweeping gesture. "This is a nice place. If I was an old guy like you, I'd stay home more often. Stay out of shelters and other dumps, stay out of the valley altogether. There's nothing down there you need to know about. Except maybe these…" He reached over and with a grin shuffled the pages still in my hand.

Then he turned and pretty much marched out the door. As he went, I noticed that the holster of his gun was unsnapped. It was too bold a gesture, too egregious an offense to be a matter of carelessness. He was threatening me and he knew that I knew that that was the case.

THIRTY-THREE

I stumbled back into the apartment, sat down and started to read.

I was shocked. There were all sorts of summonses here: notices of violations of city ordinances, overdue tax bills, even parking tickets. All of them purporting to have to do with acts against the law committed by people who lived in our village.

Topping off the mess was a handful of "homeless" tickets.

And there were also notifications of motions made by City Councilors to shut down the village on the grounds of its being unsanitary, unhealthy, environmentally dangerous and even racist!

I simply could not understand what was going on here. Had Jeffrey been grossly negligent in some way? I would not allow myself to believe that, especially after our conversation and after seeing with my own eyes that the village was in fine shape. Something else had to be going on.

I spent hours studying those papers, looking up laws on the internet, comparing facts and figures.

The numbers were all wrong. The number of people who lived in our village was nowhere near as high as reported in the minutes of City Council. The description of the sanitation we'd provided our residents was fraudulent. We had always had the best plumbing, the best water system. I was not the son of a builder for nothing. Though my father had been a *muratore*, a *brickiere*, a bricklayer, he had had a profound understanding of how a building worked. And so did Jeffrey, and so did I. The reports I was reading were clearly false, clearly intended to make the village look like some sort of careless collection of filthy hovels.

I came to the conclusion that these papers were one further step in a campaign to destroy my village. I decided I needed help fighting this harassment, and though I had every reason to expect no help at all any more from Matt West, I decided to visit him again, anyway.

When I got to Headquarters and asked for Matt, I was astonished that he came down to greet me and personally escorted me upstairs to his office. He was back to being his old friendly self. "What can I do for you?" he asked, studying me as though I were a suspect. You look a little flushed today. Everything all right?"

I was beginning to be so fed up with the police that I actually thought Matt was trying to trick me somehow. The old good cop, bad cop routine. Except I had nothing to give, no beans to spill.

"Here, have a seat. And a coffee. Two milks, no sugar, right?"

In the old days, Matt had always had a pot of coffee going in his office, unlike any other cop I'd known. He'd used it to make people understand that they could feel at home here, could talk to him and trust him. Now he had one of those coffee-makers with little individual containers of gourmet grinds. The coffee routine was getting on my nerves. I was moving past the point of trusting anybody.

He put a warm cup in my hand and pushed a button, telling his secretary to keep everybody else out.

"Okay," he said, "what's up?"

"These," I said, barely containing my anger which seemed to get worse in direct proportion to Matt's apparent kindness. "I've been handed these by one of your boys."

It was an insulting thing to say. Matt was not the type of police officer to ever refer to his fellow professionals as "boys."

But he just nodded and reached out for the papers, which I'd stuffed into a briefcase I hadn't used in years. I felt a moment's shame when I realized how shabby it looked against Matt's slick new desk.

If he noticed, he didn't say anything. He began to read the papers, and by the motion of his eyes, I could see that he was a fast reader and fast at what he comprehended, too.

But when it came to going over the papers with me, he took his time.

"Some of these tickets—a couple of the parking tickets and a couple of the homeless tickets—are legit. They can be disposed of."

"How?"

He glanced up from the papers. "By paying them!"

I relaxed and smiled. Parking tickets given to people visiting the valley and parking on the streets above were not that unusual. And Jeffrey knew about homeless tickets even though he'd only settled a few of them.

But the other papers were a different matter. "These complaints from City Council look pretty frightening, I agree," Matt said. "But I can tell you that they are not actionable—they're just suggestions that various councilors have made. They can be legally ignored, though they certainly give you a good idea of who your enemies are!"

"I don't get it, Matt. Why should I have so many enemies in the city? Why are people so against my efforts just to help a few people out? City Council is always going on about helping the poor and about citizens taking personal responsibility for the fate of their fellow citizens...."

Matt shrugged. "Whoever your enemy is, the person is clearly capable of getting a large and varied number of city officials on his or her side."

"How did Al Brownette find me?" I asked, impatient to get some inkling about what Matt was really saying here. "How did he know where I live?"

He looked at me as if I'd asked a stupid question, which I had.

"And what's with Ted Downs? I saw him at a banquet not long ago. He was hobnobbing with developers. What's his interest in my affairs?"

"Ellis, you're too keyed-up about all this. You're putting two and two together and coming up with ten. If I were you, I'd just pay the damn tickets and relax." He shuffled all the papers together and handed them to me. "And I'd lay off Ted Downs. He's a good man who's had a run of bad luck and who's trying to pick up the pieces."

He gave me a look that said that I, better than anybody, should understand how that played out.

"What do you mean, Matt? What sort of bad luck?"

I didn't expect him to get personal, but he did. "There's nothing illegal about a police officer being a real estate investor. What Downs is doing is trying to rebuild his life after the suicide of his son."

The thought of such a thing hit me hard, considering how close Jeffrey and I had become in the past few years. "What happened?"

Matt was silent for a moment. Then he went on in a voice that was pretty soft for the tough guy that I knew him to be. "It was one of those cases that you just can't understand. Everything was fine for Ted. He had a nice wife and a teenage son. Apparently the kid was real smart, a geek type. But I guess the kid was bullied by somebody. Anyway, he committed suicide. It happened really fast. Shortly after it occurred, Mrs. Downs took off, blaming her husband for her son's death...."

"Bullied? You mean at school or on the internet?"

Matt shrugged again. "Who knows?" He gestured toward his tidy desk. "Look, Ellis, I got a lot of work to do here. I hope you're clear on those papers. Just pay the tickets and put the other things aside. If somebody's against you for some reason, you'll find out who and what soon enough. You can always call 911 if you find yourself in danger...."

***

On the way home, I stopped to see Jeffrey. I told myself I needed to show him the tickets and ask his opinion on the other matters. But I really just wanted to make sure he was okay.

"Dad, I'm not surprised. I've often helped people in the village with things like this. I'm sure you realize that assisting people the way we do makes us suspicious in some people's eyes. It's a sad fact—and a strange one. But I've gotten used to it. And as for the visit from the cop, that's not unusual either."

"No? Just how long have the police have been frequenting the village?"

Jeffrey laughed. "From day one." He hesitated and I hoped it wasn't because he was afraid to reveal something that we'd failed to discuss in our recent fraught conversation. "To tell the truth, Dad, I think that lately the police have been down here far more often than in the past--on an almost daily basis. They claim that the neighbors on the rim of the valley have security issues, and I'm sure that's true. There have been so many buildings put up in the past year—expensive condos that well-heeled people are buying and moving into. I'm sure people like that would want to think that the police are keeping an eye on anything that's happening down here." He gestured upward, but I didn't need to look at all those new glass giants to know what he was talking about.

"And," he went on, "I always have to face the fact that we're not housing angels down here. Sooner or later somebody is going to piss off the cops in some way. Again, it's just something I've learned to deal with."

"Who comes?"

"What?"

"The cops. Who comes? Is it guys on the beat or special squad teams or what?"

Jeffrey thought for a minute. "Usually it's random people—I mean different officers, though I suppose they're mostly from the local station house. Once in a while, it'll be somebody from downtown on a court matter. And a couple times lately it's been that older man and younger man I told you about. They almost act like father and son, but I get the feeling they're not as nice to other people as they seem to be to each other."

"But you say you didn't get their names. Did they speak to each other, where they called Ted and Al?"

"I didn't hear, Dad. I'm sorry. All I can say is that they've been down here more than once and the last time, they sort of threw their weight around for a while and then left. You know, warning people in a general way to keep their noses clean."

"If you see them again, Son, you let me know. Right away. Phone me on my cell if you have to."

Jeffrey laughed. "Dad," he said, "by the time you find your phone, they'll be long gone."

THIRTY-FOUR

Once again I had the feeling that I had gotten nowhere and would get nowhere with this "investigation". None of the pieces fit together in any way I could understand. A man had been killed by four police officers. That had to have been what Queenie thought, or else why would she have sent me on this wild goose chase?

Of the four, two appeared to be completely harmless as far as committing murder went. Feeance Blake struck me as an unfriendly person, but she also seemed straight-arrow, as if she had no axe to grind and no interest in anything but doing her job as an officer of the law. Mark Hopequist, on the other hand, didn't strike me as having much of a police career ahead of him. He just wasn't cut out for the job. Soft. Sentimental. Maybe kids liked him. Criminals would too.

So that left Ted and his buddy Al. I had to admit that they were practically a cliché. I could have written a TV police drama about them—the old cop, hardened by years on the street and getting on as he always had by appearing to be congenial then coming down hard and heavy. And Al, the tough little puppy-dog doing all he could to learn how to bite—and when and how hard.

None of these had the one thing you needed to kill somebody. They had no motive.

Which brought me yet again to thoughts of the victim. It seemed like everybody except my Queenie had a motive to get him out of the way. He was obnoxious, argumentative, inflammable… But those negative personality traits were annoyances. They weren't motives for homicide. They weren't motives for anything except the profound desire to get away from the bastard.

I went to the window of my apartment, as I had lately begun to do often, and looked out over the valley. Directly beneath me, the trees, now stripped and awaiting winter, stood in their profusion as if guarding the river. It was still flowing, and depending on the severity of the winter, might not freeze up at all.

But if it did turn very cold very suddenly, parts of the river would solidify in days, if not hours. There had been a time when the river never froze because it had been so polluted, but things were different now. Most people respected the Don and refrained from using it as a garbage dump, though, as I said, I did sometimes see shopping carts down there as if it were some kind of challenge for a prankster to figure out how to steal one, run it to the river and heave it in.

Of course I had total contempt for such people.

But I had more important things to think about. What were Al and Ted doing down there? I was sure it was them that Jeffrey had described.

I couldn't think of anything that connected them to Jeffrey or to the village.

But after a few moments' thought, I realized there was one thing.

Me.

As I stood there, I remembered a day on which the river, or at least the part of it near the now skeletal long-term facility on its banks, had frozen solid. I recalled how on that day, I'd rescued a woman who had escaped from the facility. Not just any woman but a woman I had once loved and who had never returned my love—not even for an instant.

And I thought of my first wife, the cool blond beauty who had betrayed me.

And I thought of Queenie, my one true wife, the woman who had won my heart by her courage and her wry humor and her earthy beauty and—above all—by her kindness and her unending concern for other people.

She had been kinder to me than anyone had ever been. The last thing she would have thought of was any sort of payback.

But I owed her. And I would pay her back. At least in this one way: I would keep at it. I would find out who killed the Juicer and why. If it took me the rest of my life.

So I decided to give it one more shot. And that led me to a place I didn't really want to go: back to the domain of the infamous Johnny Dirt.

To tell the truth, when I got there I was impressed. Apparently it was clinic day at the downtown shelter that he ran. I had to come to the conclusion that Johnny was yet another of the many people that Queenie had set on the path of success. When I had known Johnny before, he had been nothing but a dirty, irritating street bum. But now, one could almost say that he had become Queenie's successor in the shelter business. Not only did he now seem remarkably organized personally, he was actually managing to run a place that—at least on this day—seemed a particularly smooth operation.

What appeared to be a professional nurse was set up in the tiny room that served as Johnny's office, and she was seeing patients who were lined up out the door of the office and into the larger adjacent room that each day served as an activity room, a dining room and, when the furniture had been shoved against the walls and the mats laid down, a dormitory for those who couldn't stand sleeping outside in the increasing cold.

I had to wait to see Johnny because he was so busy, but he seemed glad to see me, which was another remarkable thing. He had always given me reason to think he hated me in the past.

"Look, man, I already told you. Queenie put up with people that nobody else would, and to her, the Juicer was a big kid who just needed somebody to look after him."

"What about you, yourself, Johnny. What did you think? What was the Juicer's problem, anyway?"

"He was a gigantic all-round pain in the ass. But his worse problem was his big mouth."

"What do you mean?"

"He was a yapper. Wouldn't shut up once he got started. And he thought he was smart enough to run the government. 'If I was the mayor, I would—blah, blah, blah.' To hear him tell it, he should run the whole damn city, if not the world."

I had to smile at the energy with which Johnny delivered this piece of information, but there was no smiling at what he said next.

"There was one thing I don't think Queenie ever really saw. The Bruiser—I mean the Juicer--was a bully when she wasn't around. On any day, he would start with the help."

"The help?"

"Yeah, the people who worked at the shelter. Not the just volunteers but the hired workers, too. He would tease them. It was funny at first. But it got mean real quick. He'd ask them where they came from—they were mostly immigrants—then he would make fun of their countries. Like he had a name—a bad name—for every group of people. Sometimes he went at it so hard and long that one of the women would start crying. They never complained, though. Because they were afraid for their jobs."

"You mean Queenie would fire them?" I asked with surprise.

Johnny laughed. "Not hardly. They were just paranoid because of being immigrants." He shook his head.

"So the Juicer really went at them?"

"Yeah, but not just them. He liked to spout people's personal business in front of other people. Because he was always in some kind of trouble, he would run into people in jail and in the mental lockups. One of his favorite tricks was to claim that he saw somebody's friend or relative in some lock-up, then haunt the person with the fact that his brother or whatever was a criminal or worse—a loony."

"That's a pretty stupid thing to do."

"Yeah. But you'd be surprised at how much you can hurt a person by insulting someone they care about."

"Can you remember anyone in particular that the Juicer may have teased in this way?"

Johnny laughed "Shit, there have been so many that I can't remember anyone exactly."

I changed the subject. "Johnny, now that you're running things here, do you ever have to deal with homeless tickets or summonses? Do you ever have any trouble from City Hall?

He smiled. He had quite a few teeth missing. I imagined that that might soon change considering that he now had a salary—provided by the taxpayers of course.

"Trouble from City Hall? Absolutely not. I'm their sweetheart. I'm their bad guy turned good. They love me. They even had me talk in front of the whole council as a speaker to tell them how I 'turned around.'

"You should try it sometime," he added with a smirk. "You know, a little speech about how you were a judge, then a bum, then a lawyer, then a judge and now an old guy who goes around bothering people at work because he's too old to have a job himself."

I didn't know whether to laugh or to punch his self-righteous, mocking face.

THIRTY-FIVE

Mulling all this over, I came to the conclusion that though Matt West might think there was no problem with a cop being interested in real estate investment in his spare time, I wasn't so sure. I could think of a number of ways in which conflicts of interest could occur. Specifically, I could see how harassing the inhabitants of the village could lead to media attention. And that might result in a call to get us out of the valley. Since our land was privately owned, developers could acquire it directly. And if they managed to depreciate the value of the site beforehand by treating the village as a slum, they would find themselves in a very favorable position.

That might account for Ted's being down there. As for Al, aside from plain belligerence and the new notion that seemed to be creeping into the force that a good cop was a bald guy who knew how to push people around, I had no idea what motive he would have for involving himself in my affairs.

While I was pondering these facts, I got a call from Aliana. She hadn't called in a while and I had to admit that I was surprised to be happy to hear from her.

"Ellis," she said, drawing a breath and speaking faster than she usually did, "I know you as much as told me that you don't need me anymore, but I can't let a story just fizzle."

"It hasn't fizzled, as you put it, I've…"

"I know. You've been asking around. So have I. Let me fill you in."

It was more of a command than an offer. "Okay, Aliana. What have you learned?"

"I've been active on two fronts, so to speak." She hesitated, "But hey, rather than talking on the phone, why don't we meet for a coffee?"

"Don't you think that's a little dangerous?" I answered.

It was meant as a joke but I was embarrassed that the minute the words were out of my mouth, a double meaning popped into my head.

"Yeah, well, I haven't been shot at lately. Have you?" she teased.

"To tell the truth, Aliana, I can't quite get that incident out of my mind, can't convince myself that it was just some sort of accident."

"Well then let's try someplace different…"

I agreed to meet her at a Country Style doughnut shop midway between my place and hers.

I had discovered a secret cache of clothing in my size at the back of the closet in the bedroom I'd shared with Queenie. I was shocked at first. Then I remembered that Queenie was the kind of person who liked to do her Christmas shopping bit by bit all year long.

It broke my heart to look at these things, to imagine the way that Queenie would have watched my face as I opened each package, a mixture of apprehension and pleasure in her smiling eyes.

When I had first come upon the items, my impulse was to leave them in their bags and boxes and to take them down to the Salvation Army depot.

But I couldn't bear to. So I had left them pretty much as I had found them.

But now, I decided that it would be a waste to discard these loving gifts.

So I chose a dark red sweater and a gray shirt with red detailing and wore them to my meeting. And when Aliana saw them and commented that I looked great, I only felt a jolt of guilt and sorrow for an instant.

"I've been digging into the background of the Juicer. I know you're on top of this, and everybody knows how hard Queenie worked to help the guy, but the more I learn about him, the uglier it gets."

"What? What have you found out?"

"Do you remember that protest a couple of years ago when the cops more or less corralled a bunch of citizens on Spadina Avenue on a Sunday afternoon?"

I thought for a minute. "You mean the last time the city hosted a big-deal conference like the one that's going on right now?"

"Yeah. That's the one. What happened was that a few renegade cops—probably not Toronto police but guys from other jurisdictions called in to help—anyway, they went wild one afternoon and just rounded up anybody within blocks of the conference site. They wouldn't let anybody leave the scene. It started to rain, but they still made innocent people, whom they had no reason to believe were even demonstrating, wait for four hours before they released a few of them and took the rest down to the detention center that had been especially set up for the conference."

"And there they held them for many more hours...." I recalled.

"No washrooms nearby. No medication for diabetics and others desperate for them. No lawyers."

"And nobody charged for this mistreatment of the innocent members of the public."

"One guy," Aliana corrected. "One cop was charged. Even though dozens took part in the incidents surrounding the mistreating not only of innocent people caught up in the crowd, but even mistreatment of the actual demonstrators, some of who were violent professional rabble-rousers, but many of whom were ordinary citizens just offering their opinion in a public way."

"What does all this have to do with the Juicer?"

"A lot. The fact of the matter is that he was well known to the police. I checked the records. There's every reason to believe he was a vicious, often out-of-control individual. Most recently, I mean less than a year before his death, he had done a significant amount of time in remand if not in jail."

"What for?"

"He was charged with aggravated sexual assault, but pleaded down."

"Why? I had to ask. Why would Queenie want to help somebody like that?" I suddenly realized something I should have thought of a long time before. That there were aspects of her work that Queenie had never shared with me. And that one of them was the physical danger that she must have been in a good deal of the time. I wondered if she had kept things from me because she'd been fearful that I would have expressed a desire that she give up the work she so clearly loved. I wouldn't have. I never would have. But now, now that she was gone, I was devastated to think about the risks she must have taken. She had once said that if you don't help the worst, who will?

"Ellis," Aliana said softly, reaching toward my hand as it lay on the table, but not actually touching my fingers. "Are you okay with all of this? We can leave it for another time if you want."

"No," I said. "No, go on. What else?"

"During that demonstration I just mentioned, the Juicer was part of the crowd that was detained."

"How ridiculous. How completely insane to think that a guy like him would be part of a political protest!"

"Right," Aliana said. "That's the point. He was one of the ones detained just for being on the wrong corner at the wrong time. He was swept up with everybody else and taken off to the holding facility. There was no way he could even really find out what was going on. The longer his detention went on, the more frantic and uncontrollable he became. Until he finally freaked altogether and attacked another detainee—a young man whom he accused of sexually assaulting him when the kid got too close and accidentally touched him. He then proceeded to harass the boy, accusing him of a homosexual offence, for several hours in the confined presence of many other detainees.

"The cops caught the whole thing on video. Apparently, the charges against him that resulted from that incident were still pending at the time of his death, but the fate of the young man he had attacked was sealed far sooner. He committed suicide the next day. His father, who happened to be a Toronto police officer, later swore that he would get justice for his son. That he trusted in the courts to bring the matter of what he called bullying and rape to a just conclusion, but that if they failed to do so, he wouldn't hesitate to take matters into his own hands."

"And did he?"

"I don't know. It was later learned that it would have been a difficult court case because despite the huge number of witnesses, the detention center was so crowded that it wasn't clear from the video who could really have seen what. Plus, in the melee of arresting people during the demonstration, a number of important documents, including any record of the arrest of The Juicer and his victim, had been lost, if they had ever existed. Some people said that nobody even knew for sure what the boy's name was until his father spoke out."

"Do you know the father's name?"

She hesitated before answering. Then she said, "Yes, Yes, I do. Ted Downs."

THIRTY-SIX

Everything changed then. In that moment. Because now I did have a case. Now I had a motive. It didn't occur to me for one second to question the accuracy of anything that Aliana had just told me. I was beginning to see that she had, indeed, always been my friend, not just in the times of my greatest trouble, but right now.

"Aliana, I don't know what I'm going to have to do about this, but…"

"Ellis, I'm not finished. As I said, there were two things I had to talk to you about today. It's Kezia."

"Kezia?" It took me a minute to remember who she was talking about. It had only been days since we'd seen the girl but so much had intervened that I had as much as forgotten her. Besides, she was a distraction, a small problem taking time and attention from one that was much larger.

"Yes. A couple of days ago I got a mysterious phone message that it took me a few hours to realize could only have come from her. I tried calling her back, but of course, there was no answer. So I took a chance and went over there. I thought about waiting until somebody came along and opened the lobby door, but I ended up waiting such a long time that I just decided to buzz, figuring that she wouldn't answer or wouldn't let me in."

Aliana was so intense that I had no trouble focusing on what she was saying, despite the fact that my head was spinning because of what I'd just heard about Ted Downs.

"So what happened?"

"The second the buzzer rang, she answered. When I told her who it was, she actually sounded relieved. She told me just to stay there until she could come down. So I did. I only waited a couple of minutes. She didn't even take the elevator, she just ran down the stairs."

"Why? Why was she in such a hurry?"

"She seemed so glad to see me that I figured we could have a good talk. So I offered to take her downtown for a snack and a chat. But instead of responding to my offer, she just broke down completely—crying and shaking. She even let me put my arm around her. She was gasping so hard I couldn't understand what she was saying.

"After a few seconds, I managed to lead her over to the ledge formed by the radiator in front of the lobby window."

I remembered that all the furniture in the lobby had been removed for one nefarious reason or another.

"We sat and she managed to calm down enough to tell me what was wrong. She said she couldn't go out and she couldn't stay away from the apartment for long because she and her good brother were guarding it against her bad brothers. She said her brothers had warned them that they were on the way over and that they intended to set fire to all their books and notes and what she called their "writings." They told her that they knew that there was a computer hidden in the apartment and that they were going to find it and throw it off the balcony."

"The bastards."

"Kezia even mentioned her book again—the one about snow. She was hysterical. She kept saying 'It's almost done. I can't lose it now.'"

"What did you say?"

"I offered to keep her papers and books at my apartment, but this made her even more nervous. She says her brothers will follow her if they find out she's going to somebody else's place."

Aliana paused and looked out the window. We were in a neighborhood of well-kept old homes intersected by a major north-south street lined with small businesses. It would be hard to find a less dangerous-looking location. But I knew she was thinking what I was thinking. People had been shot dead in neighborhoods like this.

"I don't really get this," I said. "Why do a couple of gangsters care about a pair of kids who are studying and writing? Is it just harassment or is there more to it?"

"I asked her. I told her I couldn't understand why her brothers were so concerned about her writing. At first she clammed right up. Just sat there, silent. And then she started looking around frantically as if she thought they were somewhere near. I was beginning to think I should get help. Call social services or the Youth Bureau. But I just waited, sitting quietly beside her, and after a little while, I got it out of her that the brothers were so stupid that they thought Kezia was writing about their involvement in the cocaine trade because one day she made the mistake of telling them that the book was about snow."

"Surely they were pulling her leg!"

"I told her that, of course. But she remained unconvinced. And she kept saying, "I have to go upstairs. I have to go upstairs… I managed to keep her beside me for a few more minutes. I told her I could help her get back to school. That it would be safe and that I'd make sure she had somebody to help her at once if she felt in any danger.

"What did she say?"

"She said something that really frightened me. She said she didn't have time for school because she was still researching her book down by the river. She said she sometimes takes the subway and goes into the valley by herself. When I told her that this was dangerous—at any time but especially now when there's likely to be ice and snow down there—she said that she knew that but that if she could talk to that old judge guy, he could tell her anything she needed to know."

I didn't know whether to be flattered or alarmed. "The old judge guy being me, I suppose?"

Aliana smiled. The first smile I'd seen since this intense conversation had begun.

"That would be the old judge guy in question," she said.

"If she wants to talk, I'm completely available—as long as you can come along, too."

Aliana looked surprised for a split second. Then she realized what I was saying.

"Of course. But I don't think that'll happen. She said her brother told her that if she wants to avoid trouble, she has to 'keep things in the family'."

I got up and got us a couple more coffees. Aliana thanked me. Apparently she intended for our conversation to go on a little longer. Which was fine, except I couldn't really see where all this information about the girl was leading.

"There was one more thing," Aliana said. She took a sip of her coffee, but it was very hot and I could see that she was trying hard to control her reaction to it. I wondered whether appearing to remain in control at all times was a trick that reporters practiced in order not to lose the upper hand in interviews. I also wondered why she thought she needed the upper hand with me.

"What? What other thing?"

"She said she'd been down in the valley a lot. She mentioned that she didn't care about winter starting and that she liked the river when the ice began to form. She said that she was down there one day and that she saw somebody she knew but that she didn't talk to him because she didn't think it was safe to talk to men down there even if you knew them."

"She shouldn't have been down there at all. Did she say who the man was?"

Aliana looked me in the eye. Maybe that was another reporter trick. I didn't look away. "Yes," she said. "It was the man that Kezia calls 'that nice cop'."

"Hopequist."

"Right."

I thought about that for a moment. "Aliana," I finally said. "I know I said that I don't need your help anymore, but I see now that I was wrong."

She looked at me as if I were speaking a language she didn't understand. "What do you mean?"

"I mean that the time has come to solve this crime. Hopequist is not somebody we have to worry about. I can see now that I've fooled around long enough. There's only one person in this whole scenario who has the least motive for doing harm to the victim and that person is Ted Downs. The time has come to go after him, and I can't do it alone."

THIRTY-SEVEN

We found out where Ted Downs lived and we did surveillance on his house. I'm ashamed to admit we did this, especially since we had no experience and therefore no skill at it. But we did discover a few things about the man. We followed him a couple times when he left home. He was always alone. He dressed nicely, like a businessman at his leisure. He carried books sometimes, as though he were studying something or for something. Nobody came to his house except people that we could see were his neighbors and people we were pretty sure were other cops.

Ted Downs had no wife and no kids that we ever saw, which confirmed what we had learned before.

We actually talked to a couple of the neighbors, Aliana using her professional skills. Mostly they told us to mind our own business. But a couple people said that Ted was a great guy who had suffered a terrible loss quite recently but was doing his best to get over it and get on with his life.

Aliana made further use of her police contacts and we ended up one night at the Crooked Cookoo, located at some obscure intersection in Scarborough, a corner that I had never seen despite my decades of living not far from it. It was archetypical enough to be a parody of itself. Dark, crowded, noisy with raucous music that I thought was being piped in until I caught sight of the band that was playing in a corner of the place lit only by one red bulb and one blue one.

"How can we talk to anybody here?" I asked Aliana. I was shouting over the noise, but she didn't hear me.

"What?"

"I can't hear myself think. How are we going to get anything in a place like this?"

"You don't need to think," she said. This time she was standing so close to me that the sound of her voice reached my ear unimpeded by the ambient racket.

I had to admit she looked great in tight jeans and a black sweater that showed she hadn't lost any of the youthful attractiveness of her figure. I realized I had never really looked at her before. I've always been a one-woman man, even if it's been three different women at three different times. I could easily figure out Aliana's age, based on the difference between us that I'd known since she was a kid. But the music and the push of the crowd and the fact that Aliana was alternately shoved right up against me, then torn away was making it hard for me to concentrate.

"Just stick with me and listen," she said, leading me to a table where she was soon joined by three or four men. I couldn't see all that clearly, but they looked tall and rather muscular and handsome in a bald-headed tough-looking sort of way.

"Ted? Great guy. Shame what happened to him."

"Downs? He's retiring, isn't he?" I heard he was handing over the job to his brown-nosing little sidekick!"

This elicited a laugh from the group, a laugh in which Aliana seemed to join.

"He's got a shadow, a little shadow that goes in and out with him. That's Ted and Al," somebody said. And they laughed again.

At the end of the evening, I felt I'd learned nothing new about Ted Downs, but I learned a lot about Aliana.

She was a skilled actress. I was sure the talent had served her well over the years. I couldn't help wondering whether she'd ever exercised it on my behalf—or, come to think of it, on me.

The next thing she reported to me was that she had been doing some research at the coroner's office.

"I know you spoke to Singh, but he can be pretty tight-mouthed. I loosened him up a bit, reviewed his whole report with him. It's true that the Juicer didn't die on the street. He died in the hospital in which he'd been a patient for several days prior, due to his recurring mental problems. He passed away of a massive coronary. At the time of his death, he was heavily bruised from the take-down at the shelter—there were lacerations and contusions all over his body. That fact rendered some details of his condition incapable of analysis."

"I don't get this, Aliana. A man is beaten by the police and he dies of a heart attack and the coroner concludes he died of natural causes?"

She shrugged. "I can't argue with the coroner, Ellis. But I will say that I spoke to a nurse at the hospital who had worked on the Juicer. By the way, he had a name."

"William Collins."

"Right. He was only forty-four."

"I thought he was much older than that!"

"So did everybody else. But he wasn't. He still had a life ahead of him."

"And so did Ted Down's son," I couldn't help saying.

"Anyway," Aliana went on, "the nurse told me that the strength of people who are hysterical—even if they have no previous history of mental illness—can be phenomenal. She said you might think that a sedentary man not in top physical condition might be a weakling—and he might be until enraged. I'm sure it's hormonal. It may even have something to do with the survival instinct."

I had to smile at her despite the grim details of this conversation. "You're going all Darwinian on me, are you?"

She looked at me as though she'd forgotten that I was capable of humor. She shook her head as if to dismiss the distracting thought and pressed on. "While I was talking to the nurse, the facility's grief counsellor came in."

The mention of such a person made me suddenly uncomfortable, as if I had, for a moment, forgotten my own grief and now had had it shoved in my face.

Aliana didn't seem to notice my brief discomfort. "The grief counsellor told me that it would not be unusual for a deeply grieving person—especially one whose beloved died with issues remaining, such as the criminally-detained son of a cop--to occasionally feel homicidal rage when trying to deal with the demise of the loved one. But, she also said that in all her years of doing this work, she has never encountered anyone, nor heard of anyone, who actually committed murder out of rage at their grief for a lost one."

I thanked her for the information. And she told me that I was welcome. I told her I'd think about it all and get back to her. She stuck out her hand for me to shake it, and when I took it, she gave my fingers a little squeeze.

I didn't intend to let matters drop. Not at all. I intended to continue the surveillance on my own.

But when I went back to Ted Downs' house and saw him arriving home, probably after a long shift, I realized that Ted, like me, myself, was bearing the burden of sorrow over the death of a loved one. To pretty much ambush him on his own territory would be little short of cruel.

THIRTY-EIGHT

But if I thought that it would be easy to sneak around spying on a cop, I had another think coming.

I was, for a change, minding my own business down in the valley. I wasn't visiting Jeffrey, or even thinking about anything except the beauty of the trees covered with new snow and the sound the river makes as the fast-flowing center section slides past the tinkling ice closer to the shore.

It was as if the ice itself had sprung up and smacked me. A cold, hard, sharp slap stung my cheek and my jacket was pulled so forcefully from the side that I lost my balance and slid down onto the icy path. I struggled to get up, but when I got halfway to my feet, my shaking knees gave way under me and in utter fear and humiliation, I ended up on my bum at the large feet of my attacker.

"What the hell do you think you're up to? You're asking for it, Portal. You're going to find yourself where you've always belonged in spite of your fancy legal footwork, you common thug, you piece of shit..."

I turned away from the kick I could see coming.

But before his foot met my face, something or somebody pulled Ted Downs away

"Leave him alone," I heard Jeffrey shout. I didn't think I'd ever heard him say anything that loud before. "Just get the fuck away and get the hell out of here."

I'd never heard him utter profanities, either. But I had to admit, he sounded pretty frightening.

"Get up, Dad," my son said, lifting me by the arm and helping me to stand, which was suddenly difficult on the icy path. "We're finished here and so is he...."

Jeffrey turned in the direction from which I'd come, intending to lead me back down the path, but as soon as we turned our backs on the enraged cop, he was on me again, jumping on my back and pushing me down. This time his heavy boot met its target. I felt a searing pain in my side, heard the crack of a rib, suddenly found it hard to breathe.

I was as frightened for Jeffrey as I was for myself. Not only afraid that Downs would hurt him physically, but afraid he would arrest him—or both of us—for assaulting an officer.

"Lay off, son," I struggled to say. "He'll arrest us."

"For what? He attached you. And anyway, he can't. He's not in uniform. He's not on duty."

This opinion came not from Jeffrey but from a ragged-looking man who, with several others had suddenly appeared on the path. Despite my pain, I struggled to think where I'd seen this man before. And I remembered. He'd once been a lawyer, had even appeared before me several times. But then, like me, he had hit the skids. He'd never made his way back up though, even if he did feel qualified to give a legal opinion.

"Let's go, Jeffrey. Please, let's just get out of here now."

"I'm saying it again and this time I mean it," Jeffrey answered with a power in his voice that I suddenly realized must always have been there. How else would he have managed the village? How else would he have managed his life as my son? "Get out of here and stay out. This is private property. You have no right to be here if we are not breaking the law. And I assure you, we are not. Just go."

I thought for sure we were doomed. The pain in my side was getting worse by the second. The temperature seemed to have dropped about twenty degrees since I'd set off on my walk. I was beginning to shiver, and each quivering movement sent new spasms of wild, jabbing hurt. And bad as the reality was, I was beginning to imagine worse. Any minute now, I was sure, I would feel the frigid steel of handcuffs.

But it didn't happen. Maybe the village lawyer was right. Maybe Downs wasn't going to haul me in and arrest me for resisting arrest or something similar. Maybe he was just going to keep me there, yelling at me until I passed out.

"Lay off, Portal," he shouted. "Leave me alone. You have no right to come to my house. It's none of your damn business what goes on there. And it's none of your concern what's going on with the case of William Collins. Or with my son. Just keep your damn ideas to yourself and stop prying into my life. You got that? Because if you don't get off my back, you're going to find yourself right back where you belong—with other no-good criminals just like yourself..."

He made another lunge for me, but Jeffrey held him off.

"We'll stay away, I assure you," Jeffrey said. "Now please leave. You can see that you've hurt him. I'm going to have to attend to his injuries. I'm going to have to get him to emerg."

The way Jeffrey said this was reassuring. For the first time since before Queenie got sick, I had the feeling that somebody was watching over me. I only had the feeling for a few seconds because right after Jeffrey spoke, I passed out, and I didn't wake up until we'd been in the RAZ unit at Scarborough General for six of the twelve hours we would spend there.

When I got home, Jeffrey put me to bed. It was a strange reversal of roles and in my analgesic-induced state, I sped back in memory to the time when he was a quiet little child. His sister, my daughter Ellen, was a spitfire. Always something on the go: Girl Guides, church groups, the soccer team... But Jeffrey had always kept quiet, kept to his room reading or as he often told me, thinking. "I'm just thinking about everything," he would say. The two could not have been more different then as now. Ellen was a top-notch legal whiz, and the general feeling was that she would soon follow me to the bench, though all bets were that, unlike me, she would have a long, completely distinguished and absolutely uninterrupted career.

As I lay there floating in the sea of dreams, it seemed to me that a cloud of attendants came and went. I woke often to find Jeffrey beside the bed and sometimes Ellen and sometimes Angelo, my teenaged grandson. Once I thought I heard and saw Aliana, but decided that was a dream or a hallucination.

I stayed at home in bed for six days, until the pain in my side let up enough for me to get up and walk around the apartment. At first I was happy to be relieved of the responsibility I felt about the insoluble mystery of the death of William Collins.

But the more I got back to being myself, the more the whole thing bugged me.

And then I realized that I was bored. That was all it took to get me back on my feet and back in the game.

The next time I saw Aliana in my apartment, she was really there.

"I went back to see Singh at the coroner's office," she reported. "I just wanted to clarify some details about the state of the body at the time of death."

She sounded like a pathologist herself and I wondered whether each time she conducted research for an article she sounded like the subject of her piece for a while.

"Of course he confirmed everything we've heard a million times before, but he added something that nobody has ever mentioned." She stopped. "Can I get you anything? You look a little pale...."

"I'm fine. Don't leave me hanging here. What did he tell you?"

"The pathologist said that the Juicer was in a state of high excitability. He died of heart failure brought about as a result of stress caused by several types of injury, including possible injuries from a Taser."

"A Taser? Singh actually used the word? Nobody had a Taser during the incident."

Aliana nodded.

"Everybody's been very definite about non-lethal weapons being authorized to supervisors only...."

"I know. Anyway, Singh said he couldn't conclude decisively that a Taser had been involved. Nor would he say that had a Taser been involved it was the cause of death. All he would say was that the body showed signs of pressure injuries and of bruising consistent with being struck several times with a blunt object or objects."

"He told me that, too."

"He said the injuries were consistent with the victim having been hit with some sort of stick and that he may have been struggling against being held down by more than one person, which possibly could have resulted in the type of pressure injuries on the corpse."

"Sticks? Tasers?"

"I know. The pathologist said that even taking into consideration the effect of the victim being in a state of high excitability, the pressure wounds alone would not be sufficient for a finding of anything other than 'death by natural causes.'"

"The pressure wounds were from batons."

"Yes."

"And the Taser wounds?" Whatever the answer to this question, we were treading on new ground.

Or not.

"They may not have been Taser wounds at all," Aliana answered. "I tried to get as much out of the pathologist as I could. He would only say that the marks were different from the other bruise marks and may have been consistent with Taser wounds. I don't think he even put that in his report—the conclusion was that vague."

"Taser wounds…. Where does that leave us? Matt West told me a long time ago that no officer involved in this incident would have been carrying a Taser. Of course, being authorized means nothing if you can get your hands on something with nobody stopping you."

Aliana looked at me as if to say I was the Apostle of the Obvious. Or maybe as though she forgave me for being dull because I was in such bad shape.

"How would we ever find out?" I persisted. The pain in my side had all but stopped since we'd begun this conversation. But the minute I let my mind wander away from the topic of Tasers and wounds, it came back.

"Are you okay?" Aliana asked. "Let's leave things for the moment. A little bit is enough for you right now."

I didn't need to be babied, but I didn't mind having someone so obviously concerned about my welfare. "I'm okay. Don't worry about me."

"Are you going to have charges laid against Downs?" Aliana asked, confusing me for an instant. "For kicking you, for assault. There were plenty of witnesses to the unprovoked attack."

"To tell the truth, Aliana, I never gave that a moment's thought. There's no way in the world Downs would be called to account for knocking down an old geezer who'd be seen to be unsteady on his feet."

She smiled, but I knew she didn't think the attack against me by a younger, stronger man—especially one called upon to maintain the peace—was in any way humorous.

"You're a brave man," she said. She sounded like she meant it.

"If I could get Ted Downs charged with a crime," I went on, "it wouldn't be for the misdemeanor of having his foot slip on an icy path and ending up between my ribs."

Aliana nodded. Then she got up and made me a cup of tea. It was nice. And it didn't even hurt me to drink it. I could tell that the healing of my body was progressing. And from the guiltless gratitude with which I could accept the ministrations of Aliana's kindness, I could tell that my soul might be beginning to heal, too.

***

She waited a few more days and then she came and got me and told me that we had a mission to perform. She said she could tell that I was ready to get back at it. Though at what, I wasn't sure.

"It's Kezia. She wants to see us. I think we should go over right now."

Aliana drove like an Italian. I couldn't have said that if I weren't one myself. But I lacked the verve and the nerve as we used to say.

Kezia was waiting for us. She wasn't in the lobby this time, but she answered the buzzer so fast I was sure she'd been standing right beside it.

She looked beautiful. Her curly hair had been left to grow long. It formed a big dark halo around her pretty face with its youthful and makeup-free beauty.

She held a sheaf of papers in her hand. The package of pages was bound with a cloth band a couple of inches wide, a blue and silver band exactly like the one that held her hair away from her eyes.

"Here it is," she said with such pride that it brought tears to my eyes. I could see Aliana was moved, too. But I had the feeling that the source of Aliana's vicarious pleasure was different from mine. I had the sense she was looking at the manuscript as a job completed.

"It's heavy, isn't it?" the girl said. She hadn't moved from the door. As Aliana took the manuscript in her hand, Kezia said, "It's on the cloud, too." She wrinkled her pretty nose, "at least I hope it is. But just in case, I want you and Mr. Portal to take it now, to keep it safe. In case anything happens."

Unmistakable fear underlay the celebration of the moment. "I need you to take this out of here now and maybe not come back."

"Why, Kezia?" I asked. "What's wrong? Is there somebody else here with you?"

She shook her head rigorously, sending all those rich curls swaying. "No. Not now. But they might come back and they're real mad at us now. Even at my mom. So you take this away and someday after I figure out how to do it, I'll get a publisher to print the book and then I can sell it and people can use it."

As always, her ambition, touched as it was with latent despair, moved me to want to help her in any way I could.

Which was why I tried to contact Mark Hopequist. I knew he had helped the girl in the past, and I was sure that even though he was no longer with the Youth Bureau, he'd at least have some ideas as to how she might be kept safe from the wrath of her gangster brothers.

All I managed to do was to leave him a message. Because when I called the number of the division where I thought he worked, someone else came to the phone, and that someone else told me that Mark Hopequist had left the force.

When I dared to ask why, whoever was on the other end of the phone laughed and said, "Guess it got to be too much for him. Never did like the violence in the city. Go figure. I mean what else is a cop going to see, right?"

THIRTY-NINE

With all that was going on, I didn't have much time for television. Even for the news. So I had long ago lost track of the goings-on at the world affairs summit and of its aftermath.

The aftermath was still going on. The conference had been deemed an international success, even though there were people in Toronto who felt it had been an international embarrassment because of the totally over-the-top police presence that mirrored—in fact exceeded—the excesses of the previous world conference held in our city.

This time, as with the previous conference, the police presence was overwhelming, and though no innocent citizens were corralled and detained in a public street in four hours of pouring rain, there were plenty who complained that they had been treated with undue violence.

And one of those had managed to get a police officer charged with assault. I wouldn't have even seen this on the news had I not been watching TV because I'd been ordered—not by my doctor, but by Aliana and Jeffrey—to take it easy for another week or two until my side stopped hurting.

What I saw was a man being led away from court by his lawyer. The man had his jacket over his face, so I couldn't see who it was. But spliced into that clip was another that showed the incident in question. Two police officers were clearly beating a third man with their batons. The victim lay in a fetal position on the ground, trying only to protect his head and his face. He was making no effort to fight back or even to resist in the slightest. But the two officers were smacking him with the maximum force of their batons. The two officers were wearing protective masks, but one officer had lifted his so that his face was showing.

I saw that face fill the screen and I was shocked, though not surprised.

It was the face of Al Brownette.

I had known all along about the violence that lay so close to the surface of this man, the barely-controlled anger that expressed itself in his every movement: the cocky, jerky walk, the arms and hands never relaxed, always looking as though they could be raised with lethal force at a split-second's notice.

But he had no motive for murder. He would have to have been completely crazy to sneak into a hospital and Taser an old man for the mere sake of doing a favor for his friend Ted. He might be violent and stupid, but he was no lunatic. In the few seconds of the video in which you could see Al being led away by his lawyer, his whole body seemed that of a man who had gotten out of trouble before and would get out of trouble this time, too.

Which is what I was thinking when my entire apartment was suddenly filled with flashing red light.

It was coming from the rear parking lot and as I got to the living room window and looked down, I could see three fire trucks pulling in. Their sirens were off. Perhaps I'd heard them in the distance, but apparently there was no need for sirens now. It didn't sound as though the emergency was on our street, so I knew it must be down in the valley.

It was a little after six p.m. on a winter's evening, so it was pitch dark already. If the emergency wasn't in our building—which clearly it wasn't—then something was desperately wrong down below.

I saw almost at once that the fire crews were setting up some sort of emergency illumination. A bright white light flooded the parking lot momentarily, then turned outward. But the light was reflected off the thick branches of the trees, which, being covered with snow, acted almost like a mirror.

Whatever was going on down there could not be lighted from above. I knew that, and I knew that the fire crews were about to learn it, too.

I had been up and down the walls of our valley in every conceivable condition of weather and of light. I knew I could get down there faster than anybody else, even in my weakened condition. I'd been hurt in the valley before, and I'd still navigated without getting lost or stranded.

I had to know what was going on, and, unwilling to waste a second, I grabbed my coat and scarf and hat and boots, and I set out.

I avoided the firemen. I didn't want to be held back, to be told that I wouldn't be allowed down there. In the dark and the hubbub it was easy to slide past the fire engines and to find my usual path down.

It was slippery, but because the way was so familiar, I knew which branches I could rely on to support me when my feet wouldn't. And I managed to use the decline of the path to ease my way.

I headed for the village. I couldn't conceive of an emergency at this end of the valley that wouldn't involve its inhabitants.

And of course, I was right. Above me I could hear the shouting of the firemen and the sound of their loudspeakers, but I could only see their lights for a few steps of my journey. I soon entered the dark forest, made navigable by snowlight. For a while I heard nothing. Then I began to hear the voices raised in panic, the screams, the yelled instructions to "Hold on. We're coming. We'll get you. Don't let go."

I trudged through the wood for ten minutes before I could see the lights of the village through the trees. I approached slowly because of the ice that had formed everywhere that the villagers had walked over the past few days, except for the shoveled paths.

But no one was on those paths or even in the village. The lights were on but the buildings were deserted.

Carefully I followed the sound of the voices to the edge of the river.

There Jeffrey knelt by the bank as if to get as close as possible to whatever was happening on the partially frozen waters of the Don. "Hang on!" he shouted, though his voice sounded more like a wish than a command.

The other villagers surrounded him as he knelt there, their second-hand unstylish coats, their ragged scarves, their hockey-crested toques, marking them as a team, now a team struggling to save one of its own from the grip of the unforgiving ice.

Someone had fallen in. And though the river was shallow in some places, it was everywhere deep enough to drown a man, especially a man dressed in heavy winter clothes that would absorb the water immediately and add pounds to his weight. Especially a man who wore heavy winter boots, boots that would fill with water like a cup, like a jug. Especially a man who might be drunk or stoned or old or too deaf to hear what the people on the shore were shouting.

I had saved people from the ravages of the Don before. In fact, I had even once pulled Johnny Dirt away from certain death in its wily embrace.

But that had not been winter.

I tried to get closer to the water to lend a hand. But whoever had fallen in had already drifted out to where the current was moving with surprising swiftness in the middle of the stream. He was waving his arms, bobbing up and down, appearing and disappearing, shifting into and out of the weak light.

"Stand back!" Jeffrey shouted. And most of the gathered villagers did as he said, but one or two rushed forward.

"No!" They reached toward him and tried to hold him back.

"Get away!" he yelled. "Let me go!"

The cries of the man in the water became more strangled, more desperate. And also, I couldn't help but realize—farther away.

Without thinking about what I was doing, I pushed through the crowd on the bank and rushed toward my son. I reached out and grabbed his coat. "Jeffrey, you can't go out there. You'll drown. It's too late."

He pulled hard and got away. The shore ice crackled at his step and when he reached nearly the edge of the frozen part of the river, flat shards—wide slivers of thin ice—broke away and he was plunged into the black water.

I think I screamed then. I thought I could still hear faint cries from the distance, but I wasn't sure.

"It's too late, son," I called out. "Come back. It's useless. We'll lose you, too."

At my words the others on the shore began to call out to him. And it occurred to me just how high a stake they all had in his continued survival. He was their leader, their provider. I was linked to Jeffrey by the power of love. They were linked to him by the power of necessity. I've had a long, hard, life. Love is great. Need is greater.

The fire crew made its way down. They pulled Jeffrey out. Despite the dark and the cold and the increasing unlikelihood of finding the victim alive—or at all--in the dark recesses of the valley, they kept at it for seven hours. Until they found him and brought his body up into the village lodge, where the villagers took turns sitting with the body for fifteen hours until they took him away.

I had to go up to the apartment to get some sleep. I tried to convince my son to come up to his apartment, to spend the night with his own family, but he insisted on staying down in the village overnight. He didn't even go up to change his clothes, but put on dry items brought to him by the villagers as he sat warming beside the fireplace in the village lodge.

"Everybody's really upset," he insisted. "I have to stay down here at least until the grief counsellors show up. Tootie understands. Besides, I'll be in constant phone contact with her."

So I left him. But I went down as soon as it got light the next morning, which wasn't early. We were nearing the first official day of winter, and the light from the sky was not in our favor.

I found Jeffrey at his desk. I was sure he'd have a lot of forms to fill out now that he had lost one of his clients. But I was also sure that after the sleepless night of disaster that he'd spent, he was in no shape to handle paperwork now.

"Let me help you, son. There must be something I can do."

He looked at me for a minute as if he didn't know who I was. Then he managed to gather his wits and said, "We lost one of our oldest members—not just in age but in the length of time he spent with us."

"What happened? How could he have fallen in? I thought you had a safety course that you gave everybody. I thought you conducted an annual safety audit."

"This accident had nothing to do with safety," Jeffrey said with weary resignation. "It had to do with rivalry between two men and their constant battle to be on top of the heap."

I knew that what he meant by getting to the top was not what I meant. "You mean one-upmanship?" I offered.

Jeffrey nodded. "Always and in everything," he sighed wearily. "What happened was pretty simple and pretty stupid. When the ice started to form on the river near here a couple of days ago, some debris was washed up and stuck in the ice. We're all careful about litter and about throwing things into the water, but of course it happens all the time. People have found some astonishing things discarded in the Don."

"Yes." I remembered some of the treasures I myself had harvested over the years, jewelry, parts of machines that I had sometimes used to repair the things I used in the riverside shack that had served as my home, books I managed to dry in the sun, clothing. And photographs. As though people wanted to discard lovers and friends and family members who had betrayed them by throwing their images into the Don.

"They were fighting over this," Jeffrey said, and he held up a cloudy plastic bag that contained what looked at first like a cell phone or a little hand-held computing device. "Apparently it had washed up near the shore and the two men were having an argument about who had seen it first, who had the right to keep it."

"What is it?" I asked.

"I don't know. A phone or something. Whatever it is, it hasn't been underwater too long by the look of it. But it was frozen solid, so I'm sure it doesn't work anymore."

"So they were fighting over it? I hope you're not going to tell me that one pushed the other into the river?" All I needed was another homicide case in my life.

"No, no. Nothing like that. What happened was that one man had the thing and when the other man tried to get it from him, the first man threw it as hard as he could. It landed out on the ice. There were others around and everybody was shouting for the two to just forget the piece of garbage. But the second man ran out onto the ice to retrieve it. The object stayed where it was, but the ice under the man broke free and he was thrown into the water."

"He died for this?" Jeffrey handed me the bag. I opened it and peered in.

"I don't know what it is," Jeffrey admitted. "Do you think I should keep it in case there's an investigation or something?"

I couldn't answer him because I was stunned—no pun intended. I was pretty sure I knew what the object was.

"Jeffrey," I said. "Those cops that were down here—not just the one who assaulted me, but the others, too. Did you ever see them drop anything or throw anything away while they were down here?"

"I don't know, Dad. Right before the weather got cold there were so many people down here that I started to feel as if we were being invaded. There was even that kid. Like I said, we're careful about litter down here. So if we caught anybody throwing stuff around, even a cop, somebody would probably have noticed and said something." He thought for a moment. "But the trees are thick, even now when it's just trunks and branches. And this is a pretty isolated part of the valley. So I guess a person could throw something away easily without being seen. Why? Do you know what this thing is?"

"Let me hang on to it for a day or two son. I'll find out whether there's any reason to keep it."

"Okay."

"Now get up to your home and get some rest."

He didn't budge. Not to abandon his post. Not to take the black object from me—an object that I was pretty sure was the thing I needed most in the world.

FORTY

I wasn't sure what the charge would be if I got caught withholding evidence in a homicide case. I just knew I was willing to risk it, at least for a couple of days.

First thing in the morning, I called Aliana. "I need you. I've got to see you right away. Are you working today?"

"I'm working every day, Ellis. What's so important?"

"I have something to show you. And I want you to come here. I don't want to be carrying it around."

"What are you talking about?"

"Get over here and I'll show you the second you arrive."

She didn't say another word. Just clicked off. I imagined the countless times Aliana had dropped everything to pursue a hot lead.

Well this lead was hot—hot enough to get both of us in a great deal of trouble.

She showed up within the half hour, though it seemed to take much longer. "What is it? What's wrong, Ellis? Are you ill? Is it your side?"

I shook my head and ushered her in. Before she even had a chance to take off her coat, I had seated her on the couch. I sat down beside her, and with caution, pushed the dented black object from its grimy plastic sandwich bag without touching it.

"Do know what this is?" I asked her.

She studied it as it sat on the coffee table in front of us. Then she put her glove back on. Gingerly she picked up the object. I could tell that her cautious handling of the object was not from squeamishness but because she already understood that this was something that didn't belong here, didn't belong with us.

"How did you find this?"

I told her the story of the partially frozen river. I told her that cops had been coming and going down there for months. I told her that Mark Hopequist had quit the force. And I reminded her of two things: that the pathologist had suspected a Taser wound on the body of the Juicer. And that Mark had talked about Tasers with Kezia.

"Didn't it strike you as odd that he would tell a little girl about a lethal weapon?" I asked. "Granted she's an exceptionally bright and curious girl…."

"To tell the truth, Ellis, I didn't believe her."

"You didn't believe Mark told her about Tasers?"

"I didn't believe he told her anything. I thought she was telling us a tale to impress us. It didn't ring true and I didn't think it could teach us anything."

She looked at me then with a look of what, for lack of a better term, I might have called "self-surprise," as if she had uncharacteristically failed to note some essential fact that could make or break the piece she was working on.

"I can't blame you for thinking that, Aliana. The story didn't convince me, either. But now that I reflect on the matter, why would the idea of a Taser randomly occur to a kid—even a curious and clever one?"

"We still don't know whether she's telling the truth. And even if she is, so what? What does it prove?"

"It connects Mark to the weapon."

"Only in a very weak way."

"So we need more."

She turned the object over in her long fingers. Then she held it to her face to take a closer look. Both of us were well aware that any carelessness on our part might be damaging the evidentiary value of the thing, and as a retired judge, I should have been especially sensitive to this truth.

But I wasn't a judge anymore. And I had spent enough time away from being one to know that justice isn't always best served by her own minions and their restraining ways.

"We need a lot more," I conceded. "First we need to know exactly how this thing works. Then we need to know whether, and if so, how, such an object could fall into the hands of a police officer or officers not authorized to use it. Then we need to know whether it was Mark and Mark alone who had access to the weapon. And then we need to know whether he did, in fact, use it."

Aliana studied the Taser, staring at it as if it could speak to her and tell her the answers to all our questions at once.

"It won't be hard to find out how it works," she stated with her usual confidence. "And we can't make the assumption that it presently belongs to or ever belonged to the Toronto police. It won't be hard to find out whether there are private suppliers of such devices."

She looked up with a smile. "I've got a friend or two who can help us understand whether any Tasers have strayed in the last little while."

I smiled ruefully back. "In the old days, I could have asked Matt West a lot of these questions. But things have certainly changed with him."

"He's aiming to be chief, Ellis. I guess you must realize that by now."

"The thought has occurred to me. But be that as it may, he's not going to help us. In fact, if he learns we have something like this, he'll come after us. And if he gets his hands on it, we'll never see it again."

Aliana did something I should have expected, but hadn't. She reached into her purse and pulled out a small camera. She took pictures of the Taser from every angle, sometimes taking extreme close-ups. When she was finished, she put it back in the plastic bag.

I expected her to take it, but instead, she asked me for a paper towel and when I handed it to her, she carefully set the Taser on top of it on the coffee table. Then she went back to her purse, dug around for and found a bottle of hand sanitizer and gave herself a good washing.

"Give me a couple of hours," she said.

I used the time to go down and see how Jeffrey was doing and whether he could tell me anything more about the discovery he had inadvertently made.

"As you know, Dad, it's not the first time we've lost somebody down here. The police were here for hours last night asking questions, though there really wasn't much I could say. It was an accident. Everybody who saw what happened said the same thing."

"Who were these police? Anybody you know? Anybody who's been down here before? Were they all in uniform?"

Jeffrey thought about that. It was now early afternoon. His sleepless night showed on his face. He rubbed his unshaven cheeks and ran his fingers through his hair. For the first time it occurred to me that his blond locks were turning gray.

"I can't say I recognized anybody. It was dark during the whole rescue, and there were so many people..."

"Sure, son," I said. "I think it's time for you to go up now. I'm sure Tootie is concerned. Go and get some sleep. There's nothing more for you to do about this down here."

He took my advice.

I stayed in the village for an hour or so, making sure that Jeffrey's right-hand man down there, had things running smoothly.

I took the opportunity to ask him a few questions, and I spoke to a few other of the villagers, too. Everybody was upset, surprised, exhausted. Nobody recognized any of the firemen or police officers who had attended the scene.

But one person said that he had seen a fairly young officer strolling along the river a little while before—before the river froze. The man said he'd seen "that little girl," too, "the one that was researching her thing for school or something."

"Was she with the police officer?"

"Not on the days I saw them. They weren't together. The girl was with one of the villagers—an old guy that likes to tell stories about the river. He's harmless, but I think the kid got in trouble for being down here. I never saw her again after that one day."

"Was the cop right near the river? Could he have thrown something in?"

The villager pulled a ratty old scarf tighter around his scrawny neck. "Is there anybody alive who couldn't have thrown something in the Don?" he asked with a croaky laugh. "We get all these environmental types down here." He screwed up his face into a mocking snarl. "They come down here with their ideas. Acting like butter wouldn't melt, if you know what I mean."

I nodded.

"But I gotta tell ya, they're a bunch of phonies. They come in their big fancy cars—and act like they don't use gas or nothing. And they live in them condos—ten rooms for two people..." He gestured toward the high banks of the river, invisible from where we sat in the lodge, but as clear in my mind as they must have been in his.

"Right," I said, "I get it. But I just need to know if you saw a cop throw anything into the river right before it was cold enough for it to freeze."

"I seen that young cop down here with a couple other cops," he said. "But the only thing they threw in the river was me!"

He roared as if he'd just made the greatest joke.

FORTY-ONE

"It's a Taser alright," Aliana said, opening a little book and reading from her notes. "But there's some good news and some bad news.

"The good news is that its time spent in the frozen river probably didn't damage its data drive and we can most likely get quite a bit of information off of it still."

"What kind of information?"

"If it had a password or a code identifying the user, it should still be on the device and—with a little help from a friend of mine—we should be able to obtain and decipher that information. It should also have a clock—like a timer—that records the date, time, and on some models, the location of each time the device was discharged within a certain set time frame."

"Aliana, are you saying that Taser recorded exactly when it was discharged and by whom?"

She checked her notes again, but I had the feeling she was stalling. She hadn't told me the bad news yet.

"Theoretically," she said. "But until we get the thing to somebody who can examine it and hopefully decode it, we won't know."

"Can we do that? Can we get it to a decoder?"

"Most likely. I just got a few more strings to pull."

"So that's the bad news?"

"No, Ellis. That's still the good news. The bad news is that the Taser did not belong to the Toronto police.

"What?"

"Apparently there are all sorts of Tasers. They're made by more than one manufacturer, so of course different brands have different features. And there are different models. My source identified our Taser at once. And he knew that it was not the type used by the Toronto police."

I thought about that for a moment. "So," I said, not trying to hide the defeat in my voice, "we've hit another dead end."

"No," Aliana said firmly. "We certainly have not. We've got a discarded Taser and we've got a man who died in a high state of excitability possibly of a Taser wound. That means we've got a story. All we need now is the connecting incident."

Even in my depressed state, I had to smile. Aliana had a writer's way of looking at things. Everything was a story and all you needed was to tell it in the right way. The thought gave me an idea.

"That's not all we have," I suddenly realized.

"What? What are you thinking?"

"We've got Kezia."

"Kezia?"

"Yes. Maybe we shouldn't have dismissed her tale so off-handedly. She's the only thing we have that connects every part of this story: Mark Hopequist, the Taser, the river…"

"But not the victim."

"Wrong. If we can connect everything else, the murder will fall into place."

"But we've questioned Kezia. We've seen her again and again and we get nothing."

"Aliana, how many times do you interview a suspect—I mean a subject—before you're satisfied that you have the whole story?"

"As many times as I have to. As many times as it takes. But I don't get very far just pounding them, just asking them the same questions in the same way…."

"Of course not. So that's why we're going to try one last time. We're going to show Kezia the Taser."

Aliana shook her head. "What good could that possibly do? We'll just end up scaring her. She'll never tell us anything again."

"I'm not sure what exactly she has told us already," I replied. "One more try. One more visit…"

"I don't know. From what she told us the last time, from the way she acted, from the fact that I have the manuscript she was afraid to keep at home—from all these things, I don't think she's even there anymore."

"Let's wait until tonight," I insisted. "Let's try something we haven't done before. Let's go over there at a different time."

"I don't know. I'm not sure what that would accomplish."

"Let's give it a shot."

She almost jumped when I said that. I knew what she was thinking. I was thinking it, too, but I wasn't going to be stopped by fear of Kezia's brothers. I'd never seen them. For all I knew, they were another myth in this twisted tale of danger and deception—if it was deception and not just the over-active imagination of a child who wanted to be a famous writer.

***

When we got to Kezia's building, there were so many people coming and going in the lobby that we didn't even buzz. We went straight upstairs. Coming at night made quite a difference. First of all, there was the noise—music and shouting and doors slamming....

Then there was the smoke in the hallway. Not just cigarette smoke.

We got to the apartment, and I knocked on the door.

"To tell the truth," Aliana said. "I would be amazed if anybody answered."

I knocked again. And again.

I was about to turn away when, yes, to my amazement, the door opened a crack and a pair of wary eyes peeked out.

They were not the eyes of anyone I'd ever seen before.

"We are here to talk to Kezia," Aliana said in a tone of voice that was halfway between velvet and steel. "She knows us. We've been here before."

"She ain't here," a voice said, and the door opened a tiny bit. I could now make out the features of a black woman whom I judged to be in her early forties, though she had that tough, tired look that comes with a hard life and long hours.

"Could we speak to you, madam, then?" Aliana asked, her voice softening a little. "You see we've been helping Kezia for a little while, and we're concerned that we haven't talked to her in a few days."

"What you got to talk to my girl about?"

"We were wondering about something she told us before and we just want to check it out, to make sure we heard her okay," I offered.

The woman smiled. "My girl talk all the time. I don't know whether she make up a story or she tell the truth...."

"That's exactly why we have to talk to her again," Aliana said. "Not that we think she made up a story or anything. We just need to ask her one more time about something she said."

The door cracked open a tiny bit more. I could see that Kezia's mother was as carefully dressed as her daughter always was. I thought she must have been either coming or going from her job. She wore a black sweater and skirt, but the plainness of her clothes—which were probably part of a uniform—was set off by elaborate but tasteful gold earrings and a thick necklace, and her hair was arranged in a cascading pile of curls that ended at and set off her finely-carved jaw. It was a beautiful face despite showing the ravages of a hard life.

"Look, Mister, Miss—you already brought trouble here. Or at least you added to it. All my kids are bein' bothered by the cops all the time. The police are always at them about bein' a witness to something somebody else done. My kids don't know nothin'. They don't know no killers. They don't know no gangsters. They good kids. They friendly and everybody like them. So they don't need to talk to nobody like you."

"Mark Hopequist," Aliana said as if she hadn't even heard the good kid speech that we had both heard a hundred times before when the families of the victims of gang shootings expressed their shock on the TV news.

At the name, the woman's face changed. It dropped down a few levels of belligerence.

"He the only good guy ever come around here," the woman said. "But he disappear just like everybody else. And now my kids are disappeared, too. So if you want to talk to any of them, you're shit out of luck."

With that, she slammed the door in our face.

To the great amusement of five or six lanky, dread-headed boys who lifted their hands in a complicated salute to each other in mocking acknowledgement of our rejection.

FORTY-TWO

"How will we find her?"

Aliana sat in my living room, her notes spread before her on my coffee table. "Where have we seen her before?" she replied.

"Only at her own apartment and..."

"And down here—I mean in the valley near the village."

"Is it possible that she could have come back here—at the start of winter?"

I shook my head. "I don't think so. The only place she could have easily come down here is the village, and Jeffrey would have alerted me at once."

"And we know of no friends, no other adults..."

"There are the counsellors at the Youth Bureau. Might she have contacted them?"

A quick check eliminated that possibility.

"Mark."

"What?"

"Maybe she sought out Mark. Maybe she's with him now."

We stared at each other for a second.

"Let's go!" Aliana said.

***

We never got there. We never even set out. Because Kezia got to us first. The minute Aliana and I opened the door of my apartment, we heard frantic footsteps pounding down the hall.

The girl was running as though she were being chased, but there was no one behind her that I could see. Her face was streaming with tears and her t-shirt was dirty and ripped. A light jacket—not nearly warm enough for the weather—was hanging unbuttoned from her slender shoulders.

She ran straight into Aliana's arms, and I could see how she was shaking from crying and from the powerful fear that seemed to have gripped her.

"They're going to kill me. They're going to kill us all...."

Aliana didn't try to calm her down. I unlocked my apartment and dragged them both in, drawing the deadbolt.

I led them to the couch and Aliana sank down with the girl in her arms.

I was as shocked at the sight of them as I was to hear Kezia's frantic, inarticulate cries. The last time anyone had held someone in their arms on that couch, it was I. It was Queenie in my arms. And I was comforting her before the ambulance had come to take her away from our home forever.

I felt as though I were being thrust back in time, as though I weren't really here and it weren't really now.

I whispered a prayer. I whispered a prayer to Queenie. If there was anybody in heaven, it would surely be her. "Help me, Queenie," I said. "Help me to save this kid. Help me to keep my promise."

"Could you get us some water?" Aliana asked, and I sprang into action to do so, though the way Kezia was gasping and choking, I was afraid to let her drink.

But she gulped down the water as if she hadn't drunk anything in a long time, and within a few seconds, she was able to catch her breath and to stop shaking.

Aliana began to talk to her in a soft, soothing voice. "You're okay now. You're safe. We're here and we'll protect you. Just take it easy."

The girl's breathing slowed. She took a couple of deep breaths. She dried her eyes with her fingers, until Aliana came up with a little packet of tissues.

"You want to tell me what's wrong?" she finally said.

Slowly the girl began to tell her tale. "There's a war now," she said. "There's a gang war and I'll get killed if I say anything or tell anybody's name or like that." She drew in a deep, shuddering breath that shook her slender shoulders, but she carried on. "My one brother belongs to one gang and my other brother, he has ties to a different gang. Now there's a war and they are supposed to kill one another and they have rules and the rules say that they don't

220

have to worry about anybody who gets in the way. They could shoot them, too."

Aliana kept her arm around the girl during this exchange. It occurred to me how I had gradually seen so many other sides to her than just the hard-nosed reporter. But I kept totally silent, not wanting to interrupt or to throw things off track in any way.

"Kezia, nobody is going to shoot you. I promise you that."

"No! The girl pulled away. "No. Nobody can promise I won't get shot. I'm not afraid for me."

"Whose safety are you concerned about?" Aliana asked carefully.

There was another volley of tears and shakes. When the girl finally regained her composure, she said, "My mother. I don't want those assholes to hurt my mom!"

"They won't," Aliana insisted. "There are plenty of people who can help you. We'll call the police…"

"They can't help."

"How about Mark?" I interjected. "Would you feel better if you talked to him?"

"He isn't a police officer anymore."

Aliana and I exchanged glances.

"How do you know that, Kezia?" I asked.

"He told me. He told me the day before yesterday."

"You saw him?" I asked. "Where? Where did you go to meet him?"

Kezia smiled. "At the Youth Bureau."

"But they said they hadn't seen you."

"Oh, they got this secret policy. They don't tell over the phone to other people. It's like one of their services. You could request it. You could say that you want to have a meeting with somebody on the, like, premises and they won't tell nobody you were there and they supervise the meeting—like stand outside the door and make sure everything is okay."

"And you met Mark Hopequist like this more than once?" I asked.

"Yes. But only a couple of times. That's when he told me he would show me a Taser if he ever got one."

Now it was I who was finding it hard to breathe. "And did he, Kezia? Did he ever get a Taser? Did he ever show you?"

"I don't know if he did get one, but he did get a..." She searched for a word. "What do you call those books that have the pictures of things in it and how much the stuff costs?"

"A catalogue?" Aliana offered.

"Yeah. He had a catalogue with a whole bunch of different kinds of weapons and that in there and he showed me a few of them and how they had features and that and one feature was they could tell whoever it was who shot them off and exactly what day and time it was and that."

"Why, Kezia? Why would Mark Hopequist be showing you these things?"

She stared at me as if the answer were so obvious that she wondered why I was bothering to ask the question. "Because of my new book," she said. "Now that I finished the recipe book, I need a new book to write. And I'm going to write it about the police. So I need all the research I can have. And I think talking to people is the best research there is."

The look of fondness on the face of Aliana made me wonder why she had never had children. "You're right, Kezia. You are absolutely right."

"Did he ever say he actually had a Taser?" I asked.

"No."

"Did he ever say where he could get one?"

The girl thought about that for a minute and I wondered whether we were about to come to the end of her willingness—or even her ability—to co-operate.

"I asked him if all the police officers were going to get Tasers soon because they were like a future weapon or something. He said some officers have them but only the bosses. He said nobody even gets to touch them except them. But then we talked about guns and things and how my brothers and the gang members, they get guns from the States and steal them from each other sometimes. And Mark, he said that if a person wants a weapon, they can find a way to get it—even with nobody else ever finding out."

Aliana nodded, then caught my eye over the girl's head. "That's true, Kezia. Did Mark ever say he ordered things out of that catalogue?"

She shook her head. "I seen other catalogues, though. Ones you could buy all kinds of things from. Clothes and makeup and videos and that." Her voice broke a little. "But now I don't know if I could ever get nothing from a catalogue."

"Why ever would you think that?" I asked.

"Because either my brothers will take it or break it. That's what they say they will do." She hesitated. "Or else they will take me and break me. That's what they say, too."

"Kezia," Aliana asked, "have you ever seen guns in the possession of your brothers?"

That question was too much. The girl started to shake again, and it took us quite a while to calm her down and to get her to eat a little soup and for Aliana to run down to the nearby Walmart and buy her new underwear and jeans and a pink t-shirt with a picture on it of some exaggerated doll-like character with a big head.

We got her to lie down on the couch for a while and it was only a minute or two before she drifted off. While she was sleeping, the phone rang, and I rushed to answer it before it could wake her.

It was my daughter. "I'll call you back, Ellen." I heard her protesting voice as I slammed down the receiver.

"What should we do, Aliana? We can't keep her here. And we can't turn her out on her own."

Before she could answer, her cell phone rang. It took her a couple minutes to find her purse, and by the time she did, the ringing had stopped. But she checked the number on the display. "Ellis," she said, her fingers hovering over the keyboard, it's my contact with an answer as to what, if anything, was on the display of the Taser. Whatever he found, we're going to have to get down there and pick the thing up. And we can't keep it much longer. It's evidence. We have to turn it in."

"Evidence of what, Aliana? If there's something on that thing that incriminates somebody, I want to know who before I turn it over to Matt West, knowing I'll never hear about it or see it again. And if there's nothing on it, it's just garbage, just something somebody threw in the river because they felt they had to for one reason or another."

"Right. But what do we do? We can't take the girl with us...."

"We take her home. She may be right that she's in danger there, but she's in danger anywhere she goes. At least we can put her mother's mind at ease."

"If her mother's even there."

"If her mother is there, we'll leave her. If she's not, you can stay with her and I'll meet your contact."

Aliana shook her head. "No. He won't talk to anybody but me. He won't give the Taser to you. It has to be me."

"Then I'll stay with the girl. It can't be helped."

"What if they come after her? What if she's right about the war between the brothers?"

"Aliana, we are wasting time. We have to move one way or the other. If anything leaks, if anybody finds out that we have a valuable piece of the evidence, it's all over for us."

"Okay. We take Aliana home. If her mother's there, we leave her and we go get the Taser. If the woman's not there, you stay and I go."

"And then?"

"I don't know about 'then', Ellis. I don't know at all."

***

It was hard to wake Kezia and harder still to convince her to come with us back to her apartment. She reached a state of near hysteria.

"They'll kill me. I'm telling you, they are shooters. They will shoot you, too."

In the end, she agreed that she would go home only if Mark Hopequist was there to meet her.

"He'll keep me safe, even if he isn't a cop anymore."

The request confounded me, but when I thought about it, it seemed it might work. I had no intention of leaving the girl alone with him, not now that we might have powerful evidence against him. Nor would he provide much protection if Kezia were right about her dangerous brothers. Like me, Mark had no weapon. His police automatic was gone, and even if the Taser were his, he certainly didn't have it anymore.

"I don't know if we can get him. I don't know whether he's somewhere that he can leave to get here right away…."

"Call his iPhone. Text him." Kezia insisted, and she spewed out the number she had memorized.

The phone rang three times. I considered letting Kezia talk to him, but that didn't seem wise. It was essential that Aliana and I control this situation. "Hopequist," I said. "We need your help here. Right away."

Within minutes, we had formulated a plan. Mark would meet us in the lobby of Kezia's building. Aliana and I would go in separate cars. She'd drive Kezia home in her car, then when we got to the building, I would meet Mark and together he and I would take Kezia up. We didn't know whether Kezia's mother was home because Kezia didn't know whether she'd be at work that day and when we'd phoned, no one had answered.

So we met Hopequist. Kezia was different in his presence— easy, smiling. And he was easy in hers. Dressed in his civilian clothes, he didn't look like a cop at all. He didn't even look like an ex-cop.

I waved Aliana goodbye as she pulled out of the drive of the apartment building. I had the horrid feeling that I was sending her off to some kind of doom. But the doom of what or of whom my instinct didn't tell me.

So we turned and headed for the elevator, the three of us. I hadn't yet figured out what was supposed to happen next, because it seemed to me that everything depended on what that Taser told us. Did it reveal a killer or did it reveal that an old fool and a woman who should have known better were on a wild goose chase?

Yes, we headed toward the elevator and toward the execution of our plan to save Kezia and to bring a killer to justice.

The best laid plans.

FORTY-THREE

When we got to the apartment, the door was already open. I thought Kezia would give it a push and usher us in. At first I couldn't hear anything but the TV tuned to some sports station or other.

Then I heard a gruff, low voice sounding as though it were issuing some sort of order. I couldn't make out the words, and I was about to move closer to the door when Mark reached out and motioned Kezia and me away. The gesture was so commanding, so practiced, so effective that I knew it was a police gesture. Move aside. Stay out of danger. I'm trained to handle this. Those were the things Mark Hopequist was saying with his whole body. Despite my fear, I felt a jolt of pity for him. How close he had come to being a fine police officer. How totally he had failed.

He made another gesture, and I could see that it was a gesture he would have made had his hand held a gun.

But it didn't. We were completely vulnerable. Of course the best thing to do was to leave—and to take Kezia with us—no matter what was going on in the apartment. It had been foolish to come here. But it was clearly too late now....

"Get away you bitch. Get out of the damn way."

"He's talking to my mom!" Kezia shouted. "He's got a gun on her."

"Stay back," Mark warned.

But he had nothing. No gun. No baton. No radio to call for help.

I reached into my pocket. Once again I had left my cell phone sitting on the shelf by the door, the shelf on which I always put it so that I wouldn't forget....

"No!" Kezia shouted. And she sprinted past Mark and me, shoved the door wide open and dove into the apartment.

What happened next happened so fast that I was never sure of the order of events. Mark kept close to her, kept her from running to her mother who was standing in the middle of the living room surrounded by four men with guns drawn. He pulled the girl aside, toward the wall, and as he did so, he reached into his pocket, pulled out his cell phone and tossed it to me without a word, keeping his other hand tight around the girl's arm.

I dialed 911, but before I could say a word, a loud shot shattered the silence and the phone flew out of my hand and landed at the feet of the shooter. "Get back you old asshole. Get the fuck out"

"Stop!" Kezia shouted. "Please stop. You don't have to be enemies. You can be brothers—like you really are!"

Only one person, one of the young men, paid any attention to her, or for that matter to us. "Get out," he repeated. "For fuck sake just get the fuck out." He waved his gun in the air, but he didn't aim it at us. He could have shot us down in an instant if he had wanted to.

I saw Mark's eyes scanning the small living room for a position of advantage, but there was none. Kezia's mother had disappeared. Whether she was lying on the floor behind the couch or had escaped the room altogether, I couldn't tell. My eyes were riveted on the four gun-wielding men who faced off, three against one.

They began to shout at each other in a slang I just could not make out. They were belligerent, threatening, accusing. As their shouts rose in pitch, Kezia became more and more uncontrollable, until she finally tore away from Hopequist. Another blast of gunshot rent the air. In an instant, Mark lay on the floor, shot through the chest. And beneath him, shielded by his body, lay a screaming Kezia.

At that precise moment, the apartment door swung open.

I prayed that it might be the police. But it wasn't them. Not yet.

It was Aliana. She stood in the doorway for a moment, a look of complete shock on her face. "Go back," I whispered. "Get out."

I should have known. I should have realized that backing away from a story was not something that Aliana would ever do.

Instead she moved forward into the room.

I dashed forward and I grabbed her. I pulled her into the hallway and up against the wall.

"What…?"

I couldn't answer. She wouldn't have heard me if I'd tried. Because there was such a volley of gunshots then that all other sound was obliterated. And it stayed that way for as long as it took for the police to arrive and for a couple of them to rescue a shaken Kezia who could only say over and over, "They're dead. My whole family. They're all dead. There's nobody left. And I don't want to be left either."

FORTY-FOUR

We were taken away by the police and questioned for hours as to what we were doing there and what we had seen. They took Kezia first and we weren't given any information as to where she was going or who would care for her.

Aliana went in one cruiser and I went in another. We were, of course, only witnesses, but we knew as well as the police knew that witnesses in a gang shoot-out were few and far between.

Maybe I should have been afraid to tell what I knew about Kezia and her brothers. Maybe I should have feared for my life as other witnesses in such cases did. Maybe I should have still kept in mind the day that Aliana and I had been shot at—accidentally or otherwise. Maybe I should have kept wondering about the person who had followed me that now long-ago day in the valley—the one that had or had not left me a note telling me to mind my own business. But I was tired. I was so tired that I went home—it was now the middle of the night—and lay down and I thought of nothing until I awoke at noon the next day to the scream of the phone, followed by the buzz of my cell phone on the shelf by the door.

I couldn't get to the cell, so I answered the land line. It was Aliana. Of course it was.

"Are we done and done for?" she asked. She sounded chipper. If there was one thing in the world I did not need on that morning, it was chipper.

"Aliana, how did you make out with the police? What did they ask you? What did you say?"

"Ellis, I told them everything I knew and everything I saw. But I was careful to present the whole thing as though I were merely a friend of the family—I mean the good people in Kezia's family."

"Yeah, I guess you'd have to be careful to point out exactly what family you were talking about." Seeing people shot in front of me was not something I'd ever experienced before, and I was pretty sure that the memory of it was going to make me feel sick every time for a long time.

"It was horrible," Aliana said, "but it's over."

"Is it?" I couldn't keep the bitterness out of my voice. "Or is it just starting? I don't know Aliana, and I don't care. Sooner or later, we'll have to go to court on this, you and I. Sooner or later we're going to be forced to learn what happened to Kezia. Sooner or later it's going to occur to one or both of us that we really screwed up royally letting ourselves get involved in this mess."

"Yes, but…"

"There is no 'yes, but' about it. I'm finished. I'm finished with Mark Hopequist whoever or whatever he was. I'm finished with Kezia. I'm finished with the other three cops and I'm finished with the Juicer."

I didn't have to tell her that I was finished with her, too. She had already hung up.

Fine. And as for Queenie, I was finished with her, too. How had she let me get into this situation? How had she made me think that there was a murderer here? How had she left me to solve insoluble mysteries? How had she left me here? How had she left me? How had she?

***

I didn't call Aliana or hear from her in any way for the three weeks it took the Toronto police to arrange for the very public and very grand official funeral for Officer Mark Hopequist, the hero.

It was a bitter December day, and I hoped that what was being carried that day in the front of the procession of more than a thousand officers from all over the world as it made its way across College Street west from Headquarters, was ashes. Because I didn't see how anything could be buried in ground that was frozen, though I knew nothing about modern undertaking procedures.

I was standing shivering just inside the gates of the cemetery when I felt a hand on my shoulder through the heavy wool of my coat. I thought it might be a guard asking me to move on and not block the entrance.

But it wasn't.

"You never stuck around to see how Matt West acted when I gave him the Taser."

I didn't turn around. I didn't want to see her face. I didn't want her to see mine. Because I was glad she was there. Because I had missed her. Because we had a great deal of unfinished business between us and I didn't want to think about how in heaven's name we were going to finish it.

"I'm sure he was displeased," I said without turning around. The freezing winter breeze caught my words. I wasn't sure Aliana had heard me. That she even knew I'd answered her.

"Surprised, angry, ultimately dismissive, as if it couldn't possibly make a difference to anything or anybody whether we'd found the Taser and discovered what was on it."

I turned then. Against the white winter, she was wearing a bright red coat with a hood. Its broad red faux-fur edge set off the sparkling intensity of her dark eyes. I thought she looked beautiful, but maybe that was just because I'd gone so long without seeing her. Not that it mattered to me.

"What was on it?" I couldn't help but ask.

"There was some damage, of course, it had been under the water at least for a few days—maybe for much longer. They were unable to tell exactly how long. There was a battery in it of course and a time-keeper. Two time-keepers as a matter of fact. One was a clock and it had stopped at some time during the submersion of the Taser."

"So didn't that tell when it had been tossed?"

Aliana shook her head and the bright red hood fell away revealing her sleek dark hair. "Inclusive."

"And the other time-keeper? What was that?"

She held me in her glance for a moment, and I knew she had something to tell me that was going to put me on the spot somehow.

"The other time-keeper was a record of the instant that the Taser had last been discharged."

I held my breath. "And when was that?"

"It was at three fourteen a.m. on the twenty-third of July of last year." She looked away for an instant, then her eyes grabbed mine again and held. "Do you know what that is?"

"It's the day the Juicer died."

"It's the hour the Juicer died."

In the distance, I heard the mournful sound of a piper breathing a lament. The slow procession of the casket, borne on the shoulders of six strapping officers, made its way up the long winding drive of Mount Pleasant cemetery and came to rest at the door of a mausoleum that must have belonged to the Hopequist family. It occurred to me that I knew nothing about the deceased except the paltry facts I was able to pull together in the futile days of my investigation into his doings during what turned out to be his last days.

"If that is so, Aliana, then we have proof of his murder."

"Ellis," she said softly, so softly that I had a hard time hearing her over the pipes and then the grave-side prayers, "we have nothing. The name of the person who had registered the Taser was gone. So were all traces of fingerprints and DNA, wiped off and irrecoverable."

Before I could respond to this, before I could even think where it left me, I looked up to see three figures headed toward me. And I realized that that the crowd was dispersing, that the funeral was over.

"I don't know what they want, Ellis," Aliana said in her strongest voice, "but I'm sure you can deal with them. In the meantime, I think you have to realize that what you said the last time you talked to me was right. You've gone as far as you can. It's over."

She turned and the last I saw of her was a bright red dot mixing in with the crowd like a drop of blood against the gray stones and the black coats of the mourners and the blowing white of the December snow.

FORTY-FIVE

They were in dress uniform, all three of them, and I had to admit that they looked wonderful, Ted with his mature body, his almost noble stature; Al with his young, strong, muscular physique, and Feeance, the richness of her amazingly thick hair tamed and tucked beneath her uniform cap.

The way they came at me, I was almost forced to back up until I couldn't go any further on the path that led to the gate.

I could tell by the way they were standing as they blocked my way forward that whatever they had corralled me to tell me, Ted was the spokesperson.

"Ellis," he said in a voice I had not expected to hear from him, it was almost respectful, "I'm glad we caught you here today. We were going to pay you a call, but speaking here will be more appropriate, I think. "

The others nodded—almost as though they'd practiced this little act.

"Appropriate to what?" I didn't try to move. I didn't want to take a chance of having them push me—or even touch me. I didn't want to admit that I was afraid, but I was. "Appropriate to what?"

Ted reached out and tapped my shoulder. He was wearing white gloves, dress gloves. "We came over here to thank you."

"Thank me?" I would have been less alarmed if he had said, "We came over here to hit you." "Thank me for what?"

"For all the trust you put in Mark. For believing that he could help that girl. For letting him try."

"I don't know what you're talking about."

"I think you do. You must have realized all along what was going on with him. I tried to warn you a couple of times…."

"Warn me?" Suddenly I realized what he was talking about. That it had been Ted who had followed me that day in the valley, that it had been he who'd left me the note. But I wasn't understanding what he was getting at. What this strange speech was about.

"We've been limited in what we could say," Ted went on. "But all of that has changed now. Mark is gone. And he's a hero. He saved that girl's life."

Al and Feeance nodded solemnly.

"Yes," I said, "Yes he did. But what else did he do to 'save' a person? What did he do to save the Juicer?"

"The time has come to put that away." It was Feeance who spoke now. Slowly, deliberately, as if she'd had time to weigh those few words before she'd spoken them.

Behind her, Al Brownette stood, looking bored, but pulling himself back to the matter at hand.

"Mark was a different kind of person," Ted went on, "a different kind of man. He didn't understand that the best way to help a person is to get them to straighten out—get them to help themselves. That's why what you and Ms. Caterina have done for Kezia will be better in the long run than what Mark did for her—what Mark did for anybody."

I wasn't sure what he was getting at, what he was really telling me.

"What do you mean? What did Mark do?"

Ted put his hand on my shoulder. I fought the urge to shake it off. If he was taking me into his confidence in some way, I didn't really want to be there. "Mark hated to see anyone suffer." He hesitated. "In a way, he was like Queenie. He actually felt sorry for that old reprobate. Sorry enough to take matters into his own hands. He figured he could solve the Juicer's problems for once and for all and he knew that no one would be able to prove that he had intervened." He hesitated again. "Happens all the time in hospitals, Portal. You should know that."

He was telling me that I should forget about what I now understood Mark Hopequist had done. That it was over because the killer had been brought to a justice above even the law.

Ted Downs smiled at me. As though he could read my thoughts. As though he knew I was right.

Al and Feeance turned then toward the gate of the cemetery. I could see a cruiser parked outside and figured they were headed toward it, not that it would have been distinguishable in a minute from all the other cruisers pulling away. Ted turned, too, and he stood in the middle of the other two with his arms around their shoulders. A show of camaraderie perfectly in keeping with the spirit of the day.

Perfectly in keeping with the spirit of a brotherhood that would admit no others.

FORTY-SIX

When my so-called "case" ended, the real mourning began. I had heard that in the period immediately following the death of a loved one, a person finds so much to do, so many details to handle, that they manage to push away the real thing they are supposed to be handling.

So it was with me.

The winter months dragged on, a winter of bitter cold, but ironically, of great beauty, so that on many sleepless nights, I would rise in the dark and go to the window and see the silver of the snow caught in the cruel grasp of the cold blue moon.

There were seemingly endless days on each of which I rose with great determination, planning to go through the whole apartment and get rid of things that no longer belonged in my life.

Some days, I would find a photograph and be brought back to times that Queenie and I had enjoyed with such love, such gratitude. We travelled up north sometimes—all the way to Moosonee where Queenie came from. Here was a picture of her with a caribou. A tourist shot really, though not many tourists made it to James Bay. And here was a picture of the two of us at a Canada Day celebration at our local Scarborough park. Like everybody else in the neighborhood...

The funny thing about happiness, it started to seem to me, was that you couldn't tell the difference between simple happiness and something much more complex.

And I now knew, more than I had ever known in a long life of much experience, that the same could be said of sorrow. Simple sorrow is as deep, as abiding, as the complicated wanderings of the mind in the complexities of losing many intertwined things.

So I grieved.

And the winter melted and disappeared and spring came and the valley grew green beneath my balcony and I woke up one day and got on with my life.

I started with Jeffrey.

Over the winter, I hadn't been down in the village much, but now I decided to get down there and lend a hand.

When I got to the lodge on a day on which the small green rapids that flowed past the building were singing in their new-found release, I found my son with his nose buried in a gigantic piece of paper that I soon learned was a plan.

"A plan for what?" I asked, peeking over his shoulder but unable to see anything that made sense to me.

"Dad," he said without answering. "We have to have one of our talks…."

And he told me that one of the benefactors he had told me about before had "come through".

"It's more than a million dollars, Dad, and it's going to be matched by the city!"

"Where would we get a million dollars, son? And why would the city give us a hand when they've given us nothing but trouble for years?"

"Dad, I have to tell you who the donor is. And I don't want you to be upset. I want you to think about the people who will live down here in decent housing, some of them for the first time in their lives."

Alarm bells went off. There was only one person I knew who could blithely hand over a million dollars and also convince the ornery city politicians to dish out too. And that person was someone I had deliberately not communicated with in years. I wasn't at all sure how he always seemed to find his way back into my life, but I knew before Jeffrey even said his name that it was he and he was back.

"Look, Dad," Jeffrey reached out and put his hand on my shoulder—a rare gesture of caring, but a sincere one. "John Stoughton-Melville is in a perfect position to help us. He's retired from the Supreme Court now…."

That was news to me, not that I cared. "So? Lots of people are retired. That doesn't give them the right to interfere in the affairs of others."

Jeffrey laughed. "Come on, Dad. He's not interfering. He's enabling us to build your dream. We can upgrade the housing a hundred per cent. And we can install the latest in environmentally-friendly features. Everything. We can use natural building materials. We can landscape the whole village using plants that are native to the valley, including many that haven't been able to thrive here for years." He paused. "And we can get City Council off our back for good."

"You're going to need more than two million the way construction in Toronto is these days."

Jeffrey nodded. I knew what he was thinking. With Supreme Court Justice, Retired John Stoughton-Melville on his side, the two million was only the beginning.

"You can't be sorry, Dad, you have to be immensely pleased and gratified for our people and for our valley." He made a wide, sweeping gesture that took in the newly greening banks, the swiftly flowing water, even the bright, new blue sky, though he wasn't going to convince me that that bastard Stoughton-Melville had had anything to do with that.

***

As the weeks went by, I had to admit that I was getting caught up in the excitement down there. I spent a good part of each day helping Jeffrey in whatever way he needed, sometimes including physical work.

So I was often dead tired when I went back up to my apartment at the end of a long day.

But even so, I sometimes found it hard to sleep. So of course, I read. I had got in the habit of bringing Jeffrey's copy of the *Toronto Daily World* up with me when he was finished with it.

Which is how I discovered that Aliana was writing for them again.

She had, in the past, always written commentary on tough news stories and pressing social issues. But I saw that she had changed her focus. Her new column appeared not in the news section of the paper, but in a section I had always ignored, the section labelled "Lifestyle."

At first, I still ignored it, but the temptation to learn what she had to say about her own lifestyle—"single over fifty and being okay about it"--was too tempting, and I soon found myself digging through the *World* every day to get to her column first.

And then one day, I saw it. Aliana's interview with Kezia. The girl was newsworthy because she had just become the youngest writer ever to have secured a book contract with one of the country's biggest publishers.

I thought about that all day. I thought that maybe I could find a way to reach Kezia. I thought about how happy the kid must be. And how happy Aliana must be, too, since she had had such a big part in the girl's success and had done such a great job of interviewing Kezia.

And I thought about how well Aliana and I had worked together.

And how well we had gotten along until the very end when the stress of our unsolved mystery had finally gotten to us.

And I realized that when she had said, "It's over," she might not have meant us—not that there necessarily was an *us*. And I saw that maybe there could be.

And I picked up the phone.

Rosemary Aubert has achieved world-wide attention with her Ellis Portal series. She is a Toronto writer, teacher, speaker and criminologist who mentors fresh mystery writers and treasures classic ones.

Made in the USA
Charleston, SC
18 December 2014